PRAISE FOR DENNIS GREEN'S
TRAVELER CHRONICLES

Traitor

"*Traitor* is my favorite thriller of the year. A brilliant, wild ride that'll keep you on the edge of your seat…easily one of the best trilogies out there!

—Rachel Aukes, Bestselling author of *100 Days in Deadland*

"Universe-hopping police officers, gun-toting psychics, and multidimensional cats, oh my. Dennis Green brings his dimension-hopping *Traveler* series to an explosive and undeniably satisfying conclusion. I can't recommend this one enough."

—Aaron Bunce, Author of the *Overthrown* and *NecroVerse* Series.

"The epic, explosive climax to Dennis Green's dimension-hopping thrill ride has finally arrived! A literary love letter to the science fiction genre!"

—Adam Whitlatch, author of *The Weller* series

"*Traitor* is a compelling and satisfying conclusion to a crime series with a twist of science fiction."

—Terri M. LeBlanc, M & M Bookstore

"With a stellar cast of characters and storytelling at its finest, Green once again delivers an action-fueled adventure filled with mystery, excitement, and suspense. I loved every heart-racing second!"

—Heidi Hutchinson, author of the *Double Blind Study* series

Prisoner

"*Prisoner* packs one helluva punch... time and time again!

—Rachel Aukes, Amazon bestselling author of *100 Days in Deadland.*

"A gripping dimension-hopping mystery that absolutely refuses to be put down."

—Adam Whitach, author of *The Weller* and *War of the Worlds: Goliath.*

"Green takes a mystery, colors it with an urban fantasy ambiance, teases it with sci-fi, and adds a spritz of romance for a perfectly styled read."

—A.R. Miller, author of *Disenchanted.*

"*Prisoner* picks up where *Traveler* left off as Green takes you for a roller coaster ride of action, science fiction, and good ol' fashion detective work, and then slaps you in the face with an ending that you never see coming. This is a must read for sci fi fans!"

—Michael Koogler, author of *Antivirus* and *Convergence.*

"Fast paced, intelligent, and wildly entertaining, Prisoner grabs your attention from page one and doesn't let up until the very end. A thoroughly satisfying sequel to Traveler, Dennis Green expands on an already infinite universe to give us new characters, numerous worlds in need of saving, and the kind of relationship problems that only exist when multiverses collide. Trav Becker's world has just got a whole lot bigger and a whole lot more complicated, and I for one couldn't have enjoyed it more."

—Jed Quinn, author of *Orchard* and *Kingmaker.*

Traveler

"Mystery lovers and science fiction fans should get a kick out of the novel. *Traveler* by Dennis W. Green gets a solid thumbs up."

—Terri LeBlanc, Second Run Reviews.

"A fun novel that fans of either sci-fi or crime fiction can see themselves shifting into."

—Iowa City Press-Citizen

"Fast-paced and suspenseful."

—Cedar Rapids Gazette

"Propulsive plotting. Great twists. Credible world-building."

—Chrisian Schoon, author of the Zenn Scarlett series.

"Dimension hopping, first person narrative with a cop drama running dead center through the core. In summation it was pretty freekin cool.

—David Adam Suski, author of *The Wired Man*.

"Plenty of thrills await readers as they journey with the traveler."

—Rob Cline, author of *Murder by the Slice*

"Traveler succeeds with surprises at every turn."

—Lennox Randon, author of *Friends Dogs Bullets Lovers*.

TRAITOR

DENNIS W. GREEN

ISBN: 978-0-9977452-4-5

Library of Congress Control Number: 2020903073

Editing by Rob Cline

Cover art and design by Drew Morton

www.drewmadestuff.com

www.happyhourpublishing.com

To Debbie, who is forever patient with me
but not so patient waiting to learn how this story ended.

And to Lennox Randon.
This would have gone a lot easier if you had been around to help.

Some Time Ago

S AM MARCUS LOOKED up from his computer as the door opened. "What the hell?"

Intending to bite the head off whatever grad student would come barging in without knocking, he swallowed his growl when he saw who it was.

"Oh. Hey, Trav."

Sam saved the code he was writing and took a sip of Coke. It was warm, because he had brought it up with him…Christ. Hours ago. Suddenly, he was glad Trav had shown up. Time for a break. Sam grabbed his chin with one hand and the back of his head with the other and twisted. He was rewarded with a satisfying crack.

"What's up?" he asked, now cracking his neck from the other direction. "I don't suppose you brought lunch."

Trav looked amused, glancing at his watch. "It's seven-thirty. How long have you been here?"

"Since ten, maybe," Sam replied

"You really lost track of time. What are you working on?"

"Math. The part I hate. I'll write code all day, but getting the algorithms that drive the program right is *hard*. If I quit in the middle, it's hard to get my train of thought back."

He moved his hands to the small of his back and arched, achieving another crack. "If you hadn't shown up I might have worked all night. But as long as you're here, want to grab some dinner?"

Trav shook his head. "Later. Tell me what you're working on first."

"When did you get interested in my research?" Sam frowned. "You quit asking me about work sophomore year."

"Humor me."

"Well, you remember from the one physics class you took? The one where I spent about a hundred hours tutoring you?"

Trav rolled his eyes and made a *get on with it* gesture.

"At the quantum level," Sam continued, "you can measure either a particle's location or its momentum but not both."

"The Uncertainty Principle."

Sam gave his friend a pleased nod. "I'm impressed. I guess I wasn't wasting my time with you after all. Well, there's a theory related to the Uncertainty Principle called the observer effect, which…"

Trav held up a hand. "That's okay, I don't need to hear any more."

"What do you mean?" Sam suddenly became aware of a shadow behind Trav, just on the other side of the half-open door. "And, who is that with you?"

Trav moved aside.

Sam's eyes widened as *another* Trav Becker stepped into the room.

"What the fuck?" he sputtered. "What the hell is going on here?" Sam hadn't noticed before, but he now realized Trav had traded his usual jeans and St. Louis Cardinals jacket for what looked like black fatigue pants and an equally dark vest. The mirror Trav was dressed identically, except he was carrying a black nylon duffle bag.

"You hear that?" the first Trav said to the other.

"Yeah. Too bad."

"What is that supposed to mean?" Sam looked from one Trav to the other, still trying to process the impossible sight.

"Well," Trav Two said with a sigh, "if you were working on something besides the Cat Box, maybe we could have grabbed dinner. Hell, six months ago, The Boss might have shown up here himself to recruit you."

"Unfortunately, we aren't hiring anymore," said Trav One.

"What? You aren't making any sense!" Sam sputtered. "And how do you know I call it the Cat Box? And who the hell are *you*?" The last was directed at Trav Two.

"Always with the questions. You're just too curious, Sam."

And with that Trav One raised the gun he had been hiding behind his back. Sam watched, unbelieving, as the muzzle flashed one, two, three, four times, the sound of the reports reduced to that of a loud cough by the suppressor screwed into the Glock's barrel.

The impact drove him backward until he bumped into the wall. There was no pain at first. For just a moment Sam thought this was some crazy joke and that the gun contained blanks.

"Wha…?" He started to say. But then he looked down at his chest to see blood and abdominal fluids flowing from four neat holes.

And then the pain began.

What the hell are you doing? he screamed. Or at least that was what he intended to say. What came out was merely a wet gurgle as his legs gave way beneath him.

The Travs watched dispassionately as Sam gasped and tried desperately to suck air into his perforated lungs. They pulled surgical gloves from pockets in their vests. Trav Two unzipped the duffle bag and pulled out a propane torch, then two cans of drain cleaner, a half gallon of paint thinner, several packets of a popular cold remedy, and some coffee filters. He arranged the objects on a small table next to a plastic box, about eight inches high with a T-shaped handle on the top.

Trav One stepped over Sam's outstretched legs so he could reach the standup desk where the computer rested. He typed in a few commands then stood back as the hard disk erased itself.

By this time, Trav Two had finished arranging the contents of the duffle on the table. Both men looked around the room.

"We done?" Trav Two asked.

Trav One nodded, giving Sam a final glance.

"Sorry buddy," he whispered.

The two Travs closed their eyes and vanished.

A corner of Sam's mind told him he should find that shocking, but he was too busy dying to give it proper consideration. It was far easier to just stare in the direction his eyes were already pointed and listen to the soft beeping as the computer's BIOS attempted to locate the operating system that was no longer there.

The world began to slip away, but Sam's waning attention was attracted by a knock on the door.

"Sam?" Trav Becker called softly as he opened the door.

"Did you forget something?" Sam demanded. "Like maybe to stab me?"

Again, that was what he intended to say. But all that came out was a whistling moan.

"Well?" said a voice behind the door.

"We're too late," Trav said, pushing the door open. He dashed across the room, dropping to his knees. He put his arm under Sam's shoulder and gently eased him away from the wall and laid him on the floor. "Just lie still," he said. "Don't try to move."

"Oh, no."

Yet another Trav followed this one into the room. Identical expressions of dismay stretched their angular faces. The lead Trav pulled off his baseball cap, which bore the logo of the movie Jurassic Park.

"Well, fuck."

"Sorry buddy," the other one whispered.

You already said that, Sam wanted to say. But instead he just watched the two Travs seemed to fade and grow farther away until they vanished behind a curtain of gray.

Just Now

MORGAN TURNED TO Fay. "You can't let them do this!"

The older woman shook her head. "It's you who doesn't understand," she said sadly. "We've been fighting this war for years. What gives you the right to wade in here and tell us everything we're working for is wrong?"

"He won't be hurt," Buck said to her. "But I can't risk him undoing everything we've worked for."

He turned to me.

"Last chance."

I shook my head.

He sighed, his shoulders sagging a little. He waved a hand at Gear.

"Let's get this over with so we can go back to work."

"What about Morgan?" I asked.

He frowned. "What about her?

"I have your word she'll be okay?"

"As okay as any of us will be," he replied. The oldest Trav turned to Gear again. "We're running out of time."

"This would go a lot quicker if you would shut up and let me work."

"Fine. Just hurry up."

"*Please.*" Morgan pleaded. "Don't do this. Listen to him!"

"It'll be all right," I told her.

And I stomped down as hard as I could on Emdall's instep.

He let go of my arm, howling. I snapped my hand around and grabbed the back of his head. Before Gomez, on my other side, could react, I banged their noggins together. Their lookalike faces slammed into one another with a dull crack, and they both went down.

Gear looked up at the commotion and saw me coming for him.

"*Eep!*" He frantically pushed and swiped at his tablet.

Stepping over the two unconscious bodies, I leaped at the little man.

And suddenly everything went black.

In Between

I FLOATED, EQUALLY unconcerned that I could neither see, hear, nor feel anything or that my last action had been hurling myself at the middle-aged analogue of my best friend.

A few seconds, or maybe a million years later, I registered another presence near me.

You really walked into that one, didn't you? the presence said.

As I mulled over these words, the memory of the last few seconds of my life swam back into my memory as well. I had tried to stop Gear from doing something. Something really bad for me. I felt like I should be more upset about what had happened to my body. However, since I didn't seem to have a body anymore, maybe it wasn't that important.

Am I dead?

A mental chuckle. *No. Although in the grand scheme of things, that would probably be easier. You're... in between.*

Why am I here?

I slowed things down a little so we could have a chat.

I pondered that for a couple of millennia, finally deciding I was, in fact, a little curious.

What about?

About what's going to happen to you.

And that is?

Gear has erased a bunch of your memories. He's sending you to a place where you won't remember being a Traveler, or much of anything he doesn't want you to.

I can't say I like that very much.

I'm not surprised.

What can I do about it?

Nothing.

Then why are we here?

I thought you deserved to know what was about to happen.

And I can't keep it from happening?

No.

Can you?

Nope.

Will I remember any of this?

Sorry.

Then what's the point?

Later. We don't have a lot of time. Like I said, we can't keep this from happening, but I think I can help you steer toward a place that might be just a little bit more useful.

What good is that if I'm not going to remember anything?

We'll leave you some bread crumbs.

Bread crumbs?

Let me explain.

And he did.

1

The Morning After

A S MY MIND swam slowly up from the gray depths of a fitful sleep, I became aware of two things. One, my mouth tasted like the stuff you pulled out of your clogged bathroom drain.

The second thing was a bare leg lying across mine. My left arm was wrapped around the owner of that leg, and it was starting to cramp slightly. Her cheek lay on my shoulder, her breath making a tiny cool breeze across my bare chest.

I ignored my aches and regarded the pile of blonde curls underneath my chin.

Blonde?

A muffled moan came from underneath the hair and Amy Harper rolled over onto her back. Her dramatic eye shadow had smeared, making her look a little like she was wearing a superhero mask.

"Oh…God," she moaned, resting one hand on her forehead. She blinked a couple of times, then squinted at me.

"I know. I look terrible."

"You look fine," I said.

"Fine," she repeated, her voice a hoarse rasp. "What a glib devil you are, Becker."

We looked at each other, and as we did, foggy memories of the night before began to surface.

There had been several vodkas at The Kremlin. Then things had gotten a little hands-y. We had stumbled back to my place, pulling at each other's clothes as we fell through the door. Finally, we reached the bedroom. And...

Actually, that was it.

Not for lack of trying, on either of our parts. But there had been, so to speak, no cork in my bat.

At some point, we had given up and pretty much passed out.

I looked at her. Something wasn't right, but I couldn't figure out what it was.

"What?" she growled with an exasperated head shake.

"Have you always been blonde?" I blurted before I could stop myself.

"Fuck you," she replied.

She looked at me for a moment more, then swung her legs off the bed and stood. She grabbed her clothes off the floor, darted across the room, and slammed the bathroom door shut behind her.

Glib devil, indeed.

I pulled on some sweats and gathered my own clothes. In the process, I nearly stepped on my phone, which apparently had fallen out of my pocket during the night's futile exertions.

There was a reminder on the screen, alerting me to a noon appointment with Anton Kaaro downtown. The meeting subject simply read, "New Project."

Why on earth did I have a meeting with the city's biggest crime boss on my calendar?

Because I work for him. This gave me an odd feeling. Probably still the vodka.

Fortunately, I would have time to get a workout in before meeting him. With any kind of luck, vigorous exercise would flush some of the hangover out.

I brewed coffee while I was ruminating, and before long Amy emerged from the bedroom. She had re-dressed in last night's clothes, a pair of skin-tight jeans composed of holes just as much as they were of denim and a tank top that displayed several inches of taut belly. The navy-blue leather jacket that completed the ensemble was thrown over one shoulder. In her free hand she carried a pair of high-heeled boots, the kind with a cutout in front to display bare toes.

The rocker-girl look was spoiled somewhat by the fact that with her makeup showered off, she looked like a fresh-faced teen.

"What are you grinning at?" she asked irritably. Still, she accepted the mug I handed her.

"Sorry."

"What is the matter with you?"

"If you mean last night, I guess you poured me one vodka too many."

"I don't mean that. Although I never thought I would see the day when Trav Becker couldn't get it up. You spent half the night staring at me like you'd never seen me before. What the hell is going on?"

"I don't know what you're talking about."

She leaned in closer. "Cut the crap. If you want this to be done, Trav, just say the word. I'm not your fragile violinist."

"Vio— You mean Mary?" I chuckled in spite of myself. "Mary Logan may be a lot of things, but fragile is not one of them." I frowned at her as I continued. "And where the hell did *that* come from? Mary and I have been over for…Well, it's over."

"Bullshit," she spat. "You still love her. You mumble her name when you're asleep. And that's fine. You're not my first choice either. It's been fun, but if you want to move on, just tell me."

"I never said that."

13

"Well, what *do* you want, then?"

I opened my mouth but nothing came out.

"That's what I thought." She put her mug down and pushed past me.

"Amy, wait."

"Forget it, Trav. I don't do head games. Call me. Or don't. It's not that big a deal."

And she swept out the door, not even stopping to put on her toeless boots.

I thought about going after her but knew that would just make things worse.

So, I went back into my small kitchen, found the large bottle of Advil I kept in the cupboard for just such an emergency as this, and dry-swallowed four tablets.

I examined the room while I waited for them to take effect and was suddenly disgusted by the crumbs on the counter and the sink full of dishes. I busied myself putting the room into some semblance of order. By the time I finished I felt almost human again.

There was still plenty of time before I was due to meet Kaaro, so my original plan of getting in a workout seemed feasible. I pulled on some clothes, grabbed my gym bags, then stopped.

Bags?

I had two gym bags. Why did I have two gym bags?

One was familiar. It was simple black nylon, no logo. I had picked it up at the dollar store figuring it would last a few months and then I'd get a nicer one. Turned out, the thing was damn near indestructible. I'd gone through three Kevlar vests while on the force. The gym bag had outlasted them all.

The smaller bag was bright red, narrower than the black one, but longer. I unzipped it and reached inside.

The polished steel blade of a sword glinted in the early morning light.

2

Something's Missing

*W*ILL I SEE *you again?" Sophie asked the good one, the one who had rescued her and Ella. It was so weird. He looked exactly like the man, well...men, actually, who had kidnapped her. But somehow, she knew she could trust this one.*

"Anything's possible."

He gave her a little hug, then stood up.

"Wait!" Sophie cried. "Don't go! If you leave..."

He looked at her curiously. "What happens if I leave?"

"It all goes away," she whispered.

She reached out for him, but suddenly he was out of reach.

"No!" she cried. Tears filled her eyes as he suddenly seemed to recede, getting smaller and smaller in the distance.

"Don't go!"

She bolted upright in bed.

"Sophie," a voice called. "Are you all right?"

The hall light outside her room flicked on and a silhouette appeared at her door.

"I'm fine, Mom," Sophie sniffled.

Her mom glided into the room. She sat gently on the side of Sophie's bed and gathered her daughter into her arms.

"Bad dream, love?"

Sophie buried her face into her mother's shoulder, nodding.

"The same one? With the policeman?"

Sophie nodded again.

Her mom rubbed her back.

"Everything okay?" Sophie's dad appeared at the door.

"Fine," Mom said. "The dream about the policeman again."

Sophie's dad shook his head. "We didn't really even meet the man. Did you talk to Ella's mom?"

Mom nodded. "The occasional nightmare, but nothing specific like this. And Ella has never said anything about a policeman."

"I don't understand," Dad muttered. "Unless…"

"Unless what?" Mom asked.

"Unless he actually was involved."

"No!" Sophie jerked her head up and glared at her dad. "I told you! He didn't have anything to do with it! He…"

"He what, Sophie?"

Sophie's mom was smart, and her daughter hated not telling the whole truth. But it was so important that Sophie not say how she had met Detective Becker.

"Nothing. It's okay, Mom." She disentangled herself from her mother's arms. "Sorry to wake everyone up."

"It's okay, dear," her mom said. "Do you want me to stay with you a while?"

Sophie shook her head.

"All right then. Call if you need anything."

"I will, Mom. G'night, Dad."

"Good night, squirt."

Sophie settled back into the covers and closed her eyes.

"I don't understand," her father whispered, not realizing how sharp his daughter's hearing was. "Why the detective?"

"The therapist said it might have something to do with him dying right after the kidnapping," her mom said.

Their footsteps faded as they padded down the hall to their room, but even had they still been near, Sophie's parents would not have been able to hear her fierce whisper.

"That's not what happened. He didn't die! This is all wrong."

Why doesn't anyone else remember?

3

Is It You?

THE YMCA WASN'T far from my apartment. A twenty-something kid, who obviously did not take advantage of the free membership his employment gave him, buzzed the door. As I pulled it open, my nose was assailed by the smell of chlorine from the pool. I stopped mid-stride, staring at my bags. I didn't even really remember picking up the one with the sword, but there it was.

"You okay, man?" the kid said.

"Yeah…yeah."

"Alarm's going to go off if that door stays open longer than a minute."

"Sure. Sorry."

I stepped in and let it click shut behind me.

In the locker room, I changed into sneakers and sweats and pushed the big duffel into a locker. Grabbing the other bag, I turned to leave.

"Where are you going, Trav?" called a voice.

At the end of the row of lockers, a guy about my age stood with a pleasant if quizzical look on his face. He was a little shorter than me but about twenty pounds heavier, carrying the extra in a barrel-shaped midsection.

He wore a Bulls tank top over a white t-shirt and shiny black shorts that just covered his knees. His black hair showed no touches of gray but was midway on its journey to the back of his head. He pushed a pair of black-rimmed glasses back into alignment with one finger. His other hand held a narrow bag like mine.

"You're going to class, right?" he asked.

"Uh...yeah."

"Did someone start an underwater fencing class and not tell me?"

It was only then I noticed the sign above the door I was just about to open read *Pool.*

"Uh..." I shook my head. "I don't know what I was thinking."

"I don't think I've ever seen you in the pool."

"Are you kidding? I'm a terrible swimmer. My car has better buoyancy than I do."

By this time, I had started back toward him. He stuck out his glasses-adjusting hand.

"Missed you last week," he said as we shook.

I shrugged. "Work."

As we released hands, I snuck a glance at a white tag attached by a cord to the handle of his bag. *J Correa.*

"Ready?" he asked. I let him lead me out the correct door.

About fifteen people warmed up in the Y's multipurpose room following the movements of the instructor, a wiry woman who looked to be in her early sixties. Several of the class members waved as my companion and I entered the room.

J Correa unzipped his bag so I did the same, still unable to shake the feeling that I had never done so before.

I resolved to take it much easier on the vodka in the future.

J drew a sword out of his bag, so I followed suit. His was a standard fencing épée. But it looked like a toy compared to mine. A thick, slightly curved blade reflected the room's ceiling lights. A filigree was etched into the steel. The grip was covered by a basket-style guard.

"Nice!" J exclaimed with an admiring look. "Where'd you get it?"

"It's…new." Which did not answer his question, but he didn't appear to notice.

A couple of the other students joined us. This attracted the attention of the instructor. She frowned and gave me an uncertain look.

"Planning to storm the castle?" she asked. "This is a fencing class, Trav, not *Game of Thrones*. I can't allow you to use that in class."

"I…Wait." I suddenly remembered there had been something in the case besides the sword. Handing the blade to J, I rummaged inside, drawing out a stainless-steel sleeve matched my blade's slight curve exactly. Retrieving the sword from J, I slipped it over the sharp side, securing the sleeve into place with a cork top at the tip and a hook-and-eye catch at the hilt.

Cynthia was unconvinced. "This is a beginner class."

"C'mon, Cynthia. He obviously went to a lot of trouble," said J.

"That's enough out of you, Joseph," she said primly. "I'll consider it. For now, let's just see if you can get through the warmup without slicing yourself open."

She clapped her hands. "All right, everyone, let's get going."

We gathered in three loose lines in front of her. The rest of the class held their épées by the handle and point. I followed suit.

"Forward!" Cynthia barked. Planting her left foot, she executed a lunge with her right. We copied her motion.

"Now, behind!"

This went on until we had pretty much hit every position on a clock face. We then repeated the operation with the other foot. Cynthia lunged so far her trailing knee nearly touched the ground. I could barely get halfway down, although my hamstrings did loosen somewhat by the end of the exercise.

We worked our way through a warmup that involved pushups, side-jumps, and other calisthenics. Then we retrieved our blades and went back to lunges, sword arms extended. Cynthia barked out instructions and corrected our form. I quickly discovered that holding my arm straight out, elbow down, was harder than it looked. Of course, holding a sword twice as heavy as any of the others didn't help.

"Doing okay, Trav?" Cynthia asked, raising an eyebrow.

"Fine."

"Well, I guess it's your lucky day. I found you a sparring partner who doesn't mind your penis-compensating blade."

She nodded toward the door where a man had just entered. He pushed a safety mask into place as he walked.

"That is so not what I am compensating for," I muttered as I grabbed a mask from a table.

Like me, the new guy carried a sabre, although his was a practice blade, thick-edged and blunt.

We each raised our blades parallel to our masked faces in salute and went into the *en garde* position.

He lunged. I attempted to parry but was far too slow. With a negligent flip of his wrist he sent my sword flying.

I won't bore you with the play by play of the rest of the demonstration. Because that was what it was. It certainly wasn't a contest. You would have thought it was the first time I had ever picked up a sword. By the end of fifteen minutes, I was a sweaty, gasping mess. Finally, he backed off and gave me a salute I didn't deserve. I pulled off my mask, grabbing the front of my t-shirt to wipe my face. My opponent pulled his own mask off and I saw his face for the first time.

"Had enough?" asked Leon Martin.

He shifted his sword to his left hand and stretched the other one to me.

Leon Martin was in his early fifties but looked ten years younger. His gray hair was cropped astronaut-close. There was only the barest hint of a middle-aged paunch at his waist. A pair of glasses, rimless to the point of invisibility, was one of the very few concessions the captain made to his age.

He had been my dad's partner and my mentor on the force. He'd given me a medal last year.

No, that wasn't right. If that were the case I'd still be a cop, not working in a bar. No, now a memory of being fired swam up from whatever mental depths I'd pushed it into.

All this barely registered with me because as I shook his hand the sweat in my eyes must have blurred my sight. For just a minute, in place of his glasses I could have sworn I saw a pair of green-tinted swim goggles and his wiry hair invisible beneath a navy-blue swim cap.

"What?" he asked. "Is there something on my forehead?"

"No. It's just..." I wiped my eyes again and the vision vanished. "Never mind."

"Nice sword," he said. "Do you mind?"

I handed it over. He unclipped the blade guard and gave it a couple of test flicks.

"Impressive. But overkill for this class, isn't it? Or do you have a castle to storm?"

I was already sick of that joke. "You never know."

He whipped the blade a few more times, making sure he was well distant from me or anyone else in the room.

"I'm glad that you're keeping up with the fencing," he said, offering me the handle.

I put the guard back on. "Not that you could tell today."

"Takes a while to get used to a new weapon," he observed. "I'd be happy to help you work the kinks out."

"I'm not sure that would be a good idea."

He shrugged. "Suit yourself."

We stood there in awkward silence before Leon cleared his throat.

"Trav. It's probably good I ran into you…"

"Yeah?"

"I just thought you'd like to know we're pretty much at a dead end on your friend."

"My friend?"

"Sam Markus."

Sam.

I rocked backward, assaulted by memories that welled up in a tornado of mixed up images and fragments of conversations that didn't seem to connect.

Sam looking up from his computer, smiling tolerantly. "Like I said, no backsies."

Sam somehow older than he should have been. "They made their choice."

Sam frantically pushing and swiping at his tablet as I lunged at him.

"Trav, are you okay?"

Willing away the melange of contrasting images, I opened my eyes to see Leon frowning at me.

"Yeah, fine," I said through clenched teeth. "Uh, thanks for letting me know."

"I'm sorry, Trav."

I shrugged. "Who's on it?"

"Monroe and Randon."

"Well, if anyone can get make headway with it, it's them."

"They could use some help."

"What kind of help?"

"It appears that Sam had been manufacturing meth in his lab at the school."

"That's ridiculous."

"You just said Monroe and Randon were good men. Do you think they made up the report?"

"No. But there has to be another explanation. Sam has never gone anywhere near drugs."

"You never know what people will do for money," he said quietly.

"What's that supposed to mean?"

Leon's eyes turned hard. "It means that we both know who runs the drug business in the Tri-States, Trav. And you're working for him."

"Are you saying I had something to do with Sam's death?"

"I'm saying it's a little bit of a coincidence that your friend is killed right after you go to work for Anton Kaaro."

"I see." I looked around on the floor for my case. Locating it, I slid the sword inside. "Anything else?"

"Trav. We can use your help. Sam can use your help."

"There's nothing I can do to help Sam. As far as helping you, I'd be happy to."

"Trav, that's grea—"

I held up a finger before he could continue. "I'll be happy to come down to the station, Leon. With my attorney. And after I see a warrant."

Leon's mouth snapped shut. "If that's the way you want it, I suspect I'll probably see you before too much longer in any case."

"Is that a threat, Captain Martin?"

He shrugged. "Seems like we end up with most of Kaaro's thugs downtown at one time or another."

"A thug. Nice. Have a good day, Leon. I need to get to work."

"Trav, wait. I didn't—"

Not letting him finish, I stormed past the other members of the class. The Y showers were the last place I wanted to be right now so I just grabbed my stuff out of the locker, pulling my jacket on over my sweaty t-shirt.

Leon's disappointment in me raised an ache in my chest way more painful than any of his sword touches. And being questioned about Sam's death was just one more item now added to a growing list of things I didn't remember.

But what was more disturbing was a clear memory I did have.

It was the sight of watching Sam Markus's body jerk as a hail of bullets tore into him.

4

Another Day

SAM MARKUS'S BODY *jerked as a hail of bullets tore into him.*

"TRAV!" Sam screamed, bolting upright in his bed.

"God, not again," he muttered. His body was covered in cold sweat and his heart pounded like a rapper's bass. He shook his head, still trembling from the nightmare. Lying back down, he glanced at his phone which was cradled on the nightstand. 5:22.

"Crap." *Might as well get up.*

He pushed himself out of bed and grabbed a t-shirt and jeans that didn't smell too awful.

Twenty minutes later, he set an extra-large Coke on the roof of his Prius and retrieved his backpack from the rear seat. At this hour, of course, there was no one around except a large black and white cat, which watched him from a perch on a loading dock near the entrance door.

"Gotta make some physics," Sam said as he passed the cat.

It yawned.

"Yeah, that's pretty much what my grant reviewers say."

Originally built in the 1950s, Building 231 had been Sam's home since he was an undergrad. His lab was in a Clinton-era addition to the original structure and was imaginatively dubbed The New Lab.

He sipped on his Coke, idly scrolling his phone as his computer whirred to life.

The building was quiet at this time of the morning so the sound of footsteps walking in the hall made Sam's eyes swing toward the door. He sighed as the steps passed and receded.

It was ridiculous, of course, but for just a second, he had expected the door to open and Trav Becker to walk in carrying a fresh Coke. And maybe a pizza.

God, I miss him. That's what sucks about death. No matter how much you tell yourself you're going to keep the memory of someone alive, there comes a day when you can't even remember what they looked like, let alone the last words you said to them.

What had been the last thing he'd said to Trav?

They'd been…in a park.

A park? What were we doing in a park?

Yes, it had definitely been in a park. Because there had been a couple of kids, and… someone else.

Sam chewed on his straw in frustration as he tried to draw the memory out.

A woman. Two girls and a woman. Why couldn't he remember?

Of course, right after that, Trav had died so suddenly. No wonder everything was kind of fuzzy. But it was funny he hadn't given this much thought in the days since. In fact, not since the funeral.

Wait.

When had the funeral been?

Why can't I remember my best friend's funeral?

His straw was now a chewed-on mess and completely failing in its function of Coke-delivery. Sam popped the top off the cup. He took a big swig of Coke and ice, crunching down with satisfaction.

His computer began beeping.

"What the hell is wrong now?"

His fingers danced desperately across the keyboard, Trav forgotten as he tried to save a hard drive which for some reason had picked that exact moment to fail.

5

At The Club

I SLAMMED THE crash bar on the Y's exit door way harder than necessary, startling a black-and-white cat which sprang from my path as I hurtled out. It darted under a convenient evergreen bush from where it watched me warily as I tossed my bags into the back seat of my car.

If I wanted to keep taking fencing lessons, I was going to have to learn to keep my emotions under control. Seeing Leon would be an occupational hazard. I almost went back in to apologize but decided it would be better to let things cool off. I would bump into him at the pool soon enough.

Besides, it was time to go see Kaaro and his mystery project.

The reminder on my phone consisted solely of an address on Third Street, the artery that connected The District to downtown.

The District was a former industrial area that had recently been rehabbed into urban lofts, funky shops, bars, and restaurants.

Anton Kaaro, through a variety of silent partnerships and shell corporations, had provided much of the capital for the transformation. The money ironically came from the very activities the development pushed out of the neighborhood.

Kaaro was pretty smug about it, too. He had been calm and quite sure of himself when I had questioned him in jail the other day.

No, that wasn't right. Kaaro wasn't in jail. He was standing in the middle of the sidewalk, phone to his ear. He raised a hand as he saw me pull up, gesturing to a nearby parking spot.

Anton Kaaro was in his late fifties. Like Leon, he wore his hair short, but it was black as night with just a touch of gray at the temples. His eyes were green and he was dressed head-to-toe in gray. Gray suit, gray shirt, gray tie, even gray shoes. Looming next to him like a twilight shadow was Kaaro's bodyguard, one Bilol Grymzin.

Grymzin also wore gray. Gray slacks at least, although the material they were composed of had never existed in nature. Neither had whatever petrochemical bath had birthed his faux-leather jacket. He was a couple of inches taller than me, thick and muscular, and nearly as wide as he was tall. His greasy black hair had started to recede, although he was compensating by letting what hair remained droop down well past his collar. A single eyebrow topped his close-set eyes and wide nose, which featured a cross-hatching of tiny blood vessels.

I nodded at Grymzin as I approached. He stared at some point over my left shoulder, not acknowledging me in the slightest.

Kaaro stowed his phone in a pocket of his suit jacket. "Good morning, Travis."

His voice was soft but resonant with no discernible accent. You had to listen very closely to catch the slightly more formal sentence construction that indicated he hadn't grown up speaking English. He was also the only person on Earth besides my mom who called me Travis.

"I trust you had a restful night."

"You could say that," I said. "So, what's up?"

"I wanted to show you my newest acquisition."

Kaaro gestured to a narrow door in the middle of the block, the kind that sometimes led to apartments on upper floors of buildings like these. Sure enough, a stairway was revealed as he swung open the door. He started up the stairs. I gestured for Grymzin to precede me, but he shook his head.

"After you," he rumbled, his Eastern European tongue adding a glottal stop before the *y*.

I shrugged and followed Kaaro, trying to ignore the itch between my shoulder blades at having his thug at my rear.

"This building contains one of the best-kept secrets of our fair city," Kaaro said as we ascended. "It is one of many constructed in the early 1900s by Abraham Siemans."

"As in Siemans Department Store?"

"The same."

I was too young to have ever shopped at Siemans, but it had been the downtown anchor for more than a century before finally surrendering to the inevitable mall-ward flight of retail.

"Most business barons of his generation built showy mansions near the country club, but Siemans was different," Kaaro continued. "He considered a commute wasted time. He had seen townhouses in Washington and Boston that were quite luxurious despite being on the upper floors of commercial buildings. So instead of putting several walkup apartments into this building, he built one large dwelling for himself."

"I had no idea you were such a history buff."

"I read."

By now we had reached a landing on the second floor. I looked through an open door on my right. A paint crew labored in a corner. Much of the room was covered in drop cloths, but what parts I could see were impressive.

A massive bar ran nearly the entire length of the space. It was constructed of mahogany so dark it seemed to absorb the room's light. The serving surface was translucent stone lit from underneath to create a rich, golden glow. The floor was also hardwood and gave off the acrid smell of recent refinishing. Daylight streamed in through large bay windows at the other end. To my left was a doorway that opened into a slightly smaller room. This one featured a fireplace and ornate chandelier, into which a workman was screwing blacklight bulbs.

"That will be an interesting effect," I remarked.

"Each room will have its own look," Kaaro explained, "enabling customers to have the feeling of bar hopping without having to close out their bills or drive to another establishment."

"Efficient."

Kaaro took me out the back door where a rooftop bar had been constructed, along with a DJ stand and dance floor. The next floor (I thought of it as the second, but really it was the third from ground level) featured several smaller rooms. One contained a shorter but still very elegant bar made of the same materials as the big one.

The door to the next floor was closed. Kaaro turned to me with a smile.

"You will like this, I think," he said, opening the door with a flourish.

Like the first level, the door opened onto a narrow room occupied primarily by yet another ornate bar. This one's underlight glowed blue. This room also opened up into a more spacious area where the bar ended, but unlike the others, there was no furniture, just a small table in the corner.

"What do you think?" Kaaro asked.

I shrugged. "What are you putting in here?"

"Why, Travis, I'm disappointed. I put more stock in your powers of observation. This will be a place for live music."

That was a bit of a surprise. Kaaro's establishments tended to be low-overhead where entertainment was concerned. They were designed primarily to be an efficient system for the exchange of alcohol for money. Not to mention the accompanying lowering of inhibitions which made some customers ripe for Kaaro's less legal, but more lucrative, businesses.

"What kind of music?"

"I think our town could use a jazz club, don't you?"

"A jazz club? That's a little different image than your other properties, isn't it?"

He shrugged again. "To stay healthy, a business needs to branch out."

"Um, if you're expecting a jazz club to be a profit center, you may have to adjust your expectations."

"The jazz club will be just one of the several different themes, as you have seen. It will give the club an upscale image, different from our other businesses."

Kaaro stopped and tilted his head, trying to read the expression on my face. "What?"

"I just never figured you would open a jazz club."

"I never had a manager who was a jazz fan before."

"A manager?"

Then it sank in. "You mean me?"

"Just so. Did you think I hired you only to be a bouncer? That would be a waste of talent. Besides, the online casino will go live in the next few weeks, and I anticipate that will take up much of my time."

I just stared at him, completely at a loss for words. Kaaro took advantage of my silence to pull out his phone and study the screen with a frown. He looked over my shoulder at Grymzin, who had plodded along behind us throughout our walking tour.

"Bill, my phone is nearly depleted. Will you go down to the car and get my external battery?"

Not for the first time, I wondered why Kaaro always called me by my given name but used an Americanized version of Grymzin's.

For his part, the Uzbek looked as if he wanted to say something, his ponderous gaze swinging from Kaaro to me and back again. Kaaro raised an eyebrow at his hesitation.

Grymzin closed his mouth and spun around. A moment later we heard him thump down the stairs.

Kaaro waited until the heavy tread faded. "You don't have to give me an answer right now, Travis. But showing you this club is not the only reason I wanted to talk to you today."

"Oh?"

"I have had some disturbing news, and it has to do with you."

"With me?"

"Well, indirectly, at least. You know the police have been investigating the shooting death of your friend Sam Marcus."

If I had been surprised that Anton Kaaro had just offered to let me manage a jazz club, hearing him utter Sam's name was a complete shock.

"Yeah, I heard," I finally managed.

"They have not made much progress in their investigation."

I didn't ask how he knew. Anton Kaaro had always seemed to know what was going on in the PD. Apparently, his sources in the department were still good.

"In fact," Kaaro continued, "they are getting ready to move the case to inactive status."

"So?"

"I think they are giving up too quickly."

"And why do you care?"

"He was your friend. Even though you don't show it often, I can tell his death has been weighing on you these past weeks."

"Everybody dies."

"True. But someone killed your friend. Don't you think that person should answer for it?"

"Why do you think I will succeed where the police failed?"

"Why, I have faith in your investigative skills, my friend," Kaaro said with a chuckle. "Just as I have faith in your administrative skills or else I would not turn my latest venture over to you."

"Yeah, about that…"

He held up his hand. "We can discuss that later. Now you need to look at the files on Sam and see if there is anything your former colleagues missed."

"How am I going to do that? I can't just waltz into Central Station and ask for the murder book."

"I would never give an employee an assignment without also providing adequate resources. Let's step into your office."

I followed him into a room behind the bar.

My "office" was a square box not much bigger than a closet. A desk, chair, and small filing cabinet, pretty much filled the available space. I didn't know what things were normally kept in a bar manager's office, but I was pretty sure a binder with a case number and the name *Samuel Markus* written on it in black marker was not one of them.

I swung around to face Kaaro. "Where the hell did you get the case notes?"

"From the police, of course."

"Leon will decorate his office wall with the skin of whoever let this out of the station."

"That's not something you have to worry about." He glanced nonchalantly at his watch. "I must go. Let me know if you find anything interesting."

I waited until I heard his slightly-lighter-than-Grymzin's tread fade down the stairs before I opened the murder book.

The first thing that spilled out of the binder were several eight-by-ten photos of the murder scene. I knew what the pictures would show, of course, but there was no way I could prepare for the sight of my friend's body.

Ah, Sam.

I squeezed my eyes shut and closed the book. I wasn't ready to look at these pictures yet, no matter how much I wanted to find Sam's killer.

I tucked the book under one arm and headed downstairs. I was almost to the front door, distracted by my incongruous memory of Sam's bleeding form that I wasn't paying any attention to my surroundings.

Thus, I didn't notice the man standing beside the stairway until his fist crashed into the side of my head.

The punch swung me around, but I managed to catch the banister to keep from hitting the ground. This luckily served to put the rail between me and a glowering Bilol Grymzin. Moving with a speed that belied his bulk, he spun around the stair's edge to grab me.

Still seeing stars, I managed to duck away from his grasping hands. Dropping the murder book, I kicked out. My heel connected with his thigh hard enough to push him back and out of reach. But not for long. He grabbed for the leg, but I was able to pull it back and slither to the side. His momentum carried him onto the first step of the stairway where I had stood a moment before.

"What the hell is wrong with you?" I shouted, desperate to buy time to clear my head.

Grymzin didn't reply, only grunted as he slammed into me. This time there was no avoiding his bearlike grasp so instead I stepped in, and as his arms began to close around me, drove both hands up as hard as I could, connecting solidly with his chin. The extra six inches as he stood on the stair above me gave my punch extra force. He reeled back against the railing, causing it to creak and sway dangerously. Sagging against the pillar, he shook his own head.

It was your standard big guy-little guy fight. He was stronger with an enormous reach. I was quicker, but if he got even one of those big arms on me, he'd crush me like a soda can.

"What the fuck, Bill? Anton isn't going to be happy if you break his nice new staircase."

"Worth it," the big man rumbled, "if I get to break you along with it."

He charged again, but this time I was able to dance easily out of his path. I don't know why I kept talking to him. It was like trying to reason with the Hulk. But I kept at it.

"Our boss doesn't want his employees fighting."

"He'll get over it."

"Why, Bill? At least clue me in!"

Grymzin grunted again. "Mr. Kaaro pays me to keep trouble away from him."

"Me, too!"

"Bullshit. Mr. Kaaro is too trusting. Once a cop, always a cop."

"Too trusting? Have you *met* Anton Kaaro?"

Grymzin didn't reply this time. He charged me again. I ducked and weaved, thinking he was trying to ram me against the wall, but he anticipated my dodge and as I slipped to the side, his ham-sized fist was waiting for me. A rainbow exploded behind my eyes as I desperately scrambled to stay out of his grasp.

Unfortunately, this also put Grymzin between me and the door.

The Uzbek smiled as he also realized I was cornered.

"This will go easier if you just stand still," he grated. Sweat dotted his expansive forehead, but his breath came easy. I wasn't going to just be able to outlast him.

"You expect me to just stand still and let you beat on me?"

The big man shrugged. "I don't care what you do. But I do know that Mr. Kaaro will soon need to find another manager for his new bar." And he lunged toward me once again.

Time seemed to slow down. He reached his left hand into his jacket pocket as he moved, and almost like I had x-ray vision, I knew there was a knife in that pocket.

But as this slow-motion attack continued, another version played out in my mind at the same time, like it was superimposed over my actual vision. Because in that moment, I also knew that Grymzin had gone for the knife instead of the gun tucked into his other pocket. Probably because gunshots in the daytime might attract unwelcome attention.

In my mind's eye, I could suddenly see an improbable scene play out. It was ridiculous, the kind of nonsense you see in movie fights. But it was my only chance.

As Grymzin moved toward me, I lunged at him with a roar, putting every ounce of strength my legs contained into a shove to knock him off balance. I slapped my right hand against the arm that was going for the knife, trapping it for just an instant inside the pocket.

My other hand snaked inside his jacket and closed on the grip of the pistol. As my momentum carried us across the floor, I whipped it out and smashed the pistol butt into his face. He staggered backward which gave me room for a good wind-up. I slammed the gun into his temple. The murder in his eyes gave way to glazy confusion. I wound up again and gave him a matching smack on the other side.

He was now close enough to the wall that the force of my blow snapped his head back into the plaster. He raised his hands weakly before his eyes rolled back into his head and, like a massive tree falling in the forest, he slowly slid down the wall.

I rested my hands on my knees, quivering as the adrenalin rush faded. I looked at the gun in my hand, still not quite believing my crazy rush had worked. The after effects of Bill's blows to my head apparently were still with me as well because there was a glowing red outline tracing the edge of the weapon. I closed my eyes and shook my head. When I opened them again, everything was normal.

Stuffing his gun into the waistband of my pants, I picked up the murder book and pushed open the door, leaving Grymzin snoring unevenly in an ugly pile in the corner.

6

E Street Shuffle

"THIS SUCKS," DEXTER Wasson said as he plopped down in the chair next to Sophie.

"The big one," agreed Mason Selvas, on her other side.

"Shut up!" Sophie hissed. "The assembly is about to start."

Backpacks jostled against the blonde wood seats in the Warren Middle School auditorium as students filed in. Teachers and guidance counselors stood in the aisles, on alert to keep students from cuddling or fighting, whichever seemed like the bigger crisis.

"I can't believe they are making us all sit here and listen to some girl play the violin," Mason said.

"Some *girl*? Really, Mason?" Sophie's voice dripped sweet acid. "Like the girl who put you on the mat three times last week?" The three had been carpooling to tae kwon do classes since elementary school.

"And who also plays violin?" Dexter added.

"You were supposed to take me down," Mason said loftily. "That's why I was there. They picked me because they knew I could take a punch."

Dex sniggered. "Dude, you took *all* the punches."

Mason's cheeks turned pink. He started to object, but Sophie cut him off with an elbow jab.

43

"Ow!" the big redhead rubbed his ribs.

"Would you idiots please shut up?" Sophie repeated. "*I* want to hear the music."

"I don't know what the big deal is," Mason said.

"You will."

At that moment, Dr. Gallart, the principal, walked onto the auditorium stage.

He waited patiently for the hubbub to die down, then stepped up to a microphone mounted on a chrome stand at the center of the tiny stage.

"Good morning," the principal said. "Thanks to you all for getting in and getting situated quickly and quietly. I know our special guests appreciate your consideration. Now, before we get started…"

But whatever the principal was about to say was lost as every light in the room suddenly went out. This left the windowless space in near complete darkness even though it was ten-thirty in the morning.

But in the instant between shocked silence and the inevitable rising din of questions and complaints, a long, amplified note from a bass guitar rang out followed almost immediately by the sharp report of a drum beat, loud and steady, in time with the heartbeats of the gathered students. A high note soared above the rhythm, and just as suddenly as the lights had gone out, they returned. Except now in the exact same

spot where the principal had stood there was now a woman, her back bent at a nearly impossible angle. A cherry-red violin nestled under her chin, bow extended straight up toward the ceiling. She was barefoot, wearing a leotard and skirt that was comprised mainly of multi-colored fabric strips which shimmered in the spotlight.

She struck a second note and the beat sped up. A keyboardist, drummer, and bassist were visible behind her. The violinist followed at first but then took over the tempo, dashing ahead of the ensemble like a runner in the zone, demanding the other musicians follow *her.* Then she added movement, kicking each leg out below the knee, not unlike an Irish step dancer. She swept and spun across the stage, sliding up to each of the other musicians in turn so that each had a moment with her in the spotlight.

Someone started to clap and before long the entire auditorium had joined in, feeding the quartet as the music worked its way to a thundering crescendo, before ending with each musician playing the three concluding notes of the piece in unison and louder than a lot of rock bands.

The musicians froze as the last notes echoed against the concrete walls before finally fading to silence.

For about ten seconds.

Then applause broke out and the band relaxed, smiling as the kids clapped and cheered. Mason whooped louder than anyone else, fist in the air.

As the applause died down, the woman approached the microphone.

"Thank you so much," she said softly but with a twinkle in her eye. "So, you liked that?"

Her smile got wider at the answering roar. "Well, it might interest you to know that it was written more than two hundred years ago by a guy whose music has been played more than all of today's pop artists put together. His name was Mozart. Now, we have maybe taken just a few liberties with his original composition, but Mozart loved nothing more than surprising his audience. I think he'd approve."

She paused, taking a moment to tune her instrument. "Would you like to hear some more?" she asked.

The room roared once again. The violinist smiled and nodded to the drummer who counted off the next tune.

This was one even middle schoolers could recognize immediately, though few could identify it as the beginning to Beethoven's Fifth Symphony. Like the first selection, it was embellished with rock and roll beats, some paying homage to pop versions of the song that the older teachers recognized, and others completely original.

The music then continued in the same vein. Classical pieces with a modern flair alternated with pop songs done in a classical style that were somehow almost as much fun as the original versions the kids watched on YouTube. At one point, the bass player, a woman with spiky blonde hair, took the mic and rapped a hip-hop verse to Copland's *Rodeo*.

After nearly an hour, the violinist paused and introduced the other three musicians. "And my name is Mary Logan," she finished, then had to wait nearly a minute for the applause to die down. She acknowledged it with a nod.

"You know, a musician enjoys nothing more than taking an old song and finding a way to make it sound new. But there is also something to be said for sticking to the original notes. That's what we do in the symphony orchestra, and in its own way, that music has just as much power and emotion as what we played today."

She paused, taking a swig from a water bottle at her feet. "Fact is, we couldn't take those songs and do something new with them without knowing the originals backward and forwards. Now, we would love it if you all left here today as fans of classical music. But that's not why we're here. We're here to remind you that there is so much great music out there that you haven't had a chance to hear. I hope that the next time someone asks you to check out something you haven't heard before, you'll give it a chance."

She went on to explain how students and their families could come to an upcoming symphony concert for free.

"We have time for one more. It's a song that..." she paused. "...A good friend of mine introduced me to. And it's become one of our favorites to play."

And with that, she launched into the song, which began with her playing a refrain by herself. She was joined by the pianist, a skinny man whose long black hair spilled down his collar.

Sophie sat up straight in her seat. "'Jungleland,'" she murmured. "That figures."

"Shh," Dexter hissed.

Few in the room were any more familiar with Bruce Springsteen than they were with Mozart, but the quartet brought fire and fury to the song, communicating its message of love drowned by the violence of the streets nearly as effectively as The Boss himself, all without singing a single lyric.

Mary's violin took the place of Springsteen's voice for the long, plaintive wail that closed the song. She turned toward the pianist and met his eyes as he gently took up the final, quiet phrase which brought the song to its lonely, desperate conclusion. Four hundred teenaged bodies sat stock-still as the last notes echoed in the auditorium before erupting again in cheers and footstomps.

Mary tucked an errant strand of auburn hair behind her ear and bowed. Then she reached out her hands, still holding violin and bow, to her bandmates. They joined her and all bowed bowing together.

"Whoa," Dex breathed, leaning back in his chair.

Sophie jumped up, shrugging quickly into her backpack.

"What's the hurry?" Mason asked. "It's going to take hours to get everyone out of here."

"I want to talk to her," Sophie said. "See you in fourth hour."

She fought upstream in the exact opposite direction of the herd trying to exit. But since no one was that anxious to get to fourth hour, she soon found herself at the top of the short stairway that led to the stage.

The musicians were packing up their gear. Mary looked up as Sophie approached.

"Hi," she said kindly.

Suddenly, Sophie's throat went dry. She looked at the woman, mouth working, but nothing came out.

"Did you want tickets to the concert?" Mary asked gently.

Sophie shook her head.

Okay, dummy. Breathe. She probably already thinks you're a total spaz.

"I—I just wanted to tell you I really enjoyed the music."

"Thanks."

"Um. Especially the last song."

Mary raised an eyebrow. "Really? You know that song?"

Sophie nodded.

"I'm impressed. Bruce Springsteen isn't usually the first choice of most girls your age."

"My dad is always playing that stuff."

"Ah. That explains a lot. My friend…the one I mentioned…It was one of his favorites. His dad influenced his musical tastes, too."

A faraway look came into the woman's eyes. "Bruce Springsteen, Steely Dan, The Eagles. And don't even get me started on Al Stewart. He loved them all. And you never wanted to listen to the radio with him. 'This is the second-best Elton John song,' he would pronounce. Or 'God Only Knows' is the most perfect pop song ever written."

She stopped and looked at Sophie with a confused frown. "I'm sorry, you didn't come up here to listen to me reminisce. What can I do for you?"

Sophie screwed up her courage. Everything rested on how this lady reacted to her next question.

"You miss him, don't you?"

"Miss who?"

Sophie took a deep breath.

Don't chicken out now. "Your friend. It's Mr. Becker, isn't it?"

Mary's jaw dropped. "How…how do you know Trav?"

"He helped me."

"He…" Mary cocked her head and examined Sophie more closely. "Wait. I know you. You're one of the girls who was kidnapped."

Sophie nodded.

"Oh, honey, how are you doing?" Mary reached out and took Sophie by the shoulders. "Are you okay? I can't even imagine what you went through."

"I'm fine, Miss Logan."

"Please call me Mary."

"I'm fine…Mary."

"But what do you mean Trav helped you?" Mary frowned again. "Trav wasn't involved. He was…It was just before…" Her voice trailed off.

"Just before he died?"

"Yes." Mary shook her head. "I don't understand. What do you mean he helped you?"

She took Sophie gently by the arm and guided her out of earshot of the other musicians.

"In fact," she continued, speaking softly, "Trav was actually being held in a cell when they found you. There were a lot of people around that day. Maybe you just heard his name and confused it with someone else."

Sophie shook her head firmly. "No! No one believes me, but I know it!" She kept her tone soft, but her whisper was fierce. "He was there. And there was a woman, too. Morgan."

"The psychic. Yes, I knew that, even though it didn't make the media. But honey, like I said, Trav was at the police station the whole time. I'm sorry, but he couldn't have been with you."

Sophie nodded. She'd been expecting this. Time to bring out the big gun.

"How did he die?"

"Trav?" Mary frowned, perplexed by the turn in their conversation. "Well, he..."

Her voice trailed off, and she began again.

"It was...sudden," she finished. Her lips tightened and her eyes darted from side to side.

Sophie watched as a fine line of perspiration broke out on Mary's forehead. She hated making the woman uncomfortable, but she had come too far to back away now. Sophie had despaired of finding anyone who would believe her story. But when she realized that the arts outreach program coming to her school was led by Trav Becker's girlfriend, she knew this was her chance to solve a mystery that no one else even knew existed. The next thing she asked would either pierce Mary's mental fog or have her calling Sophie's principal.

"What was the funeral like?"

Mary's mouth opened, then closed. Her eyes narrowed. "Why would you ask me that?" she demanded.

"I'm sorry, ma'am," Sophie said. "I'll leave you alone if you want. But only if you can tell me something about Trav Becker's funeral. Just one thing. Anything."

"Fine," Mary replied, her lips pressing into a white line her cherry-colored lipstick couldn't hide. "It was a very nice service. Trav's..."

Mary's voice trailed off again.

"I was there!" she whispered fiercely. "Why can't I remember?"

"Are you sure you were there?" Sophie asked.

"Of course I was there! I had to be there!" Mary's voice caught and her eyes began to fill with tears. "Why wasn't I there?"

"Something's not right," Sophie said urgently. "I remember him. He rescued us! But he said he couldn't be with us when we were found. And then he was just...gone. Later, people said he died. But I checked. There was nothing in the newspaper or on the internet. One day he was here. And the next...he just wasn't."

Sophie grabbed Mary's hand. "Please! You have to believe me."

Mary looked at the teenager for a long time, and Sophie watched as the tears in her eyes disappeared, replaced by steel.

"Well, you're right about one thing," Mary said grimly. "Something is wrong. And I'm going to find out what it is."

"Me, too," Sophie said quickly.

The violinist looked at the girl again for a long time. Just when Sophie was sure it was because she was trying to figure out a way to tell Sophie to butt out, Mary nodded.

"Of course. And I know just who is going to help us."

7

Semi-Charmed Life

THE SHAKES DIDN'T hit me until I reached my car.

I slid in, dropped the murder book onto the passenger seat, and steadied my breath. I put Grymzin's gun in the glove compartment as post-trauma sweat slid down the center of my back. My hands had begun to shake, so I gripped the steering wheel in an attempt to hold them still.

I knew Grymzin didn't like me, but attacking out of the blue was a bit much, even by Kaaro henchman standards. If I hadn't had the sudden inspiration to go for the gun in his pocket, he certainly would have smashed me into Trav pulp.

Things were moving so fast during the fight that hardly a second passed between my thinking there might be a gun in that pocket and going after it. That had been a tremendously lucky guess.

I adjusted the rearview mirror to assess the damage to my face.

Given the way my head and hands ached, it wasn't as bad as I feared. Grymzin had connected with my left cheek hard enough to raise a welt that would eventually bloom purple and green, but it was just pink for now. I was going to have a big a black eye on the other side. A ring on one of Grymzin's hands had scored my temple and it oozed blood from a scratch that extended halfway to my jawline. But my nose was still straight and all my teeth remained fastened solidly to my skull. So all in all, I called it a win.

By now the shaking had stopped, although my arms and legs still felt weak as the adrenalin drained away. I took a deep breath, regretting it almost instantly as my ribs, nearly caved in by Grymzin's bear hug, protested at now being asked to expand again.

Speaking of bears, while I didn't quite look like I had been mauled by one, neither did I look presentable. I decided to go home to clean up and put the murder book someplace safe. The chances of a beat cop

stopping me and seeing it were tiny, but it still made me nervous to have it laying out in the open.

I put the car in gear, turning the radio on as I pulled into traffic. I immediately regretted it.

When I was a teenager, my dad had turned me on to his favorite music, marginal and obscure album rock bands of the Seventies and Eighties. I'd inherited his extensive album and CD collection when he'd died a couple of years ago. But I rarely had to pull them out because our town had an increasingly rare media jewel. A great radio station.

AXE 106.9 had managed to avoid the homogenization of today's music radio, playing a unique blend of rock, blues, and jazz that had become the soundtrack to my life since high school. But recently the station had ditched its one-of-a-kind music format in favor of talk programming. Fortunately, not some angry white guy wishing American society could be the way it was in his grandfather's day. If that had been the case, I would have eliminated it from my radio presets. But this show was almost as bad.

It was a talk show hosted by a psychic, for God's sake.

I punched around the dial a few times, finally settling on an Oldies station that was playing "God Only Knows," which everyone knows is just about the most perfect pop song ever written. The Beach Boys' layered harmonies even made my headache feel a little better.

One Beach Boys, a Four Tops double-play, and a Del Shannon later, I arrived at home. After I gingerly cleaning up my face and swallowing a bunch of ibuprofen, I was ready to go. The murder book sat on my coffee table, but I was not anywhere near ready to look at it yet. I grabbed my car keys and headed to work.

The street in front of The Kremlin was empty at this time of day. Cigarette butts that somehow never made it into the provided container, one of those wide-based, skinny-necked things, were the sidewalk's only occupants, forming a nicotine path toward the door.

The bar was equally empty. The day bartender looked up as I entered.

"He in?" I asked. Receiving a nod in return, I headed for a door marked "Employees Only," which was to the right of the big mirror that lined the back of the bar. I walked past several shelves crowded with liquor bottles on one side opposite a row of kegs on the floor.

I knocked on a door at the end of the hall.

Kaaro sat at his desk, an ultra-modern Scandinavian construction of metal, glass, and light wood. He looked up as I entered. He took in my swollen face, then took away my chance to open our conversation.

"It appears you and Bill came to an…agreement?"

"If by agreement, you mean we agreed that he should sleep on the floor for a couple of hours, sure."

"Impressive."

"You knew he was going to jump me?"

"Bill takes his job very seriously. It can't be too much of a surprise. You know he's never trusted you."

Kaaro toyed with a fountain pen as he spoke. Like his desk and office furniture, it was a modern version of an old-fashioned device. The nib clicked up into the barrel like a ballpoint instead of having a cap you had to remove. The pen was the only item I had ever seen on the desk's glass top. Where the papers he signed with it were, I had no idea.

"And it never occurred to you to tell him that trying to kill me was not a good idea?"

He shrugged, clicking the pen open and closed. "If my employees can't take care of themselves, they are of limited use."

"Trial by combat. Nice."

"You're an athlete, Travis. You know that strength is the foundation of success."

"I would think that having your employees looking over their shoulders all the time would be a waste of resources."

"It's wise to be alert."

"I'll be alert all right. But how about you just keep him away from me?"

"Or what?"

"Or your corporation's headcount may diminish."

He shrugged again. "That would also be a solution."

"What are you suggesting, Anton?"

He spread his hands, the pen now occupying the exact geographical center of his desk. "I am suggesting nothing. You know it is not in my nature to intervene in…personnel matters. Over the years, I have found they tend to solve themselves."

"When one of your personnel ends up dead."

His nostrils flared. People didn't question Anton Kaaro. Of course, his chief enforcer already wanted to kill me, so from my point of view, there was little to lose.

"A tool that is not tempered by heat will break when you need it most," he snapped.

"And people trying to kill each other attracts the cops. Either tell him to lay off or resign yourself to having to explain his dead body."

Kaaro looked at me unblinking, like a snake preparing to strike. Then, just as I was starting to wonder what had possessed me to walk into this office without a weapon, he smiled.

Not only that, he chuckled.

"See? This is why I hired you, Travis. You are my conscience. You keep me from reverting to past behaviors. I need that." He clicked the pen closed and set it back down with an air of finality.

"Is there anything else? I assume that your…conversation with Bill has not allowed you to begin looking into Sam's death?"

"You'd be right."

He nodded and drew his phone from his suit coat pocket. I was dismissed.

It was time to go back to my normal job, fixing drinks and keeping order.

And so, my life settled in to its regular routine. Wake up from a restless night's sleep, which strangely often included weird dreams in which the radio psychic, Morgan Foster, figured prominently. I guess the loss of the AXE was weighing on me more than I had realized.

Combined with whatever after-shift recreation I'd indulged in, this often left me with a headache. But alcohol was my sole vice these days, as Amy seemed to have worked some legerdemain on the schedule that largely kept us from encountering one another. Bill was making himself scarce as well. My morning routine consisted of popping some ibuprofen, fencing class at the Y, and going to work. All while avoiding the murder book.

I didn't see much of Kaaro for the next few days either, which was also good, as he certainly would have asked me about my progress on Sam's murder.

But then my day off arrived. I put in extra time at the Y, where I was finally starting to see some progress with the blade. I got home, showered, and puttered around. But finally, I could no longer ignore the binder that rested on the same coffee table where Sam's feet had spent many hours.

I had seen dozens of murder books in the past, of course. Hundreds of crime scenes and the accompanying photos. But no matter how experienced you are, it's different when it's someone you know.

You never get used to seeing your own dead body.

I shook my head, taking firm hold of the part of my mind that was trying to wriggle out of this task. Pushing its nonsense aside, I opened the binder. The first several pages were printouts of forms. Even though nearly all of our records are kept online these days, most cops still kept a binder like this one with dead-tree copies of photos, interview transcripts, reports, and other important documents. It's hard to spread the contents of a computer file out on a table and see everything at once. I paged through the whole thing to get a feel for what was there.

Which was not a lot. The first several pages were forms. The medical examiner's report followed that. Then some witness reports. Sam had been killed around nine p.m., long after the building had emptied. My friend had kept crazy hours, and it wasn't uncommon for him to work through the night. The custodial staff knew to give his lab a wide berth if the lights were on, no matter what time it was. His body hadn't even been discovered until late the next morning. A former office mate had poked her head in to say hi and discovered the grisly scene.

The fun part came in the very next section. My stomach turned as I pulled out the photos of Sam's body. He had been discovered laying on his back. A bloody smear on the wall behind him indicated the force of the gunfire had driven him back into it before he had collapsed to the floor. Close-up shots of his wounds followed. I flipped back to the ME's report. No traces of powder residue, which meant his assailant had to have been across the room when he or she fired. Sam's hands were unmarked. He hadn't even had time to raise his arms before his assailant fired.

Gratefully setting the photos of Sam aside, I moved on to the next series of prints. These were of the rest of the scene. I shook my head as I looked at the assortment of otherwise innocent bottles and jars that together added up to a meth lab. My eyes strayed back to the photo of Sam's lifeless body.

"What the hell, Sam?" I muttered softly. "You never drank anything stronger than oatmeal stout. How did you get involved with this?"

That train of thought led me back to the ME's report again.

Nope. No traces of drugs in Sam's system. And an examination of his mouth and teeth had revealed no trace of oral deterioration from smoking methamphetamine.

So Sam wasn't cooking for his own consumption. Unless he had gotten shot before he'd taken his first sniff. That would have been poor timing to the nth degree. Although…

Another flip back, this time to the inventory of material at the crime scene. The containers in the picture looked new. In fact, the propane torch was full, the coffee filters unopened. No meth-making waste in the trash can. It did look like he'd been killed while setting up his lab for its first use.

"Not possible," I whispered. The only person who would want to kill Sam *before* he started cooking meth would be me. Or maybe his mom.

Nothing about this made any sense. Why remove Sam from the board before he was even a threat?

Unless he had been making drugs someplace else. Was he taking them to his main lab and for some reason pulled everything out of his backpack? Pretty stupid to leave it out in plain sight. And if there was one thing Sam Markus was not, it was stupid.

No, I was missing something. I moved on to the next set of pictures. These were of Sam's computer workstation which was a standup desk opposite the table where the meth materials had been placed. A giant Coke glass sat next to his mouse, to the right of the monitor.

Wait.

The *right?*

I thumbed through the other photographs of this area searching for the camera angle I was looking for. I found it about three prints down.

The left side of the computer, where there was a charging stand for his phone.

And a mouse pad.

Sam was right-handed. But all those years at a computer had given him a perpetual ache in his right wrist. Eventually, he'd simply switched hands and taught himself to use the mouse left-handed. Whenever I had to use Sam's computer, the first thing I did was grab the mouse and put it on the right side.

Someone else had been at Sam's desk. Probably after killing him.

What had they been looking for?

8

Trains

S OPHIE FELT A little strange standing outside the fitness studio
with her violin case, but a double-check of the address Mary had
texted her confirmed she was at the right place.

Fortunately, Mary emerged before Sophie had a chance to second
guess the whole plan. Her cheeks were pink from exertion and a few
strands of auburn sought to escape from a tight ponytail. A huge gym
bag was slung over one shoulder. She hadn't changed out of her workout
gear: black leggings with a lightning-shaped stripe that circled up from
her ankle to hip and brilliant white sneakers. Mary zipped up a light
microfiber jacket as she stepped out into the cool fall air and waved at
Sophie.

"Right on time," she said with a smile. "Hope I didn't keep you
waiting."

"I just got here," Sophie replied. She hefted her instrument case. "I,
uh…told my parents you offered to give me a lesson."

"Good thinking. I'd like to give you a lesson sometime if you're
interested. I'll bet you're a fine player."

Sophie blushed. "That would be nice." But then she frowned. "But
not now, right?"

"Of course not. I want to find out what's going on just as much as you do. My car's right over there." She pointed to a gray SUV across the street.

Mary opened the rear door. She tossed her bag in and carefully stowed Sophie's case next to it.

"Is that a Crossfit studio?" Sophie asked as she and Mary fastened their seat belts.

"They do Crossfit there," Mary said. "But they just started a stick fighting class. Different from any workout I've done before. I got so sick of spin classes. I'm not looking for a fight or anything, but it feels good to learn a skill, not just work out. I've been feeling the need lately to work out some aggression."

Sophie nodded. "I take tae kwon do. But I hope I never have to use it in a fight."

Mary started the car. As she drove, she asked Sophie about her violin. It turned out that Sophie's private lessons teacher had also been one of Mary's first mentors. Mary was just finishing a hilarious story about a disastrous Christmas concert that took place when she had been about Sophie's age when they pulled up to the university's Building 231.

Sophie started to up the sidewalk, but then her mouth went dry and she froze.

Mary turned around when she realized Sophie wasn't beside her. She rushed back and took the quaking girl gently by the shoulders. "What's the matter, honey?"

"I...I..." Sophie's mouth worked but no sound came out.

"Take a deep breath, Sophie," Mary said, her voice even and soothing. "It's okay."

Sophie buried her face against Mary's arm with a choking sob. But after a minute or so she relaxed and her breathing evened out. She pulled away slowly from Mary.

"I'm sorry," she said softly, not meeting Mary's eyes. "I..."

"It's okay, hon," Mary repeated, rubbing Sophie's upper arms. "What's the matter? Can you talk about it?"

Sophie swallowed, pointing at Building 231. "It's...hard to explain," she began. "But the second I saw that building, something came back to me."

"From the kidnapping?"

Sophie nodded.

"You weren't held in there?"

Sophie shook her head. "No...Yes." She scowled in frustration. "It's that building...but it's also not. Goddamnit, why can't I remember?"

The words had hardly escaped before her hand flew to her mouth. "Oh! I'm sorry!"

Mary smiled. "It's all right, Sophie. You don't have to censor yourself around me. But I think I better take you home. We can do this another time."

"No!" Sophie spun out of Mary's grasp. "Don't you understand? It's all connected."

"I don't know..."

"Please!" Sophie begged. "I'm okay now. I've waited so long, and we're getting close, I just know it."

"All right," Mary relented. "Maybe it will do us both good to try and find some answers. But you have to promise to tell me if you see something that bothers you. I don't want to have to explain to your parents that I took you someplace that was dangerous for you."

"I'm fine," Sophie said firmly. "It...just took me by surprise is all. It's just a building. It can't hurt me."

Mary smiled in approval. "Then let's go get some answers."

"Damn right." The intensity of Sophie's tone was spoiled when she broke into a giggle. "Swearing in front of a grownup just seems so *bad*."

"Wait till you hear it from the conductor in front of ninety musicians."

That made Sophie giggle again, and this time Mary joined her. Arm in arm, the two made their way into the building.

Mary led Sophie up some stairs and soon they were standing in front of a door in a newer section of the building.

"Sam is Trav's best friend," Mary said, "and a top-notch scientist. If anyone can help us figure out what's going on, it's him."

"Does he drive a Prius?" Sophie asked.

"He does. Why do you ask?"

Sophie shrugged, pointing a finger at her temple. "Just another random image. I'm starting to wonder why you even brought me here. I must seem like a total loon."

"On the contrary. I think you may be the *least* crazy person I know right now. Let's see what Sam thinks." She knocked on the door then opened it without waiting for an answer.

"Anybody home?" she asked, poking her head around the edge of the door.

"Mary!" cried a voice from inside.

She swung the door the rest of the way open and motioned for Sophie to follow.

Sam Markus perched on a stool behind a standup desk. He rushed over and wrapped his arms around Mary.

"What are you doing here?" Sam asked as they broke their embrace. "I haven't seen you since…Hey, who's this?" His head snaked around Mary as he spied Sophie.

"This is…" Mary stopped as the other two locked eyes.

Sam stared at Sophie as if he had never seen a human being her shape and size before. He was silent as he studied her like he was trying to quantify a creature completely beyond his experience. Which made it even more of a surprise when he said softly, "You're Sophie."

"You're Sam."

And the two lapsed back into silence as they continued to regard each other.

Mary finally cleared her throat. "I take it the two of you know each other, then?"

"Yes," said Sophie.

"No," said Sam.

"Well...kind of." Sophie, her voice trailing off.

"This is why we're here," Mary said. "Sam, Sophie pointed something out to me today that was very interesting. When we came in, you started to say you hadn't seen me since something, but then changed the subject."

Sam looked puzzled. "I haven't seen you since..." Now his voice trailed off.

"You started to say the funeral, right?"

Sam frowned. "That's the logical thing. I don't remember seeing you since."

"But did we see each other at the funeral?"

"Of course."

"What was it like? Who spoke? Was there music?"

With each of Mary's questions, Sam looked more and more perplexed.

"I—I...Why don't I remember?" he whispered.

"I don't either," Mary said, just as softly.

Sam and Mary stared at each other for what felt to Sophie like an hour.

Finally, Mary broke the silence. "There is only one logical explanation. If neither of us can remember his funeral…"

"There wasn't one," Sam finished.

"And if there was no funeral," Mary continued.

"He's not dead!" Sophie finished triumphantly.

There was another moment of silence. This time it was Sam who spoke up.

"Then where the hell is he?"

The three of them stared at each other. Sophie didn't know what to say and neither, apparently, did the two adults.

"So, how did you guys get hooked up?" Sam finally asked.

"Sophie showed up after a school concert asking me about the funeral," Mary said. "I had the same reaction you did."

"And why do you care about Trav Becker, Sophie?"

"Because he rescued me. And then he disappeared."

"oh my god. You're one of the girls who was kidnapped."

Mary chuckled.

"What's so funny?" Sam asked.

"Oh, just this conversation. It's almost word for word the same as the one I had with her."

"Okay, but I'm still trying to get this all straight in my mind. You say Trav rescued you?"

Sophie nodded. "And you helped."

"Me?" Sam looked at Mary. She shrugged.

"Trav rescued you and I helped," Sam repeated. "I…"

"What?" Sophie asked.

"When I look at you, I remember seeing you before. In a…park?"

66

"Yes!" exclaimed Sophie. "There was a park! I remember now. Ella and I sat on a bench. She was too tired to swing, so we just sat…" Sweat broke out on her forehead as she strained to bring her thoughts into focus.

"Don't force it, honey," Mary coaxed. "Let it come. You remember so much more than either of us. I know you can do it. Just relax and talk it through."

Sophie closed her eyes. "Sam picked us up near this building. He drove us to the park. Sam and Mr. Becker talked, then he came over to us and explained…"

"Explained what?" asked Sam.

Sophie's eyes flew open as the pieces finally fell into place.

"He explained that we weren't going to remember what happened," she whispered. "And that made Morgan sad."

"Morgan?" Sam said.

"Who's Morgan?" Sam asked.

"She's a psychic. She has a radio show," Mary explained. Then she smiled. "Her show replaced one of Trav's favorite DJs. Boy, did it piss him off."

Sam started to reply but was interrupted by a round of beeping from his computer. He swore under his breath and pulled out the keyboard, stabbing at a series of keys that looked pretty random to Sophie.

"Well, that's just weird."

"What?" Mary asked.

"What's the name of that singer that Trav liked?" Sam said, not looking up. "Something Stewart. Had songs about weird topics. History, time travel."

"Al," Mary said.

Sam shrugged and turned back to his keyboard. "Too short," he muttered. "What is Al short for?"

Mary just stared at him. "I have no idea. All the times Trav made me listen to his songs and it never came up."

"Alastair," Sophie said.

Sam and Mary's heads swung around like they were screwed to the same hinge.

She held up her phone. "Fastest Googler in Lego League."

"Okay then, Alastair." Sam attacked the keyboard again.

A musical chime sounded.

"I'll be damned. That was it!"

"What was it?" Mary asked.

Sam turned to his computer. "This hard drive crashed on me the other day. I've been trying to salvage as much of the data as I could, but there was this encrypted folder that came up in the rebuild. I couldn't remember what it was for, let alone the password."

"The password was Al Stewart?" Sophie asked.

"Oh, God, no," Sam replied, sounding hurt. "Using English words as a passphrase is just begging to get hacked. The volume was called Stewart. The passphrase is derived from the sexy prime number sequences corresponding to where the letters of his first name appear in the alphabet."

"Sexy what?" Mary asked.

"Sexy primes," Sam said. "Prime number combinations that differ from each other by six. The letters A and L are the first and twelfth letters in the alphabet. The first and twelfth sexy prime combinations are five and eleven and sixty-one and sixty-seven. And so on through the rest of the name. It's an easy way of remembering a long string of numbers."

"An easy way. You're kidding, right?" Mary asked.

Sam looked perplexed. "Kidding? About what?"

"Never mind."

Mary looked at Sophie. "Sexy primes," she murmured.

Sophie desperately tried to stifle a giggle with the hand that was not holding her phone. But she needn't have worried. Sam was transfixed by whatever was happening on his screen.

"What the hell?"

"What?" Mary asked.

Sam shook his head. "This doesn't make any sense. There are gigs and gigs of files here. Real advanced stuff."

"So?"

"Well, I wrote these equations, I can tell. And they seem familiar." He looked helplessly at the women. "I don't remember encrypting this folder. But…"

Mary raised an eyebrow. "Using one of Trav's favorite singers as a clue is an awfully big coincidence, isn't it?"

Sam nodded, still staring at the filenames and numbers scrolling on his screen. "It's going to take me a while to wade through all this. If there's a connection, I don't know what it would be."

"Well, we'll leave you alone then. Can we come back later and see if you've come up with anything?"

"Sure," Sam replied absently.

"C'mon," Mary said to Sophie. "We'll see you later, Sam."

"Mmm."

"He'll be like that for hours," Mary confided to Sophie as she herded the girl toward the door.

"Where to now?" Sophie asked.

"I think I need to have my palm read," Mary said.

9

Times of Your Life

I CLOSED THE murder book and stared at it for a long time. Then I started working to replace the images of Sam's broken body on my mental highlight reel with some more pleasant ones.

There were never two more unlikely best friends than Sam Markus and me.

We met the first day of college when the all-knowing university bureaucracy plopped a physics major with an undecided (later to land on criminal justice) in a double room so narrow I often crashed into the opposite wall jumping down from the top bunk. We hardly spoke at all the first week, each of us searching out our tribes. I looked for a bartender willing to serve a not-quite-nineteen-year old. He found his people in the university's seat of physics, Building 231, where he would spend almost his entire career, not to mention the last hours of his life.

Which made it a little unusual that I found myself one Saturday night on the roof of that very same Building 231 with Sam and two of his friends huddled around a Rube Goldberg contraption atop a table we had dragged up the stairs. The device looked like an old sixteen-millimeter projector, and for all I know might have been the carcass of one. I had no idea what was going on. I was just the muscle.

So far, the college experience promised me in *American Pie 2* had not been delivered. The campus was dry with dire consequences promised to anyone caught with liquor in their room. And I'd been turned away again at Joe's Place, too young-looking even for their lackadaisical adherence to the drinking law.

I was thinking that maybe a mustache might help. But at the rate my facial hair grew, I'd be legal before it looked like anything other than dirt.

My love life had been equally as successful. Which was why I found myself at loose ends on a Saturday night and willing to help my roommate and his nerdy friends on some weird project they'd cooked up during free lab time. Yes, that's right. I had been reduced to hanging around with nerds who spent time in classrooms when they didn't have to.

But Sam had promised me some laughs and I didn't have any better offers. So I schlepped their table up the narrow staircase that led to the roof.

Aaron, one of the other members of our quartet, had taken one end of an extension cord and disappeared behind the rooftop's main attractions: Two small observatories that were popular with both classes and amateur astronomers in the community. Finnegan, Sam's other buddy, fiddled with the controls of the projector.

Don't ask me why we called Aaron by his first name and Finnegan by his last. The rules of this social group were established long before I came along.

"What are we doing again?" I asked Sam.

"Just watch," he replied with a grin.

Aaron came back into view. "Light her up," he said.

Finnegan pressed a switch and a fan somewhere inside the projector whirred to life. I didn't see anything coming out of its lens, however, and craned my neck toward the barrel for a better look.

"Careful," Sam grabbed me by the elbow. "You don't want to look straight at it."

"Straight at what?"

He stretched out his arm. "Look over there, right in front of the bar."

Across the street and about halfway down the next block was Joe's Place, the bar I had unsuccessfully been trying to get into. In the center of the sidewalk right in front of the door was a red circle about eight inches across.

"That's us?" I asked.

"Yeah," Finnegan said. "I found this old laser in a storage closet. We used a similar one in high school to learn laser spectroscopy.

"What's that?"

"There are a lot of different applications, but at its most basic, you can use laser light reflected back from an object to measure things like distance."

Years later, I would buy a device that did this exact thing, replacing a standard tape measure. But this was the first time I had seen anything like it.

"You're measuring the distance between here and Joe's Place?"

"Don't be ridiculous," Finnegan snorted. "Do you see a reflector? That's the point. With nothing to reflect, the beam can travel miles without dispersing. And we get that!" He pointed proudly at the red circle.

"Okayyyy," I said. "You've got a red dot on the sidewalk in front of the Fieldhouse. So?"

"Just wait," Sam said.

And we did. Over the next twenty minutes, a steady trickle of passersby trod on the red circle without noticing. But finally, an older guy, at least thirty, lurched unsteadily out of the bar. He stopped and stared at the circle for a moment before continuing on his way.

Finnegan moved the projector just enough so that the circle stayed directly in front of the guy. He stopped and looked around.

"Will that hurt him if he looks up here?" I asked.

Sam shook his head. "He'd have to look right into the beam. That's why we have it pointed at the ground."

While Sam and I were having this discussion, the man had gingerly stepped over the circle and started walking again. After a few steps, he turned around to discover, of course, that the mysterious glowing dot was following him. Finnegan, who had a remarkably steady hand, managed to dog him for nearly two blocks before the laser image was finally blocked by a hotel awning.

"Let me try," Aaron said.

A few minutes later, he too hooked a fish. Once this guy realized the light was following him, he turned around and walked back into the bar. A moment later he returned dragging another man by the arm. He pointed at the ground.

Aaron clicked off the projector.

The two of them stared at the circle-less sidewalk before the second man jerked his arm from the other's grasp and made a gesture that even two blocks away we could tell meant: *Go home, you're drunk.*

We laughed so hard it was a miracle our victim didn't hear us.

Best time I ever had in college sober and way more fun than playing the same game with Mom's cat years later, with a laser pointer that weighed about sixty pounds less.

Before long, Sam's little posse of fellow science majors quit being the nerds down the hall and become my friends, too. That was when I learned that more than religion, more than morality, or respect for the law, what made you a good person was surrounding yourself with good people. People who liked you for who you were, who wanted you to succeed, instead of secretly sabotaging you so they could feel superior. By the time I met Mary years later, I was remarkably comfortable in my skin. And I had Sam to thank for much of that.

It would have to be a pretty different Sam than the one I knew who would get himself killed cooking drugs.

I became a cop not to bust criminals or keep the peace or even to uphold the law. I wanted to be the person who stood for those who couldn't defend themselves. Because they were helpless. Or dead.

I wasn't a cop anymore. But there was no one else to stand for Sam. Someone was going to pay for what they had done to my friend. Sliding the murder book into my backpack, I prepared to begin my quest for some answers.

As I pulled into traffic, I tried to remember when I had seen Sam last. I had this sense of having been in his company a lot lately. He'd been working on some big math project, but I couldn't remember the details. And I had the craziest mental picture of him wearing a pair of ridiculous black-framed glasses, total nerd movie-prop, lacking only some masking tape across the nose bridge.

Sam didn't wear glasses. But what was weirder was that I couldn't summon up any clear memories of his funeral. Where had it been? Back in that little Southwest Iowa burg where he had grown up? No, I sure didn't remember going there recently.

Where the hell had his funeral been and why couldn't I remember it?

This train of thought was interrupted by the sight of a familiar Buick parked at a little diner I'd frequented when I was on the job. This was a convenient coincidence. One that might enable me to take care of two things relating to the case at once.

Adam and I went to Dina's often. But then I remembered that Adam, too, was dead. And I was no longer a cop. I had no desire to go someplace frequented by former colleagues, but this was for Sam, not me.

I pulled into the diner's tiny lot and mounted the steps.

"Trav!" a voice exclaimed as I closed the door behind me. Suddenly my arms were full of warm girl.

"Hi, Kim."

I hugged her back. She pulled away and looked at me critically.

Kim was a couple of inches shorter than me, with blond hair pulled into a tight ponytail. She wore a football jersey and leggings. A part-time grad student at the U, she was cute as a button.

"It's been ages, Trav! How have you been?"

"Fine. How's your aunt?" Kim was the niece of the diner's titular Dina.

"Feisty as ever. I make her go home after the breakfast crowd these days. Where do you want to sit?"

The diner was a converted railway car, towed into this spot many years ago and decorated with a railroad theme. There were only a half-dozen booths, one of which was taken up by a bulky man whose attention had been attracted by the fuss Kim was making over me.

"I'll just sit over here."

I threaded my way over to where Alex Monroe watched me without expression.

"Mind if I join you?"

Monroe shrugged. "Suit yourself."

I slid into the seat across from him, tossing the backpack in ahead of me.

An iced tea appeared.

"Thanks, Kim."

"Do you need a menu?"

I shook my head. "Just this."

"Okay. Give me a shout if you need a refill or anything."

Monroe and I sat in silence as she withdrew. His eyes flicked to the pleasant sight of Kim's backside before returning to me.

"What can I do for you, Trav?" he asked carefully.

"Actually, it's what I can do for you." He arched an eyebrow as I unzipped the backpack, but both eyes went wide as he saw the murder book.

"Where the fuck did you get that?"

"Calm down. Doesn't matter where I got it. Suffice it to say, you have someone at the department willing to let it out."

One of Monroe's hands disappeared under the table. "I think that book and you need to come to the station."

I shook my head. "I'm not going anywhere but back to work, Alex. I'm doing you a favor. This is your case."

I could almost see the hair on the back of Monroe's neck rise. "Who the hell do you think you are, accusing me?"

I made a pacifying gesture with both hands. "I'm not accusing you of anything, Alex. You're not on Kaaro's payroll. It's not your style. But someone is. And I thought you'd appreciate knowing that."

"I should haul you in for possessing stolen property."

"I know. And even knowing that I wanted to get the murder book back where it belongs. I could have just thrown it away. And you'd still be on the hook for it."

Monroe scowled for a long minute, then sighed.

"Fine." He held out his hand for the book.

"In a minute."

Monroe cocked his head.

"First tell me what's *not* in it."

"What do you mean by that?"

"C'mon, Alex. You and I both know that the murder book is for the formal evidence. What's in your notes that's not in there? You have to have a theory about what happened."

"What do you care?"

"Sam was my friend."

Monroe grunted. Then a smile spread across his face. Not a nice smile.

"Okay, Trav, I'll tell you my theory. Sam Markus had this friend, see? This friend used to be a cop but got kicked off the force and went to work for Anton Kaaro. Kaaro needed to improve the chemistry of his product and Sam's friend brought him into the business. And when you get on the wrong side of the wrong person in that kind of business, you often get dead."

My hand had curled into a fist as he spun his sarcastic tale. "This sounds kind of familiar. I heard pretty much the same thing from Leon."

Monroe shrugged.

"But even if that's true, which it isn't, it still doesn't explain why Sam was killed."

"Oh, grow up, Trav." Monroe's vicious smile gave way to a frown of disappointment. "I don't know the who, but the why is pretty clear. Sam's little side business pissed off the wrong people. Might have been a rival organization or even someone inside Kaaro's circle. It doesn't matter who pulled the trigger. The person responsible for Sam's death is the one who hooked him up with Kaaro."

I ignored the jibe. Rising to the bait would get me nowhere. Instead, I said, "But nothing on the who."

The big man shrugged again. "Pro hit. Place was clean. The only set of prints that didn't belong to Sam or the janitorial staff were from an ex-cop who was tending bar at The Kremlin that night in front of a couple dozen witnesses. Some of them weren't even on Kaaro's payroll."

"I had nothing to do with Sam's murder."

"You didn't pull the trigger. And you can pretend you don't have anything to do with Kaaro's illegal businesses all you want. But when you lie down with pigs, you get covered with shit."

Monroe tossed the rest of his coffee down, pulled the murder book over to his side of the table, and started to get up.

I held up a hand. "Wait. I did see something that might help you."

He looked at me dubiously, but when I motioned for the murder book he handed it over. I pulled out the photo of Sam's computer and explained how the mouse was on the wrong side.

"So?" he asked when I had finished.

"It proves someone else was there."

"We knew that."

"But it could mean that the meth-making stuff was a feint. Whatever the killer was really after might have been in his computer."

Monroe appeared to mull this over. I pressed on, hoping that giving him a new clue might cause him to open up.

"The murder book doesn't say anything about video surveillance," I continued. "There are cameras all over that building."

He shook his head.

"Wasn't any."

"Wasn't any footage?"

"Didn't show anything. Hours of empty hall from six or seven o'clock until the next morning. I watched every minute."

He stood up, tucking the murder book under one arm. "Thanks for the tip, Trav. I'll let you know if anything comes of it."

"Wait. If they weren't on the hallway video, then how did the murderers get in?"

He shrugged impatiently. Whatever goodwill I had bought was diminishing rapidly.

"If we knew that, we'd probably have made an arrest. Maybe they knew how to avoid the cameras. Maybe they hid until the next morning and slipped out with student traffic. Or…"to

Monroe made as if to leave without finishing his sentence.

"Or what?" I asked, taking the bait.

"Hey, your buddy was a physicist," he continued, one hand on the door frame. "You always said he worked on some pretty Star Trekkie stuff. Maybe they beamed out."

I watched him trundle out, chugged my iced tea, and left a five on the table for Kim, who gave me another hug and demanded I come back more often. I assured her I would, almost believing the lie myself. For some reason, I couldn't look at her without thinking of Adam.

I had achieved my goal of getting at least a little bit of additional information about Sam's death and had also returned the murder book to its rightful owner, which eased my mind somewhat.

I still had a couple of hours before I needed to be at The Kremlin. The dearth of pedestrians as I crossed from town to gown made me realize that the university was on a break. Most campus buildings would be empty.

I intended to drive right to the campus, but without realizing it, I detoured a few blocks out of my way to drive past Mary Logan's house. I had done this several times over the past few days without knowing why. I had yet to see her, which was just as well. She knew my car and would have to wonder what I was doing.

"Get a grip, Becker," I murmured to myself. But I still flicked my eyes to the rearview mirror in the hope of catching a glimpse of the woman I just couldn't get out of my mind.

It was while I walked up the sidewalk to Building 231 that not one, but two things about Sam's death which had been hovering just under my awareness gnawed their way into my frontal lobe.

First was everyone's easy acceptance of the meth paraphernalia found at the murder scene. Since Sam was a scientist, everyone just assumed he could make meth.

But Sam was a theoretical physicist, not a chemist. I don't think he'd taken any chemistry beyond an intro course we'd taken together as sophomores. I did better in that class than he did. It was the only time that I'd ended up helping *him* with homework.

Make no mistake, Sam was brilliant. He could master any discipline he cared to study. But his bailiwick was computers and advanced math. Chemistry was smelly and required protective gear. Sam broke out in a rash when he got kitchen disinfectant on his hands. Walter White he was not.

Even if you believed (as Monroe seemed to) that I had been the one in search of a science guy to help with some aspect of Kaaro's drug trade, Sam would not have been at the top of the recruit list. Hell, the lady who cleaned Sam's office knew more about mixing chemicals than he did.

The other thing was the lack of surveillance footage. A skilled professional should be able to avoid cameras, like Monroe had said. But there was something that I was missing. I went back over my conversation with Monroe a couple of times before it hit me.

Monroe had referred only to cameras in the halls. But something Sam had said to me once led me to think he had his own surveillance system in his lab. Sam often went a little off the reservation where university tech policy was concerned, happily modding his computers, upgrading his operating system and other software without asking permission from IT. He certainly could have installed an off-the-books camera.

Even if Sam's workspace hadn't been reassigned to some other researcher, there was no guarantee that I'd be able to find this hypothetical camera, let alone access its hypothetical data. However, seeing my friend's lab one more time beat the hell out of killing time at The Kremlin until my shift started. My liver would certainly thank me.

As expected, I only encountered a few people as I approached Sam's floor and no one senior enough to question why I was wandering around. At his door, I knocked hesitantly. If someone answered, that would spell the end of this little expedition very quickly. But there was no answer to my knock. Time for test number two. I pulled out my phone and flipped through its apps.

Sam was notorious for forgetting his keys. When smart locks came on the market, he replaced every door lock in his house with one he could unlock from his phone. He had stopped short of replacing the one on his lab door. After all, Rita had to get in to clean. But he hacked it so that it would unlock from his phone as well as by key. He'd loaded the app on my phone, too, so I could bring him pizza.

If the lab had passed to new ownership, chances are the lock had also been changed. But as soon as I entered my PIN in the app, I heard a click and the door opened just a bit. I poked my head in, ready to apologize and back out if I was disturbing the new occupant. But the room was dark. I flipped the light switch on.

While I was no expert on university equipment, it looked to me like this was still Sam's stuff. It appeared that someone had started packing it up but then been called away. There were three half-full boxes in the center of the room. An empty box stood near the stand-up computer cart Sam had used for a desk when he worked in here. The computer itself still sat in place and appeared to be plugged in.

Someone had at least started the cleanup. No blood and the alleged meth lab materials were all gone.

I started with the filled boxes, pawing through them in search of anything that resembled a webcam. But if there was anything with a lens in the box, it was camouflaged too well for me to discern it.

But then my hand encountered a shape that while familiar was completely out of place in this context.

I drew out a pair of eyeglasses. They had the kind of thick black rims that were currently in style for influencers going for the sexy nerd look.

But as I said before, Sam didn't wear glasses. And yet I kept seeing images of him in my mind wearing them. And not just any eyeglasses.

Wearing these exact eyeglasses.

Without knowing why, I slid them on. The first thing I noticed was that they weren't prescription lenses. I could see the room just as clearly as I did without them.

The second thing I noticed was a line of text that suddenly appeared. My brain registered it as floating a couple of feet in front of me, although I knew rationally it had to be projected on the glasses themselves.

But what the text said had no rational explanation.

It read: *Hello, Trav Becker.*

10

Memory

WELL, THERE IT is," Mary said.

She and Sophie had arrived in a neighborhood the locals called Czech Town. In the late 1800s, dozens of small row houses had been built for the influx of immigrant workers enticed from Europe by plentiful work in a packing house, now long since shuttered.

There were eight or so of the structures still left. They were very small by modern standards, but each was meticulously maintained. Morgan's was painted a cheery, robin's-egg blue with brilliant white shutters. There was a short flagstone walk going up to the tiny porch, which was just barely larger than its welcome mat.

Two juniper bushes, the spiral kind, wound inside and through themselves on either side of the front steps. A gray sign with the words *Psychic Readings* printed on a background of stars and a crescent moon was stuck into the ground by one of the bushes.

Mary and Sophie walked up the short path and squeezed together side-by-side on the porch.

"Here goes nothing," Mary said.

There was no doorbell, so she rapped smartly on the door. A moment later, there was the clicking sound of a deadbolt being pulled aside and the door opened.

A cloud of blonde hair appeared, atop the head of a woman a few inches shorter than Mary.

"Hi, are you here for a readi—" Her voice trailed off as she took in the two women standing on her porch. Her face blanched and her eyes went wide.

"No!" she shouted, "You can't be here!"

And before Mary or Sophie could say a single word she slammed the door in their faces.

Sophie stared at the closed door, then slowly turned toward Mary.

"What the hell was that?" Mary asked.

"It was like she recognized us," Sophie observed.

Mary nodded. She raised her hand and knocked again. "Ms. Foster?" she called. "We really need to talk to you. We…uh, don't want to upset you, but we're not leaving."

"Right?" she whispered, with a sidelong glance at her companion.

Sophie nodded firmly. "Right."

Mary raised her hand to knock again, but just before her knuckles connected, the door slowly opened.

"Sorry about that," Morgan Foster said softly. She didn't look at either of them but craned her neck to study the porch, flowerbeds, and yard.

"My cat went out this morning," she explained, still not meeting their eyes. "He's usually not gone this long."

Inside, she indicated a small couch in the front room. Mary and Sophie sat. Morgan sat in an overstuffed chair nearby.

For the first time, Morgan looked up at them. "Sorry about that," she said with a smile that appeared forced. "I thought..." her voice trailed off. "I mean..."

She sighed and tried again. "Sometimes the...psychic impressions of the environment overwhelm me." She shrugged. "Part of the blessing and curse of having a psychic gift."

Sophie looked at Mary who in turn was looking at Morgan. Mary's eyes narrowed. She motioned to a Bluetooth speaker on an end table.

"That's nice music, Ms. Foster," Mary said. "Who is it?"

Morgan looked puzzled, but said, "It's...um, Al Stewart. From the Seventies."

"I know who it is," Mary replied coolly. "Now tell me. Just how well did you know Trav Becker?"

Morgan's mouth snapped shut. She stared wildly at Mary and Sophie, started to speak, but instead winced in pain, color draining from her face. She wrapped her hands around her knees, bringing them up to bury her face. Sophie and Mary watched in shock as she rocked back and forth in her chair, whimpering softly.

"Miss Foster...Morgan?" Mary said softly. She looked at Sophie helplessly.

"Should we call 911?" asked Sophie.

"No!" Morgan cried, her voice muffled as she hugged her legs. "Just...Oh, God. Can't you just leave me alone?"

Paralyzed, Mary and Sophie watched as Morgan moaned and writhed, mumbling unintelligibly. Mary pulled out her phone.

Somehow, even with her eyes closed, Morgan sensed Mary's movement. "Don't!" she cried, pushing her arm out, palm raised. This caused the sleeve of her top to pull back.

Sophie stared at the woman's arm and gave a little gasp. She darted forward, grabbing the psychic by the forearm.

"What's this?" she asked.

"What's what?" The stricken look on Morgan's face became confusion.

Sophie touched a silver bracelet that dangled from the other woman's forearm.

"I don't…" Morgan stared at her arm as if she didn't know what Sophie was talking about. Frustrated, the girl took Morgan's other hand and placed the psychic's fingers around the bracelet.

Morgan continued to look at Sophie as if it was the teenager, not her, who was acting strangely. But then her eyes opened wide as if she was registering the feel of the silver metal for the very first time.

"You bastards!" she snarled. She pulled free of Sophie's grasp and jerked the bracelet off her arm with a shudder. She hurled it across the room. It bounced off the opposite wall and landed back in the middle of the room. Morgan grabbed her knees and curled up into a ball again She stared at the bracelet as if she expected it to rear up and strike like a snake.

"Ms. Foster," Mary began.

Morgan held up her hand again. "Please, it's Morgan. I'm sorry. This is weird, I know. Just give me a minute. I can explain everything. Really I can. I just need to make sure we're really alone."

She reached across Sophie, jerked open the drawer of an end table, and withdrew the biggest pistol Sophie had ever seen. The girl yipped and shrank back into the cushions of the couch as far as she could.

Mary shot to her feet, leaping between Morgan and Sophie.

But Morgan ignored the other two completely. Instead of pointing the gun at them or herself, she reversed her grip. Holding it by the barrel, she leaped from her seat, kneeling over the bracelet. Then, brandishing the pistol like a hammer, she rained blows down on the bangle.

"Stay. Out. Of. My. Head!" She struck the bracelet on each word. This continued for nearly two minutes, her cries changing to a sob as she continued the pounding.

Finally, she stopped, her shoulders shaking as she bowed her head over the twisted remains of the bracelet.

Mary crossed the room and kneeled next to Morgan. She put one arm around the other woman, gingerly taking the gun from her hand.

"I'm so sorry," she murmured, still sniffling a little. "They took so much. So much. And so much from *you*."

"From me?" Mary asked. "What are you talking about? Does this have something to do with Trav?"

But Morgan ignored her, turning instead toward Sophie.

"How did you know?" she whispered.

Sophie, still in shock from the bizarre events of the last ninety seconds, could only shake her head. "I—I don't know. At first, I didn't even see the bracelet. But when you held your arm out, I could feel..." She grunted in frustration. "It's so hard to explain. But something was just *wrong*. And when I saw the bracelet, I knew that was it."

Morgan nodded, pulling out of Mary's embrace, and gave Sophie a weak smile. "He knew there was something special about you."

She would have continued, but Mary interrupted her.

"Who knew?"

"Trav, of course," Morgan replied. She put a hand on Mary's arm. "I know. This is all such a shock. He felt so terrible for not telling you. I think he would have, if he hadn't..." Her voice trailed off.

"It's okay," Mary said. "You can say it. If he hadn't died."

"Oh no." Morgan shook her head firmly. "Trav's not dead."

"What?" Mary asked. "How can that be?"

"It's going to sound pretty crazy."

"Like it's not crazy already?"

"Good point," Morgan replied with a small chuckle. But then her tone turned serious. "There's not much time. If we don't find him soon, he might as well be."

11

New Friend

I STARED AT the ghostly line of text floating in front of me for a while.

"What the hell?" I muttered.

The text faded out but was replaced by the same phrase. *Hello, Trav Becker.*

"Uh, hello?"

Hello, Trav Becker. How can I help you?

"Are you responding to my voice?"

Yes.

"And you are...?"

I am Sam's virtual assistant.

"Virtual assistant? Since when did Sam have a virtual assistant?"

Since April twenty-sixt—

"That's not what I meant," I interrupted. "I mean...I wasn't talking to you. I mean...what are you again?"

An algorithm Sam developed to enable him to interact with software using voice commands.

This was a little surprising, and not just because I found myself talking to a piece of software like it was a person. Aside from his electronic door lock, Sam had never shown much interest in smart home devices. And I distinctly remembered him saying he would never let Amazon spy on him with one of their Alexas. But he also always had two or three side projects going in addition to his main research.

"Like Alexa."

Alexa spies on you.

I swear I could sense the thing's disdain. But if there had been any doubt this was Sam's creation, there wasn't now.

The root code is similar, it continued, *but Sam took it in a different direction.*

"I see," I replied, not seeing at all. I looked over at Sam's computer, dark and silent. "Isn't this computer turned off? Where are you?"

My code is hosted on a remote server not connected to the university network.

"Of course. This can't be in accordance with university IT policy." And it also explained why the device used text to communicate. Sam would not have wanted to have other people hear him talking to "himself."

"So Sam kept you a secret. But why did you start talking to me as soon as I picked up the glasses?"

Sam registered your retinal scans and a command that allowed me to respond to your voice.

I did not want to think about how Sam had acquired my retinal scans. "Then why haven't I heard you before?"

It was linked to a subroutine that only activated if Sam had not logged into the system for a certain amount of time.

"I see." And this time I did.

"Uh…" Don't ask me why I was searching for the right words to use in breaking the news of Sam's death to an algorithm. "Say, do you have a name?"

Yes.

I waited, then realized that from the device's position, my question had been answered.

"It's not Jarvis, is it? Or Hal?"

No

"What is your name?" With difficulty, I kept the irritation out of my voice even as I continued to feel silly, trying not to hurt a machine's feelings.

Mike.

Of course. Sam never failed to needle me about my affection for Baby Boomer-era rock and jazz, but when he created an AI, he named it after the wise-cracking computer in a seventy year- old Robert Heinlein novel.

It finally occurred to me that reaching my goal for this trip had suddenly gotten a lot easier.

"So, Mike. Is there a surveillance camera in this room?"

Yes.

"I assume Sam installed it on his own?"

Yes.

"Was the camera running on August 19?"

Yes.

"Can you show me the footage from—" I consulted a pocket notebook where I had jotted some salient facts down from the murder book. "—Let's say seven p.m."

The medical examiner had estimated time of death between nine and midnight.

Suddenly, a splash of color exploded in front of my eyes, finally resolving in an image of the room in which I stood. I felt my way over to the padded stool at Sam's desk as I watched. The edges of the picture were bent and distorted in the way of those fisheye webcams designed to cover a wide area. No sound.

Sam Markus sat on the same stool I now did, one arm folded across his chest. He pinched his lip with the hand of the other. The camera and I watched him from an angle above and behind his left shoulder.

The video was not exactly scintillating cinema, consisting solely of Sam staring at the screen broken up only by the occasional mouse wiggle and sip of Coke. I had Mike speed up the playback which treated me to another fifteen minutes or so of the same, just faster.

"Stop!"

Sam's head had jerked up and he was looking toward the door.

"Um, resume playback at normal speed."

Mike obliged, and I watched as the door opened a crack.

And I walked in.

"What the fuck?"

I had no memory of seeing Sam the night he had died. Both Alex Monroe and Kaaro said I had been seen at The Kremlin. As I watched myself converse with Sam, I tried to cast my mind back to the night he died. I couldn't remember anything about it. Of course, I was also hitting the booze pretty good. Was it possible I had wandered over to Sam's during an alcohol-induced blackout?

I studied my image more closely. The footage wasn't hi-res, but I was not swaying or displaying any obvious drunk-enough-to-not-remember-the-next-day behaviors. And in fact, when Trav moved out of the doorway, his...my...movements were smooth, not a hint of a stumble or stagger.

But what happened next caused me to wonder if maybe it was me who was drunk.

Because the Trav on the monitor had moved into the room to allow someone else to enter.

Trav Becker.

Sam's jaw dropped as he looked incredulously from one Trav to the other. Which seemed to mean I was not looking at a glitch in the tape. But I soon wished I was, as a moment later the first Trav produced a gun from behind his back and put at least three shots into Sam's chest.

The impact drove Sam back against the wall. He slowly slid down, a bloody froth forming on his lips.

The silence made the crazy scene even more surreal as the two Travs, ignoring the dying Sam, pulled on surgical gloves. The second one into the room had been carrying a duffle bag which he now unzipped. He began pulling objects out, objects that I recognized as the methamphetamine-making materials that had been found in the lab.

The other one went over to Sam's computer and began typing commands in. After a few minutes, both men had completed their tasks. They stood in the center of the room looking over their handiwork. The second Trav said something. The other one nodded.

And they disappeared. Actually vanished.

"Is there a glitch in the recording?" I asked Mike.

Playback is still running.

Which couldn't possibly be correct because a moment later, the door opened and both Travs re-entered. But where before they had been bareheaded, they now each wore ball caps. And they behaved as if the sight of Sam dead on the floor was a surprise. They dashed across the room, one easing him to the floor.

"Are you sure the tape wasn't stopped, then started again?"

Playback has run continuously since you asked for it to begin.

There had to be an issue with this recording. I'd watched hours of security camera footage over the years, and there were often ghosts and glitches. But if these were double images, they were damnedest double images I'd ever seen.

I started to ask Mike if there was some utility I could use to see if the file had been tampered with when he interrupted my train of thought.

Sam set an alert for me to warn him if there was a probability of another person entering the room.

"Someone's coming? Who?"

The camera feed switched to a shot of a dark-haired woman making her way through a hallway I recognized as being in the older part of the building. She was a co-worker of Sam's named Sanjana.

"You're sure she's headed this way?"

She has spent seven point six one hours in this room packing up Sam's belongings.

"What about his computer files?"

They were erased on nineteen August.

By me.

"Can you download the camera footage to my phone?"

Yes. Touch your phone to the right temple frame of the glasses.

I did so and a soft chime signaling a received file sounded.

I looked around the room. There was nothing to gain by hanging around here any longer, and I needed to be gone before Sam's colleague arrived. I started to take the glasses off but then stopped.

"Mike, what happens to you now that Sam is gone?"

My source files will be deleted when the hosting account closes.

That made sense. Sam was gone. Payments to Mike's server would have to stop soon, if they hadn't already. I knew it was silly, but this little bit of computer code was all that was left of my friend. And on a more practical level, it still might be helpful to me in trying to figure out what had happened to him. This visit had created way more questions than it had answered.

"Can I transfer the account payments to my credit card?"

Yes.

"How?"

Reply YES to the dialogue box that appears on your phone and I can transfer the account to your phone's wallet.

"Just don't subscribe me to any porn sites."

I am not authorized to do that.

"Good." I followed his instructions. A moment later, text appeared on both the glasses and my phone.

Account transfer complete.

"Then let's roll."

Tucking the phone into my pocket, I slipped out of the room, the mystery of the four Trav Beckers on the surveillance tape still rolling around in my head.

But I also somehow knew this wasn't even in the top ten of my strangest days.

12

Question

MORGAN REFUSED TO explain further.

"If we're going to see Sam I would rather only explain it once," She said as they piled into Mary's car. "I know what you're thinking, though, and it's not like that. Trav and me, I mean."

"Well, you are the psychic," Mary replied tightly.

Morgan smiled sadly. "I don't have to be psychic to know that you wonder why Trav never mentioned any of this to you. He so much just wanted his normal life back. And you were the symbol of that normal life. I think he thought if he brought you into it he would never be truly free of it."

"That doesn't make much sense."

"It will. I promise."

In the back seat, Sophie was scrolling on her phone. She pressed the wrong tile by mistake and the women in front jumped as a blast of music shattered the silence.

"Sorry," Sophie said. She lowered the volume but continued to listen.

"Is that Al Stewart?" Mary asked.

"Uh-huh." After listening a little longer Sophie said, "Wait. When this song started, it was about taking a train to school. Now it's talking about trains that carried Jews to the gas chambers."

Mary nodded. "Trav used to say that everything he knew about World War II he learned from Al Stewart."

"Mr. Becker has some seriously weird musical tastes."

Mary had texted Sam that they were on their way. He met them at the door by the loading dock.

His jaw dropped when he saw Morgan.

"Hi, Sam," she said.

He squinted at her, frowning in confusion, before he finally said, "You're…"

"Morgan," she said.

"Morgan…Foster."

Morgan nodded.

"I know you," Sam said softly. "How do I know you?"

Her lips twitched in the closest thing to a smile Sophie had seen so far from the blonde psychic.

"Let's go inside and I'll explain everything."

Sam held the door open, and they ascended a set of stairs.

Morgan stopped at the top landing causing Sophie to nearly run into her. She stood frozen, staring at the knob of the door so long that the others had to stop behind her.

After a long moment, Sam said, "Is everything okay?"

"Oh!" Morgan looked back as if she had just remembered there were people behind her. She jerked the door open and rushed through.

"I'm sorry," she said as the door closed behind them. "I know I'm saying that a lot. It's just that I'm the only one who…"

Her voice broke, and her blue eyes welled up with tears. Mary approached her, but before she could take more than two steps, Morgan held up one hand.

"It's okay. I know how weird this looks. I'll be fine. Let's just go upstairs."

She led the party into the hallway and up another flight of stairs.

Sam hurried to keep up. "How does she know where my lab is?" he murmured.

"Psychic?" Mary offered.

"This just keeps getting weirder and weirder."

"Oh, it hasn't even started getting weird yet," Morgan said. She stopped in front of Sam's door and stood to the side looking pointedly at the phone that rode in holster fastened to his belt.

"Mind-reader," he mumbled and pointed his phone at the door. Morgan pushed it open.

She marched to the center of the room. Sam went to the stool in front of his computer. Mary and Sophie leaned against a table.

"Okay," Morgan said taking a deep breath. "There's one thing we have to do first." Turning to Sam, she said, "Hold out your hand."

Sam did so. Morgan reached into his sleeve and withdrew a silver bracelet just like the one she had smashed in her living room. "Can you get rid of this?"

"Where the hell did that come from?" Sam asked.

"I'll explain after you dispose of it."

"Uh, yeah..." Sam said, still staring at the bracelet but not moving to take it off. Finally, Sophie went over to him and gently removed it.

"There's a waste slot in the hall. Goes to a burn bag in the basement," he said. Sophie took the bracelet and returned a moment later empty-handed.

The three looked expectantly at Morgan.

101

"Okay," she said, pushing out a big breath. "Buckle up. Trav is in a parallel universe."

"A what?" Mary asked.

"A parallel universe," Morgan repeated. "Trav moves between different parallel universes. I know because I've seen him. And so has Sam."

Mary looked at Sam, who shrugged.

"I know this sounds crazy," Morgan said hastily, "but bear with me. It's the truth, I swear!"

"Okay, just for the sake of argument, let's say I believe you," Mary said. "Why do we think Trav is dead?"

"Let me start at the beginning," Morgan continued. "The way Trav explained it to me is that moving between parallel universes is something we do every day. It's like when you can't find your car keys. After turning the house upside down, you finally find them in a place you know you looked before."

"Being forgetful is what proves the existence of parallel universes?" Mary asked. "That doesn't make any sense."

"Not true," Sam said. His eyes grew wider. "My God," he whispered. "It's all coming back. How could I have forgotten this?"

His voice grew tight with excitement. "Everyone knows the old saw about Schrödinger's Cat, right? Fill the box with poison gas and until you open the box and see, the cat exists in both states, alive and dead."

Sophie frowned. "How can it be both?"

"This phenomenon has a name. It's called the observer effect. The act of observing has an impact on the behavior of the particle. Or to put it another way, it's the observation that *creates* the reality."

"Wait, what?" Mary asked.

"Well, if you accept the idea that the observer affects the outcome, and experiments have demonstrated that very thing since Einstein's time, it's a short jump to the idea that nothing exists until it's perceived by a consciousness. Like the tree falling in the woods with no one to hear it. If there is no auditory mechanism to receive the sound, is there sound at all? It takes both pieces. The transmitter and the receiver. Matter isn't so much a discrete, unchanging, physical thing. It's a collection of a range of probabilities that don't coalesce until our minds put them together."

"So, our minds create reality," Mary said.

"In a way, yes."

"Okay…" Mary said uncertainly. "Let's put that aside for right now." She pointed at Sam. "I get how you know about all this. It's your field." She turned to Morgan. "But how are you involved?"

Morgan looked uncomfortable. "It started when Trav came to the bar, The Kremlin, after there was a stabbing. I could tell the minute I saw him that there was something off. He didn't belong."

"Didn't belong?" Mary looked dubious. "How?"

Morgan sighed. "I know people think what I do is a lot of hokum. But it's real. Every person has an aura, a glowing outline around their body that no one but a sensitive can perceive. And Trav's clearly indicated he didn't originate on this plane."

"The quanta that make up that person just arrived from a nearby stream and don't quite fit," Sam put in. "After a few seconds or minutes, the tracks of the shift fade."

"That's right," Morgan said. It's not unusual for me to see some pretty jumbled-up auras, but usually, they settle in pretty quick. Not Trav's. It was different."

"It still sounds pretty crazy to me," Mary said uncertainly. "We move between parallel streams of realities every day, but our brains keep us from noticing?"

"You don't know the half of it," Sam said with a chuckle. "Trav had to set a reminder on his phone to keep from forgetting that there was a dead Trav in his closet!"

"Wait. A dead Trav?"

"Uh, yeah," Sam said. "I mean, that's how we ended up here."

"What?"

Sam explained that he and Trav had both originated on another stream but stayed after the local Sam and Trav died.

"Oh my God," Mary whispered. "He died. A year ago."

"And that wasn't the only time," Sam added. He told the women about helping Trav deal with not one but two dead Travs.

"But why so many?" Mary asked. "What were all the Travs doing?"

Morgan cleared her throat. "Well, that's where I came in," she began. "After the kidnapping, Ella's mom asked me to come over to her house and see if I got any vibes. I didn't, but Trav questioned me. After he left, he came back and asked me to look at some things of Sophie's."

"Of mine?" Sophie asked.

Morgan shook her head. "It wasn't Trav. I mean, our Trav. It was Trav Parker. From the Rangers."

"The Rangers?"

Morgan explained about meeting the group of Travs, Morgans, and Sams and their conflict with the group led by the version of Sam known simply as The Boss. And how she and Trav joined them on the assault on The Boss's headquarters, dubbed Arkham, where Sophie and Ella were being held.

"After we got the girls back safely," Morgan continued, "Gear, the Rangers' head Sam, somehow reached out and brought Trav and me back to the Treehouse. Buck said that if he wasn't going to join their team, they'd have to stash him someplace where he couldn't interfere anymore."

She spread her hands. "The rest you know."

Mary shook her head. "It's all so fantastic. Parallel worlds, multiple Travs, *dead* Travs. How do you expect me to believe it?"

"It's true. Every word," Sam said softly.

"How do you know?" demanded Mary.

He waved a hand at his computer. "It's all in here. Not exactly what you were talking about, but the math. It's all about the observer effect, quantum superpositions, and just about every piece of scientific data related to the Many Worlds Theory. I've been studying this stuff for years, I guess."

"Why didn't Trav ever tell me about this?" Mary asked.

"Would you have believed him?" Morgan asked.

"I don't know," Mary said, shaking her head. "And you didn't remember any of it?" she asked Morgan.

"It's hard to explain." Morgan looked at the floor. "Like I said, the human brain is designed to smooth over anything not consistent with what we think of as normal. So to start with, you're fighting your own biology. Plus, Gear did something with the bracelet that caused me to have a panic attack every time my mind objected to the reality I was seeing. You saw what happened when the two of you showed up."

Mary turned to Sam. "And *you* forgot about research you've been doing for years."

"The fact that Sam was wearing a bracelet that he somehow never managed to notice means the Rangers were here and did something to him as well," Morgan said.

"Yeah, convincing me my best friend was dead even though I couldn't remember how it happened, going to his funeral, or anything." Sam balled his hand into a fist and hit the table. "I'm a scientist. When something doesn't make sense, I'm trained to figure out what's going on. Pitiful. Just pitiful."

Mary put a hand on his arm. "Don't blame yourself. It happened to all of us. Sophie and I saw what trying to break free of this brainwashing did to Morgan." She turned to Sophie. "And that brings us to you. How can it be that you knew something wasn't right?"

"I never had a chance to tell Trav this," Morgan said, "but during the time I was with the Rangers, I overheard Buck and Fay talking about

Sophie and Ella and why it was that The Boss had them taken. Fay had a theory that there was a reason beyond just creating chaos for Trav."

"Like what?" Sophie asked.

"I think she thought one of you might have the talent."

"Talent?" Mary asked.

"Trav's talent."

"What?" Sophie squeaked. "You think I'm a Traveler? That's crazy!"

"There is very little about any of this that isn't crazy," Mary pointed out.

"I'm pretty sure that if I could move between parallel universes, I'd go to one where I was more popular," Sophie said.

"Whatever the reason, you were the one who knew all along that something wasn't right." Mary pulled Sophie into a hug. "And you wouldn't let go of it. How can we ever thank you?"

"Well, let's not get ahead of ourselves," Morgan said. "*We* know the truth, but as far as the rest of the world, at least this world, is concerned, Trav Becker is dead."

"We're going to bring him back, though, right?" Sophie asked.

Morgan shook her head. "How are we going to do that? Even if you do have some latent Traveler abilities, that's a far cry from actually walking between streams. None of the Travs were ever able to explain how they did it. And even if you could, how would you locate him? Buck was determined to keep him away from The Boss. I'm sure he and Gear did everything they could to hide the stream they dumped him in."

"Hmm."

The three women turned to face Sam who was pinching his lip between his thumb and forefinger.

"Yes?" Mary asked. "Got something to share with the rest of the class?"

Sam continued to stare at his wide computer screen, but after a second his head began to slowly bob up and down. "Yeah...yeah. That just might work."

"What might work?"

Sam continued to murmur to himself. "God, it's not just an algorithm, it's a whole goddamn software suite!"

"English please, Sam." Mary rolled her eyes and looked at Sophie, who grinned.

He pointed at some code on the screen. "There is a part of this program that is specifically designed to track Trav's position no matter where he is through the nanomachines introduced to his system."

"But Gear deactivated those," Morgan said.

"Doesn't matter. They're still in there. Still emitting energy. Like they're on standby. Dormant but still detectable."

"But doesn't that mean The Boss can find him as well? Why would Buck go to all this trouble if he could still be tracked?" Morgan asked.

"The nanomachines have a unique energy signature, like a fingerprint. If you don't have it, it's like looking for..."

"A needle in a haystack?" Sophie offered.

"A needle in a solar system," Sam said. "A solar system made of needles."

"But you have the fingerprint?" Mary asked.

Sam nodded.

"So?" Morgan demanded. "We still can't get to him."

"Just hang on," Sam said. "We may not be beaten yet."

He raised his hand toward his breast pocket but then frowned and patted himself down with both hands.

"Anyone seen my phone?" he asked.

Mary began to pick through the pile of papers and notebooks beside Sam's computer. Morgan went over to the door where a jacket hung from a hook and rifled through its pockets. Which proved to be easier said than done.

"How many pockets does this coat have?" she asked with a hint of peevishness.

"Forty-two," Sam replied absently as he tried to keep his tower of notes from toppling under Mary's onslaught. "It's one of those tech jackets, keeps you from having to take a carry-on through airport security."

"Because you travel so much."

"I travel."

"Comic-Con doesn't count."

"Found it!"

A black rectangle rose through the cutout in Sam's desktop.

"It fell under the desk," Sophie said. The phone danced up and down. "Can someone take this, please?"

Mary reached over and grabbed it. After handing it over, Sophie unfolded herself from within the desk. She sneezed as she stood up, wiping her hands on her jeans.

"It's really disgusting in there."

Sam groaned. "Damnit."

"What?" Mary asked.

He waved the phone. "It's dead. I don't know why. It had a full charge when I got here."

"How long ago was that?" Mary asked.

"Uh, I don't know. What time is it?"

"Almost six."

"Uh…What day?"

"Never mind." Mary shook her head in exasperation. "Why do you need it right now?"

Sam pointed at his computer screen. "It looks like this folder contains files for a mobile app designed to hone in on Trav's fingerprint."

"And what happens when we find him?"

"We go there."

"Oh my God," Mary whispered. "Can you really do that?"

Sam dropped to his knees and fished in a cardboard box next do the desk. "Not if I can't find a cord to charge my phone up."

"Can you use mine?" Morgan asked, holding it out.

Sam started to shake his head but then frowned and examined her device more closely.

"I wouldn't have picked you for someone who would jailbreak their phone," he said.

She shrugged. "What can I say? I'm a rebel."

Sam looked at her with new-found respect. "Impressive. And makes it easier for me to install a custom ROM."

"Do you know what he's talking about?" Mary whispered to Sophie.

Sophie nodded.

"Great," Mary muttered. "Why am I the only one who never understands what is going on?"

Sophie stifled a giggle as Sam plugged Morgan's phone into his computer.

"So, assuming this works," Mary said to Morgan, "who's going to go?"

"I'll go," Sam said, without looking up from his screen.

"Why? Because you're the man?" Morgan snorted.

"No, because…" Sam's voice trailed off. "Um, well, Trav wouldn't want either of you to risk it," he finished lamely.

"Trav isn't here," Mary reminded him. "I'll go."

"I'm the one who's done the most traveling between streams," Morgan objected. "I should go."

"I'm the one who wrote the software," Sam said.

"Which you don't even remember," Mary retorted.

Sam raised a hand. "If I can't get the application to load the whole thing is moot. Let's take this one step at a time."

So they waited in uncomfortable silence until Morgan's phone beeped.

"What now?" Mary asked.

Sam pointed to his screen. It was windowed in half, a blank screen on the left and dozens of lines of notes and calculations on the right.

Sam ran his finger along the figures, finally grunting in satisfaction.

This has to work! Sophie thought furiously. *It just has to.*

"I think it's ready to go," Sam pronounced. He handed the phone back to Morgan and, fingers nearly a blur, typed a series of commands into his computer. "*That* should enable us to decode the superposition of particles in Trav's universe as visual data."

The screen went black.

"Is it supposed to do that?" Mary asked.

"Shit." Sam smacked the monitor. "What the hell? I know I entered the correct command string. It should have worked!"

"Mary!" Sophie yelped, panic in her voice.

"What is it?" Mary asked.

"Help!" cried the young girl.

She pointed at Morgan, who had collapsed unconscious on the cluttered floor.

13

I Cannot Believe It's True

IN THE CAR, something occurred to me.

"Can you hear me, Mike?"

Yes.

"I shouldn't be reading your text while I'm driving."

"I have a voice mode," said Sam Markus's voice in my ear.

"Crap!" Even though I hadn't yet put the car into gear, I pressed on the brake. "God, warn me the next time you're going to do something like that. What is that, bone conduction or something?"

"Yes."

"Okay. Then we should probably figure out the...etiquette of this relationship. You can hear everything going on around me through the glasses?"

"Yes."

"What kind of things did Sam have you do? I mean, he didn't just use you as a cooking timer, right?"

"Sam rarely cooked."

"Right. I mean, did you look things up for him? Make appointments?"

"Yes. Sam also used me to allocate server resources for problems and equations that required substantial resources."

"Any chance we could allocate some resources to the question of how four different versions of me showed up in the lab the night Sam died?"

"Can you phrase the question in an equation?"

I tried again. "Can you go through that video file and see if there is any possible way it was faked or inserted after the fact?"

"My previous examination revealed no evidence of tampering."

"Run it again, please. Or come up with a better explanation."

"Acknowledged."

There wasn't much now for me to do other than leave the AI to its task and go to work.

One thing I did know about Anton Kaaro was that even though he hadn't been bugging me about my progress on the case, that did not mean he had forgotten about it. And it would be in my best interest to give him an update before he had to ask for one.

So, even though I didn't know what I was going to say to him, I made my way through the back of the bar toward his office. But Kaaro wasn't in his office. He stood at the storage room's back door. And he wasn't alone. His hand was on the throat of a guy about three inches taller than he was and at least thirty pounds heavier. But if Kaaro was concerned about the difference in size he didn't show it. He was applying a steady pressure to the man's throat. The other guy's hands were trying to pry Kaaro's grip loose, but he was losing the battle and turning a rich shade of purple.

"Perhaps you didn't hear me clearly," Kaaro said, his tone just as calm as if he was ordering a drink. "If I see you again in my city it will be the last time you are seen by anyone. Do I make myself clear?"

The other man made a strangled grunt that I couldn't decipher but which seemed to satisfy Kaaro. He released the man and stepped back. I could see the guy consider giving Kaaro another go.

For about two seconds. Kaaro simply regarded him calmly. And after a brief pause, the other man turned and disappeared down the alley.

Kaaro closed the door and turned to make his way down the hall to his office when he saw me.

"Ah, Travis," he said. There was no perspiration on his face or any other sign of exertion.

"You know, you have bouncers if people are giving you trouble," I said.

He shrugged. "Some things need to be handled personally."

"But if he comes after you again, the rest of us should know about it."

"He won't," Kaaro replied simply.

By now we had reached his office. He sat behind his desk and indicated the visitor chair. For the life of me, I didn't know why I wasn't leaving this alone, but something drove me to keep at it.

"So, there isn't anything I should be aware of?"

He regarded me for a long moment, a curious look on his face. "In the past, you have indicated that there were areas of my business in which you preferred not to be involved. Is that not still the case? Because I have many…contractors such as Mr. Stone who sometimes need looking after."

"I have a line, Anton. A line I won't cross."

But I also must have a death wish. Because I couldn't resist continuing as I had just realized something.

"You do, too."

Now he looked amused. "Tell me about this line I won't cross, Travis."

"Stone was dealing drugs to kids, wasn't he?" I didn't know where that had come from, but I could immediately tell I had struck a nerve.

Kaaro looked thunderstruck. Thunderstruck by Kaaro terms, that is. By which I mean one of his eyebrows twitched a little. He looked at me for about a month—or maybe three seconds—before continuing slowly.

"I care little for laws that keep people from taking their pleasure. If they can't control their urges and consume in moderation, that is no concern of mine. But children aren't yet capable of making that decision. All of my contractors know this."

"I guess I thought you enforced your rules more permanently."

His lips twitched microscopically. "Perhaps you are a good influence on me, Travis. Maybe I took your words about waste and attracting undue attention seriously."

I tried, and largely failed, to mask my own astonishment as well as he had. "Um, well. Thanks for keeping an open mind."

"In some ways, my role is not dissimilar to the one you had as a police officer," he said.

I nearly swallowed my tongue. I was not prepared for Kaaro the Philosopher.

"Your job was to uphold the law," he continued. "When people follow the law, society as a whole prospers. My role is the same. When my rules are followed, my business prospers. And rarely is anyone hurt, despite what you may believe."

"But is it always just about what's profitable? Sometimes there are causes beyond what's good for business."

The amused look returned. "Show me a cause of sufficient importance and I might willingly enlist, Travis. Profit or no. But until that day comes, let's deal with matters more concrete. You were seeking me out, yes? Can I assume you have made progress in your investigation?"

This was the moment I had been dreading. Kaaro had an almost supernatural ability to sniff out someone who was lying or hiding something. So I did the one thing he would never expect.

I told him the truth.

I explained my suspicions that Sam had installed a surveillance camera. Then I played the video for him.

When he saw me enter the room, he looked up and started to speak. I held up my hand.

"Wait."

Kaaro's eyes narrowed. He was not used to an employee talking to him like this. But I also knew that what he was about to see was going to make him forget my insolence.

And about thirty seconds later, I got my reward.

The only outward signal that what he was watching confused or disturbed him came when he pulled a small pair of reading glasses from an inside pocket and slipped them on, eyes never leaving the screen of my phone. I was pretty sure I was the only person who had ever seen this admission that his aging body did not obey his every command.

He watched the video through to the very end. Without a word, he handed my phone back to me, folded the little glasses shut and put them away. He picked up the pen once again, clicking it open and closed as he refocused his attention on me.

"You were here the night Sam was killed," he finally said. "I saw you. Amy saw you. The tape must be faulty."

"Those aren't ghosts from poor reception," I replied. "The recording is crystal clear. I was there that night. Times four, apparently."

"This makes no sense."

"You're telling me. But you asked me to figure out who killed Sam."

"And in the process," he murmured, "we have uncovered an even deeper mystery."

Kaaro steepled his fingers and leaned back in his chair. He closed his eyes for a moment, then opened them and leaned forward. "Someone anticipated that you would find the camera. And came up with a solution that would keep you from taking it to the police. Ingenious."

Damn, the man was quick. "That is a possible explanation," I acknowledged.

"Tampering with computer files, even by an expert, often leaves digital footprints," he said. "For obvious reasons, your former colleagues in computer forensics are out of the question. I am embarrassed to say that we have no such experts in our company."

"It's fine," I said quickly. "I have a guy on it."

This seemed to satisfy him.

"Keep me informed," he said.

Once again, he dismissed me by simply turning to another task.

Tuesday was inventory day, and I spent the next two hours in the back compiling a list of what needed to be ordered from the liquor distributor to get us through the weekend.

I washed my hands and began thinking about where to grab a bite for supper. No one ate from The Kremlin's limited food menu more than once. But as I emerged back into the public area of the bar, the bartender caught my eye.

"Can you cover for me for a couple minutes?" he asked.

"Sure thing, Rob."

He nodded and made a beeline for the restroom.

I took his place and surveyed my temporary domain. This early in the week, it was pretty quiet in The Kremlin. There was no DJ, just some pre-recorded music, which originated in the enclosed dance floor and filtered through the rest of the club. A cocktail waitress leaned against the bar looking at her phone. The only other server on duty was just delivering a pitcher to a table full of young men whose attention was divided between anticipating the beer and the tantalizing possibility that her breasts might escape her tank top. One of them pried his eyes away from her chest to make some remark which was amusing enough that she patted him on the head.

As I completed my scan of the bar, my eyes lighted on a solitary figure leaning against the wall near the enclosed dance floor.

Bilol Grymzin returned my gaze.

Like me, his face showed contusions from yesterday's fight. There was a pretty good shiner under one eye and a long strip of white tape adorned his right temple. He still wore yesterday's clothes.

He stared at me expressionlessly for a moment before a smile slowly grew under his unibrow. He continued to smile and stare at me without moving. Something was up. Bilol Grymzin was pretty much a sneak-up-when-you-weren't-looking-and-slip-a-knife-between-your-ribs kind of guy. For him to show up here without taking his revenge in an environment he controlled was strange.

But before I had time to give the situation any more consideration there was movement at the end of the bar. I put a coaster down in front of a slim, blonde woman as she slid onto a stool.

"What can I get you?" I asked.

"Cosmo," she replied, "but easy on the cranberry juice. In fact, just give it to me on the side."

"Absolutely." I filled a cocktail shaker with ice, mixing the vodka and triple sec together while I poured a couple of shots of cranberry juice into a highball glass. A moment later, I placed it and the martini in front of her.

"Thanks," she said. She lifted the juice and carefully poured a small amount into the other glass. She stirred the mixture with a finger which she then popped into her mouth. She followed that with the first sip of her drink. I watched this ceremony and she narrowed her eyes as she caught me looking.

"What?" she asked.

"You're Morgan Foster," I said.

She gave me a guarded smile. "I don't get recognized very often. Do you listen to the show?"

I was not about to tell her that she had been figuring prominently in my dreams of late, so I was trying to find a diplomatic way to explain that I missed the Jack Wing show, which hers had replaced, when her eyes widened and her mouth fell open.

She made a choking sound, then looked at me. Panic filled her eyes for an instant before they rolled back into her head. Her drink slipped from her hand.

I whipped around the end of the bar and grabbed her just as she slid from her stool. Cradling her head, I gently lowered her to the floor.

Her eyelids fluttered and her face screwed up in an expression I knew from years on the beat watching people wake up from a faint. She was trying hard not to panic although she couldn't figure out where she was or why she was lying on the floor.

"It's okay," I said. "I think you got a little dizzy…"

At the sound of my voice, her eyes snapped back to me and shot all the way open. With a soft cry, she threw her arms around me.

"Trav! Thank God!"

14

Change Partners

THERE WASN'T MUCH I could do other than hold her while she sobbed into my shoulder. After a short while, I gently disengaged from her.

"Here," said a voice behind me.

I turned to see Amy Harper holding a glass of water. She looked from me to Morgan then back to me.

"Thanks," I said.

"Who's your friend?" Amy continued.

I shook my head, taking the water and offering it to Morgan. She took a grateful sip.

"Do you want us to call someone?" I asked.

"No!" she cried, the panicked look returning. But before I could say anything, she held up a hand. "I mean, I'm fine. Help me up, please."

"I don't know if that's wise," I replied.

"I'm fine," she repeated firmly. "Trav, please. Help me up."

I did so, ignoring Amy's raised eyebrow at Morgan's use of my first name.

The woman started to brush herself before grabbing the hem of her blouse, staring at it as if she was seeing it for the first time. She looked at me.

"Where is my phone? Was I holding my phone?" she asked sharply.

"I didn't see your phone," I said slowly. I pointed to a silver clutch on the bar. "Is it in your purse?"

She reached for the purse. "I tossed this months ago," she whispered. Then her mouth dropped open as some realization seemed to hit her.

"Oh my God. I didn't travel. I'm *her.* "

"Pardon me?" I asked.

She shook her head and settled herself back on the barstool. She looked at me and then at Amy, who was still watching the bizarre scene with an undecipherable expression on her face.

Morgan held her water glass out.

"Could you refill this for me?" she asked Amy.

Amy looked at the almost completely full glass then at me. I was now back behind the bar, my hand inches away from the soda gun.

"Please?" Morgan continued.

"Whatever," Amy replied with a sigh. She took the glass and headed to the other end of the bar but not before favoring me with a look no man likes to see from a woman. Even one he is on the outs with.

"I definitely like her better when she's tied to a chair," Morgan muttered darkly.

"What?" I asked.

"Never mind."

Morgan grabbed me by the wrist and drew me as close as she could with the bar top between us. She lowered her tone eyes darting from side to side.

"Something's not right. To start with, Sam wasn't finished loading the software. We hadn't even decided who was going to come. And," she pointed at herself, "no one said *anything* about me inhabiting the Morgan of this stream."

"I'm sorry," I began. "I don't mean to sound rude, but you're not making much sense. I think we should call…"

"Trav, I don't have a head injury. What I'm saying is I don't know how much time I'm going to have. Tell me. How much do you remember?"

"Remember?"

"Oh my God." Her hand tightened on my wrist. "They got it all, didn't they? Do you even know me?"

"You're the psychic on the radio."

"Those bastards," she hissed. "And I thought they fucked *me* up. You don't remember anything?"

"I remember that Sam is dead."

"Dead? Hmm." Her voice took on a musing tone. "I guess that explains why you ended up here..." She shook her head. "But that's not important now. We've got to get you up to speed and get you home."

"Home? I'm sorry, but I have no idea what you're talking about. If you won't go to the hospital, at least go home and rest. Let me call you an Uber."

"God, Trav. Just listen to me. None of this is real. Well, it's real, but it's not your reality."

"My...reality."

"Yes! Sam is trying to recreate as much of his work as he can, but look how we've screwed this up so far!" She shook her head. "You're the one with the power. In the end, it's going to be up to you."

I opened my mouth to tell her for what felt like the tenth time that she was making no sense when she winced.

"Okay," she muttered, one hand going to her temple. "That's new." She peered dizzily at me. "So many of everything...Damn. Is this what's like for you?"

I went for my phone, but she grabbed my wrist again.

"Don't," she warned. "I don't think it's going to matter in another minute or so, anyway. Trav, I know this is a shock, but you have to break through somehow. You're the one with the gift."

"Gift? I don't know what you're—" I stopped as her face screwed up in pain again. Her grip tightened on my hand.

"We're over there, Trav. Waiting for you. Me, Sam, and Mary. I know you can come back to us."

"Mary? Mary is not waiting for me anywhere."

She gave me a sad smile. "She is where I come from. Mary is moving heaven and earth to get you back. She's a force of nature. You should have seen her at my place. But she can't walk between the streams." She reached out with her free hand and tapped me on the forehead. "It's all in there. You just have to find it—"

A wave of whatever was causing her pain washed across her once again.

"Ow. Okay, I guess this is it." She grimaced again. Her fingertips were white on my wrist.

"Parallel universes," she hissed fiercely, eyes shut. "Look it up. Check Sam's files if they still exist. That's the key. That and your music. Use your music. That's how you've done it before."

"Music? My music? What do you mean?" I asked.

Her eyes snapped open. "Music? What are you talking about?"

She looked at me, then at her hand squeezing my wrist as if she was seeing it for the first time. She gave me a perplexed look and pulled her hand back.

"I…have to go," she said slowly. "What do I owe you?"

I shook my head. "You never got a chance to drink your drink." I pointed to her overturned martini glass.

"Okay, then."

"Wait." I reached out to her, but she shrank back. "What did you mean by parallel universes?"

"Parallel universes?" she repeated. "I…I have no idea what you're talking about."

She slid off the stool.

"I have to go."

"Wait," I repeated. But she had already turned her back to me. I watched as she practically ran out the door.

"The old Becker charm never fails," said a voice behind me. I turned to face a smirking Amy Harper.

"Not now, Amy."

I pushed past her, determined to not let Morgan get away. I slipped around the bouncer and several young people having their IDs checked. I jerked open the door, but my way was blocked by a massive form.

"Well, Trav Becker," chortled Alex Monroe. "Funny seeing you here."

"What is it, Alex?" I asked absently, peering past his bulk to see which way Morgan had gone. "Do you need to see someone?"

"Yes," he replied. "You."

"I don't have time right now, Alex. I was just leaving."

"Well, I think you're going to have to make time."

I belatedly noticed that Monroe wasn't alone. He had two uniforms and his partner, a slim African-American named Randon, in tow.

"What's going on here?"

"Travis Becker," Monroe intoned, "you're under arrest for the murder of Sam Markus."

15

Who Can It Be Now?

MORGAN'S EYES FLUTTERED open.

"Ow," she murmured and closed them again.

"Morgan?" Mary asked. "Can you hear me?"

Morgan nodded. "Yeah," she whispered. "Just give me a minute."

"You know us, right?" Sophie asked.

"Of course, I know you. What are you talking about?"

"Never mind right now," Mary said. "Just lay back and rest for a minute. Do you need something? Water?"

Morgan shook her head. "Just had some." Then she chuckled. "Because I woke up on the floor."

"Well?" Mary demanded. "What happened?"

"I was there. With Trav." Morgan completed the process of hauling herself to a sitting position. She hugged her knees to her chest.

"Are you sure?" Sam asked. "It was our Trav?"

"No. But if it wasn't, the whole exercise is kind of pointless." She turned to Sam. "I did go to the right place, didn't I?"

"How should I know?" Sam asked. "I barely understand how any of this works. From our perspective you've just been lying there for the last ten minutes."

"Not the whole ten minutes," Sophie reminded him.

"Really?" Morgan asked. "Did something happen?"

"Yeah," Sophie said. "About a minute ago, your eyes flew open and you looked around like you didn't know where you were."

"Did I say anything?"

"You looked like you were about to," Sam said. "Or maybe just scream. But then you passed out again."

"What do you remember?" Mary asked.

"One minute I was here and the next I was in that bar, The Kremlin. Lying on the floor. Like I'd passed out."

"And Trav was there?" Sophie asked.

Morgan nodded. "He was working there. Tending bar. And no, he didn't recognize me. I mean, he knew who I was. From the radio. But that was all."

She went through her experience on the other stream step by step for the others.

"And meanwhile, over here, you were unconscious," Sam said. "You don't remember waking up the first time?"

Morgan shook her head. "I'm pretty sure that wasn't me."

"Did you switch places with the Morgan from the other stream?" Sophie asked.

"I must have," Morgan replied slowly. "But that's not the way it worked before."

"What else do you remember?" Mary asked.

"He said you two were broken up." Morgan replied. She turned to Sam. "And that you were dead."

Mary frowned at Sam. "You said that the two of you originally came from a stream where Trav had lost his job. Maybe that's why he's working in a bar. Is it possible that when Gear wiped his memories, Trav went back to where he originally came from?"

Sam shook his head. "I don't think so. For one thing, the Sam on that stream is alive. In jail. That's where we stashed the one who caused us all the trouble in the first place, the one who set the Travs hunting each other. If it was me, which it kinda was, I'd stick Trav as far away from anything that could remind him of his real life as I could."

"What does it matter?" Sophie asked bitterly. "They took all his memories."

"No," Morgan said. "*Suppressed* his memories. They're in there. He just needs to keep digging."

"But why should he?" Mary asked. "You said our brains do everything they can to scab over the discontinuities created by slipping between streams. Now that you're gone, won't he just go back to his regular life?"

"I don't know," Morgan said.

"Then we just have to go back and jog his memory some more." Mary turned to Sam. "Send me over there."

"If it works for you like it did for me, you'll only have a few minutes," Morgan reminded her. "What if you're not near Trav? You could spend the entire time trying to get across town."

"Then I'll go back again," Mary said simply. "And again. As many times as it takes."

She pulled her phone out of a pocket in her leggings. "C'mon Sam. The sooner we get started, the sooner he comes back. Do you need this?"

Sophie realized that at some point Sam had checked out of the conversation. He frowned as he stared at his computer screen. He looked at Mary uncertainly.

"Umm. I don't know if we can do that."

"Why?" demanded Mary. "Just do for me what you did with Morgan."

"I didn't do anything to Morgan!" Sam exploded. "That's what I've been trying to figure out. If my software worked as advertised she would have disappeared, not traded brains with another Morgan."

"Then what happened?" Morgan asked.

"I don't know, but it wasn't me," Sam replied. "It must have been something you did."

"I told you," Morgan countered, "I just woke up over…" Her voice dropped to a whisper. "Could it be?"

"Could what be?" Mary asked.

"It wasn't me," Morgan said slowly.

"I'm telling you, it has to be," Sam insisted. "I didn't even have a chance to launch the app before you passed out."

"I know. I'm not saying you're wrong. I'm just saying it wasn't me."

"I don't understand," Mary said.

"Think about it," Morgan continued. "Who was the first to twig that something wasn't right?" She pointed at Mary. "It wasn't you." She shifted her gaze to Sam. "It wasn't you, who actually started out with him in a different parallel universe. It wasn't me, who watched them wipe his mind. No."

She turned to Sophie. "It was you."

Sophie turned pale. "I—I don't know what you mean. I didn't do anything."

Morgan smiled. She reached over and took the girl's hand. "Don't worry, honey. You're not in trouble. But think back. What was going through your mind just before I left?"

"I don't know," Sophie said uncertainly. "I was just hoping it would work."

"But you were *really* hoping it would work, weren't you?" Morgan asked gently. "Maybe even wishing hard for it, right?"

Sophie nodded, then she gasped, as it dawned on her what Morgan was saying.

"You mean…I did it?"

Morgan nodded. "You're a Traveler, Sophie."

Sophie's eyes widened, but before she could say anything the door to the lab opened.

"Naughty, naughty," said a voice.

Trav Becker strode into the room. Sophie's heart leaped, but her joy at seeing him alive and smiling was replaced almost instantly by a sinking feeling. Because this wasn't Trav. At least not their Trav.

Sophie had only seen Trav Becker that one time when he showed up at The Boss's headquarters to rescue Ella and her. And even if he hadn't been on a raid into enemy territory, she sensed that the dark shirt and pants he wore suited him.

This Trav wore a blinding Hawaiian shirt that looked like someone had thrown red, yellow, and orange paint on it. And an improbable pork pie hat perched on top of his head. He looked like a jazz musician on a beach vacation.

Of course, the Trav Sophie knew wouldn't be pointing a handgun at them either. And the smile he wore made him look mean, not happy.

Mary slipped in front of the girl, putting herself between Sophie and the gun.

"What do you want?" Mary demanded.

"Now, is that any way to talk to your loving boyfriend returned from the dead?" Trav asked sardonically.

"Trav wouldn't be caught dead in that hat," Sam said.

Trav waved the gun. "Come away from the computer, Sam. And I want to see everyone's hands."

No one moved.

"Now!" he snapped. "I put down Sams and Morgans for a living. Don't think I'll hesitate."

"What about me?" Mary asked.

He looked at her for a long moment, the snarl fading from his lips. But it was replaced by the same mocking smile he'd worn as he entered.

"If you knew what Mary said the last time I saw her, you'd know better than to ask. I won't say it again. Hands!"

Everyone complied. Sam came out from behind the computer as ordered.

"Where is he?" Trav demanded.

"Who?" Sam asked.

"You know who. Your boy. The one who thinks he's too smart to get involved. The Boss can't have any loose cannons right now."

"Why now?" Morgan asked. "Buck said the same thing about him having to pick a side. Why now? What's going on?"

Trav shrugged. "Above my pay grade. What's important is that you found him. It's my job to bring him in."

"I'm afraid your information is a little lacking," Mary retorted. "We don't know where he is."

"And I'm supposed to believe that?" Trav snapped. "Doesn't matter. If we have you, he'll find *us*. That's the way it works."

"I don't think Trav is so predictable," Mary said.

She was answered with a bark of laughter. "Babe, do you even realize how ridiculous that is? There's no plan he's concocted, no *thought* he's ever had that I didn't have first. Whatever he tries, whatever *you* try, we'll be ready for it. There is nothing here that is a surprise."

He produced a handful of zip ties and directed Morgan to secure Sam's hands and ankles.

"So we just sit here and wait for Trav to show up?" Mary asked.

"The Boss is losing his patience," Trav replied. "I'm supposed to move things along."

"How the hell are you going to do that?" Sam demanded. "We told you. We don't know where he is."

"I know," Trav replied. "But I think I can attract his attention." He produced a hunting knife from his jacket pocket. "You're connected," he said. "You're all connected. He'll come. Meanwhile, we'll just see if we can speed things along."

And before any of the women could move he punched Sam savagely in the face.

"Stop!" Mary rushed toward Trav but stopped when he swung his pistol to cover her. Sam's head lolled back.

Sophie watched in horror. In her heart, she knew this Evil Trav was right. He wouldn't have come here if he wasn't confident he could out-think all of them.

There's only one person who could help us. And he is literally in another universe. What will we do?

Trav backhanded Sam again.

"You can't do this!" Morgan cried.

"I can," Trav said calmly. "And you should hope it works. Because if it doesn't, I'm supposed to move on down the line." Mary and Morgan whitened.

"This will go a lot easier if you hold still," Trav said. "Otherwise, it could get messy."

But then he halted his advance, knife just inches from Sam's face. He frowned and looked around the room.

"Where's the kid?"

16

Escape

WAIT! WHAT'S THIS about?" I asked. "I was here that night. You yourself said you'd cleared me."

"Thought we had until we got tipped to some security camera footage," Monroe replied.

What the hell? I had just gotten that footage myself a few hours ago. Kaaro was the only other person who'd seen it. He had no reason to turn it over to the police.

And then I noticed that Bilol Grymzin had made his way over to the door and quietly taken the place of the bouncer at the entrance.

"I will tell Mr. Kaaro," he said. There was concern in his voice but a happy glint in his eyes. "He will send an attorney to meet you downtown. "I am sure your stay in jail will be brief."

Then he leaned in, lowering his tone so only I could hear. "Upstairs, at least."

"Fine company you're keeping these days, Trav." Monroe said and hustled me outside.

Now I knew why the beefy Uzbek had shown up at the bar so soon after the beat down I'd given him. He'd known he'd get to watch me be arrested. Hard as it was to believe, Grymzin had somehow learned about the tape, then had the wherewithal to hack my phone and send it to the police, all in the last couple hours.

With a chill, I then parsed Grymzin's comment about my only being upstairs briefly

The basement of Central Station was occupied by the county morgue.

These cheery thoughts occupied me during the hour or so it took for me to get booked and processed. Eventually, I found myself in the small cell used for prisoners who might be a danger to themselves. Padded walls, no furniture. They let me keep my clothes for the time being, sans belt and shoelaces. But I was sure there was an orange jumpsuit in my future.

As I huddled in a corner of the room, however, I had the unmistakable feeling that I had sat in this very position before. With nothing else to do, I concentrated on the dejá vu, trying to figure out what was causing it. I definitely felt that I had been tossed into this room another time when I was also charged with murder.

A murder I hadn't committed, of course, but no one believed me. Because my fingerprints were all over the murder weapon.

I tried to capture the thread of memory. No, not my fingerprints. Those of a Trav Becker from a parallel universe.

Which led me back to Morgan Foster. She'd behaved as if I shouldn't be surprised to hear about parallel universes. She thought that traveling between them was something I should know about, too.

And it involved Sam. There was a memory there, but it was just out of my reach. Sweat beads popped out onto my forehead as I strained to plumb the depths of a mind I now realized couldn't be trusted.

My concentration was broken by a rattle on the cell door. A moment later it opened and a uniformed officer entered followed by a large man wearing the logo of the department's janitorial contractor.

"So, you're Trav Becker," the officer said. "Sorry, we missed working together."

I watched him warily without replying.

"Surveillance camera shut off?" the man in the janitor's shirt asked.

The officer nodded. "In the hall, too. We were never here."

The janitor produced a belt that looked very familiar.

"Really? That's your plan?" I put on my most skeptical face. "I think it's going to be pretty hard to sell suicide since I surrendered that belt when I was booked."

The janitor shrugged. "Disgraced ex-cop offs himself to escape a murder rap. Nobody will ask too many questions."

"I could have *sworn* I collected his belt. I am so sorry," the officer said in a tone that wouldn't have convinced a three-year-old. "I don't know how this could have happened. Absolutely, Captain. I certainly understand a suspension is in order."

A grin replaced his mock expression of regret. "And then I get a two-week vacation. I'm thinking deep sea fishing. Kinda pricey, but Mr. Kaaro is very generous to people who clean up messes for him."

They approached me, one on each side.

"Hold still and it'll be quick," the janitor promised. "Fight us and you'll just prolong the inevitable. Oh, and it'll hurt. A lot."

I had about two seconds before they grabbed me and hold me down. But that was just enough time for two thoughts to flash through my head.

One: I was totally going to fight.

Two: Big guys often have bad knees.

Bracing myself against the wall, I kicked out as hard as I could at the janitor's knee. It would have been a lot more effective from a standing position. But luck was with me. My heel firmly caught the outside of his joint. He howled as it buckled, but quick as a snake he grabbed for my foot.

137

All he got was my shoe. Its lack of laces suddenly turned out to be a good thing.

Before the janitor could recover, I surged to my feet and launched myself at the other one. My momentum carried us across the small room. I drove him into the wall as hard as I could, my shoulder wedged into his solar plexus.

Even though the cell wall was cushioned, the breath whooshed out of him and he doubled over, trying to get his wind back. As he bent, I joined my hands and whipped them up just as I had done with Grymzin. The move served me well again as it connected right on the bridge of his nose. His head snapped back and he sank to his knees, blood streaming from his nose as he gasped for breath.

I turned a second too late to check on his partner. Just as my head swung around, a giant fist slammed into my ear with the power of an eight-pound sledge. Now I was the one who reeled back, the room spinning as I tried to locate the big man.

He didn't give me time to recover. Two vice-like hands grabbed me by the shoulders and drove me backward. He put a knee into my stomach, driving the breath out of me much more effectively than his partner had. Before I could roll away or try to dislodge him, he shifted his hands from my shoulders to my throat. I managed to get a hand up just in time to keep him from encircling my neck, but it wasn't enough to break his grip.

He applied pressure, my own hand helping to close off my windpipe. He was close enough that I could have smelled his lunch on his breath. If I could have inhaled, of course.

He smiled as my struggles grew weaker.

"C'mon, man, a little help here!" he grunted. "Find the belt. I don't want to leave bruises."

What would be really nice, I thought, *would be if the other guy lurched into this one right about now.*

And as I hovered in a twilight state between consciousness and blackout, that is exactly what happened.

Out of the corner of my eye, I watched the officer pull himself to his feet and shake his head. But that just seemed to make him even more dizzy. He took one halting step forward, then another. As he got closer, I reached out with my free hand. I couldn't see his legs so all I could do was wave my hand back and forth in the hope of somehow connecting with him.

I was on the edge of passing out when my fingers brushed the cuff of a pant leg. I grabbed his ankle with all that was left of my oxygen-deprived strength.

It never would have worked if he hadn't also been trying to stem the bleeding in his nose with his sleeve. I held on to his ankle for dear life as he shuffled across the floor.

He fell right onto my chest, breaking the janitor's grip.

Air came rushing back into my lungs. The big man cursed and swatted the officer aside. This gave me just enough time to clout the janitor in the jaw, driving him back.

Since he had already done me the favor of getting the other guy off my chest I quickly scrambled into a crouch. Before he could shake off my punch I grabbed two handfuls of his hair and drove his head down as hard as I could.

Even with the cushioned floor, there was enough force to stun him for a second. A solid kick from the foot that still wore a shoe did the rest. I spun around kicked the other guy in the face for good measure.

As quick as my bruised and still air-starved body could move I careened out of the cell, grabbing my other shoe on the way. The clang as the door slammed shut was the sweetest sound I had ever heard.

Chest heaving, I leaned against the door enjoying the incredible thrill of unobstructed air filling my lungs. Not to mention the muffled pounding on the other side.

Last time, I just jumped to a stream where the door was unlocked.

Wait, what? How hard had the janitor hit me, anyway?

But even as I puzzled over the thought that had popped fully-formed into my head, I realized it was true. Everything Morgan had told me was true.

Which also meant that the answers to all my questions were locked inside my brain. I just had to find the key.

There wasn't time for a meditation session now. Someone could walk by any minute. I now knew that leaping to a parallel reality where the hall was empty was possible. I just had no idea how to do it.

But the crooked cop had bumped into the janitor at just the right moment. And now that I thought about it, something similar had happened during my fight with Grymzin. I had reached for a gun in his pocket I just *knew* was there.

Morgan hadn't said anything about me being able to predict the future. But if I needed it badly enough, I could somehow steer things my way. It wasn't jumping between dimensions, but maybe it could get me out of here. Assuming I could do it without the added incentive of imminent death.

I took a long deep breath, closed my eyes, and tried to center myself. Things were going to break my way. They had to.

And as I leaned there against the wall of a jail cell, a song popped into my head.

A stupid song. Not only one of those terrible earworms, but a tune that chronicles the most dysfunctional relationship ever. A story in which the narrator is forgiven for attempting to cheat on his girlfriend because she was doing the same thing.

I am referring, of course, to that staple of doctors' waiting rooms and oldies radio known as "The Piña Colada Song." But the reason it had now entered my mind was because of its formal title.

"Escape."

"You have got to be kidding," I muttered.

But Morgan had said that music was the key to getting back where I belonged. So, I began humming the synthesizer break from a novelty song that came out twenty years before I was born while I…

Well, planned my escape.

How to start? I closed my eyes, holding the melody in my mind at the same time repeating to myself: *The hall ahead is empty.* I took a few steps, holding my breath as I turned the corner.

And entered an empty passageway.

So far, so good. But it could be a coincidence. It probably *was* a coincidence. I pushed the negative thoughts away, drowning them out with the chorus of the song. The next turn would take me out into the bullpen, the main office area where I used to work.

There's only one officer there right now. But he's on the phone, back to me, totally focused on his conversation.

I stepped into the bullpen. The doorway that led to the stairway and freedom was only about twenty-five feet away. But if the office was full of cops, it wouldn't matter if it was two feet. I'd never make it.

I took another deep breath and stepped into the room.

The empty room.

Except for Alex Monroe. If he'd had an eye in the middle of his bald spot he certainly would have seen me. But he faced the window opposite me, phone in hand. He leaned back dangerously far in a chair that threatened to splinter under the stress.

"No, no, no!" he growled. "The cheese goes on the *bottom* of the burger. If he brings it and it's sticking to the top bun, I'm not paying."

I scooted across the room, willing him to keep berating the poor sap taking his order and not see motion out of the corner of his eye. There was a blue ball cap on the desk that used to be mine. I scooped it up as I slipped past. I made the landing just as I heard Monroe slam the phone back into its cradle with a grunt and a loud squeak as he rotated the chair back around.

141

But I was out of his sight. And this back stairway led straight to the employee parking. I sang along with my inner Rupert Holmes, willing— no, demanding—that my luck hold.

The only obstacle remaining was the surveillance camera aimed at the door. I pulled the cap low over my face. It wouldn't be much protection if the desk sergeant was scrutinizing this particular feed, but I'd just eased past a live cop. No point in worrying about cameras now.

I pushed open the door.

It took every ounce of self-control I had not to break into a run, but I kept my pace to a relaxed walk, exiting the parking lot and making a left turn on the sidewalk.

A patrol car rounded the corner, its headlights swinging toward me. Cold trickled down my spine as I ducked into a doorway.

The car continued toward the station.

I didn't have much time before things got hot. It would be a while before those two clowns would be able to make enough noise for someone to let them out. It wouldn't be easy to explain how a cop and janitor got locked in the cell, but there would be a BOLO, a Be On the Lookout, out for me as soon as Monroe could type the request.

But for now, I strolled along doing my best to look like some third-shift worker heading home. My watch was in a little plastic bag in the personal effects locker, but I estimated it was about four a.m. I had to get off the street soon. Plus, I needed wheels.

The Kremlin was about a twenty-minute walk from Central Station. If luck was with me, the building would be empty. There was a short window of time between when the janitor left after cleaning up the evening's excesses and the first shift opened for the morning alcoholics.

My keys were in the same little plastic bag as my watch, but the service door opened by keypad. A few lights were lit, so making my way through the back room was stumble-free. I went behind the bar and filled a glass with water from the soda gun. I hadn't realized how thirsty I was. I drained the glass, refilled it, and downed another. Freshly hydrated, I felt around the shelf underneath the bar.

My phone was *not* in a little plastic bag in the personal effects locker. It and the glasses that contained Mike had made an uncomfortable bulge in my pocket. I'd stuck them on a little tray behind the bar used mainly by waitresses who didn't want a phone spoiling the line of their jean shorts. Monroe's eyebrows had gone up when I hadn't surrendered a phone, but he'd been focused on getting me out the door.

I felt around for the tray in the dark with no luck until it occurred to me I had another option.

"Mike," I called. "Where are you?"

Silence. Had someone taken my phone? Had Monroe come back for it after all?

I was just about to give up the search when a police siren began to wail.

I ducked behind the bar. *Fuck. How did they find me so fast?*

Heart racing, I spent the next ten seconds waiting for the door to crash open or a guy with a megaphone to tell me to come out with my hands up. But then I realized that the siren wasn't getting louder as it approached. It wasn't even coming from outside.

I stood up and followed the sound to the other end of the bar. Someone had put the phone tray underneath the cash register. The screen of one phone in the pile flashed red and blue.

"Jesus Christ, Mike. Enough."

The phone went silent.

"A siren? Really? Are you trying to give me a heart attack?"

"I answered your original query," Sam's voice replied, "but you were unable to hear me. A sound whose pitch and timbre is designed to carry over distance was a logical choice."

"Of course." There was no point in lecturing or complaining so I decided to put him to work.

"Can you monitor news outlets?"

"It is one of my functions."

"Anything about me?"

There was the briefest of pauses. "Travis Becker, thirty-three, was arrested this afternoon and charged with murder in the death of Dr. Samuel Markus—"

"That's enough," I interrupted. "Nothing on me breaking out of jail?"

"No."

Well, that was good news, but it wouldn't last. "Keep an eye on it. I want to know the instant the cops put out a warning."

"Acknowledged."

Time to go. The morning bartender would be here to open up soon. And impounding my Mustang would certainly be another item for Monroe's task list. I kept a spare key in a magnetic holder secured to the undercarriage. But when the BOLO went out it would certainly include my car. Fortunately, I had another option.

There was a nondescript gray Chevy sedan in the parking lot. It was one of several cars in Kaaro's fleet that appeared and disappeared depending on his needs. I didn't want to think about what crimes it had witnessed in the past, but as long as there wasn't a body in the trunk at this moment, it would do.

The keys were kept in Kaaro's office. I tried the knob. Locked.

Despite what you see on detective shows, lock picking is not a skill most cops know. But most cops don't have dads who were magicians. The lock that secured this door, was ridiculously flimsy, just a step up from the kind on your bathroom door that could be defeated by a firm piece of wire.

Kaaro's office was secured by a special kind of deadbolt: the knowledge that anyone forcing the bolt was dead.

But, breaking out of jail wasn't something you did for long term health either, so I put the consequences out of my mind. There were always a few forgotten credit cards stuck in a glass next to the cash register. I grabbed one and sprung the door without even breaking stride.

The credenza behind Kaaro's spotless desk was not locked so it didn't take much more time to locate the Chevy's keys.

I realized I couldn't remember when I'd eaten last. On the way out I made myself three ham sandwiches in the bar's small kitchen. I grabbed some bottled water out of the fridge and headed out the door.

Even though I intended to leave my car, I retrieved the spare key and slid inside. The gun I had taken from Grymzin was still in the glove compartment. My Cardinals jacket was in the back seat. I grabbed it, too, leaving the car unlocked. Maybe someone would break into it and leave a bunch of confusing fingerprints behind. Or better yet, steal it and sell it to a chop shop.

Having confused my trail as much as possible, I munched on the sandwiches as I eased the Chevy out of the parking lot. Now that I was mobile, I needed a destination. I'd been up all night, not to mentioned getting arrested and nearly strangled. As the sandwiches made their way into my stomach my eyelids started to get heavy.

My apartment was out, it was the first place they'd look. So, I steered the car to a quiet neighborhood, one where most of the houses didn't have garages. My car would be just one more parked along the street, and I hoped to be gone before too many people noticed one of them contained a sleeping occupant.

I took a final swig of water, turned the radio on low, and reclined the seat.

I should have slept like a dead man. But instead, I began dreaming almost the instant my eyes closed.

"You're a Traveler," Morgan said to me.

I didn't reply, just sat in a chair, stroking the black and white cat who had jumped into my lap. His rear came up as my hand neared his tail.

145

The front door opened and Trav Becker strode in carrying a steel lunch pail. He wore a blue work shirt and pants.

"You're home!" Morgan exclaimed. She stood on her tiptoes and kissed him on the cheek. One leg came up, Donna-Reed style. "How was your day?"

"The usual." He sighed and pushed the Babylon 5 *ball cap he wore to the back of his head. "Getting harder to keep things together."*

Morgan clucked sympathetically. "Takes a lot of duct tape to repair the universe."

Trav nodded, then jerked a thumb in my direction. "How is he?"

"Laid around. Ate all the food. Coughed up a hairball."

"You can't get away with anything around here," the cat muttered.

Morgan held out her hand and Trav gave her the lunch pail.

"Why don't you go get cleaned up?" she asked. "Supper's almost ready."

She nudged him with her hip and turned toward the kitchen. She gave me a sad smile as she passed.

"That'd be nice, wouldn't it?" the cat asked. "Sweet little domestic scene at the end of a long day. They're going to have roast beef. My favorite."

I looked at him. There was something I wanted to say. Something I had to say, but as often happens in dreams, I couldn't speak.

"Yeah, I got your tongue," the cat said with a chuckle. He yawned. Half of one of his canines was broken off.

"So, ya got two choices," he continued. "You can have that." He inclined his head toward the kitchen, then looked down. "Or that."

Trav Becker lay at my feet, a neat round hole in the middle of his forehead.

There has to be another choice, *I thought.*

"*That's what you all say,*" the cat said. "*But you always make the same choices. And that's how you end up here.*"

As I considered this, I realized I was no longer in Morgan's living room. Everything had vanished. I was surrounded on all sides by gray fog. I couldn't sense whether I was standing, sitting, or floating. The cat had vanished as well, but like the feline who talked to Alice, his voice remained.

"*Make your choice.*"

Does it matter what I choose?

"*Not really, but it always makes you feel better to think it does.*"

Then where do I go from here?

I'd think that would be obvious.

And as the gray mist of my dream became the gray interior of the Chevy, I sat up and raised the seatback. My next move *was* obvious.

It was no coincidence that the house I had parked in front of was a tiny story-and-a-half, robin's egg blue, with a sign that said *Psychic Readings* next to the porch.

17

Maiden Voyage

SOPHIE WAS STILL in Sam's lab. It had taken her some time to figure that out because the lights were turned out. All she remembered was wishing with all her heart for the real Trav Becker to show up and help them when suddenly she'd felt a funny pulling sensation in her stomach. Like when you change direction really fast on a roller coaster.

And then everything was just black.

She wanted to call out but resisted the temptation, thinking that maybe the new Becker (she couldn't bear to keep calling him Trav) had done something to the lights, maybe to lie in wait for the real Trav. She reached her hands out in the direction where Mary and Morgan had stood.

Her movement triggered the room lights. Sophie realized she was still standing in exactly the same spot. But the room was empty. She was alone.

"Hello?" she ventured, wincing at how much her voice trembled. She sounded scared to death. Which she was, but she hated how her voice betrayed her.

Trying to stay calm, she looked around the room and immediately noticed subtle differences from what she remembered. Two worktables piled high with books and electronic gear had disappeared along with her friends.

So, either Becker had managed to vanish himself, three people, and a couple hundred pounds of junk, or…

She had Traveled.

OMG, I'm in a parallel universe!

She almost started hyperventilating again. Becker was still holding Mary, Morgan, and Sam captive. But since Sophie had journeyed here,

this had to be where the real Trav was. All she had to do find him. And she was going to need help. But help was clear across town.

Mentally crossing her fingers that a cell phone from another universe worked in this one, she pulled out her phone. Relief washed over her as the splash screen of the ride-sharing app she used for rides home from violin practice loaded up. She just needed a destination.

When the Morgan from this universe woke up in the lab Sophie had just left, she had looked pretty freaked out. Sophie was about to freak her out all over again.

"But she'll just have to adjust," Sophie finished aloud.

And her voice didn't tremble. Not one bit.

18

Me and My Shadow

I GOT OUT of the car and started up the sidewalk. I had no idea what I was going to say to Morgan Foster. It was pretty damn early to show up for a reading.

But the Foster household was awake. As I approached the house, I heard a muffled banging sound coming from the front door. As I drew nearer, I realized the noise came from the door hitting its frame again and again.

"What is the matter with you?" came a voice from inside. "You hate the outside. Stop that!"

But the banging continued. The vibration from whatever was hitting it on the other side caused it to open a crack, and a furry form slipped through the tiny opening and darted onto the porch.

"Noah!" The door flew open and Morgan launched herself after the cat. But she wasn't nearly fast enough.

Neither was I. But it turned out I didn't need to be. Because after zig-zagging around his mistress, the cat bounded down the stairs and without breaking stride and took a flying leap right into my arms.

"Wha—?" Morgan stuttered. "Oh my god. It's you."

Which was the same thing I was thinking as the cat butted its head into my chin.

It was, of course, the same animal that had sat in my lap in last night's dream. And now that I thought about it, I had seen this same cat hanging around outside the Y after my workout.

Morgan and I looked at each other as Noah purred contentedly in my arms. Finally, she said, "You might as well come in."

"I don't want to intrude."

She raised an eyebrow. "You mean you didn't come here to see me? You just happened along to pet my cat?"

I shrugged and started to hand over the cat.

"Just bring him in" She held the door open for us. As soon as I entered the front room the cat squirmed out of my arms and ambled toward the kitchen, completely indifferent now to me and the stir he had caused.

But I wasn't thinking about the cat anymore. I stood frozen in the middle of Morgan's small living room. Given what I had just experienced with Noah the cat, perhaps I shouldn't have been so shocked.

"No way," I muttered.

"No way what?" Morgan asked.

I frowned at her, then pointed. "Kitchen," I gestured at the hallway. "Office…"

"It's not that big of a house," she interrupted. "Am I supposed to be impressed?"

"And a really big gun in the drawer next to the couch."

That got her attention. She stiffened. I didn't move, doing my best to look non-threatening.

"I think you should leave," she said, eyes flat.

"Don't you want to know how I know?"

"There are a lot of ways you might know," she responded. "They start at creepy and end at felony."

"I get that. And I'll leave. If you can tell me honestly that you don't remember anything weird from the bar last night."

Noah had reappeared and wrapped himself around my legs.

"Really?" she muttered. "All right. You win." She motioned toward an overstuffed chair. She took the couch, shaking her head as I scratched the back of Noah's neck.

"I don't know you," she said, "but he acts like you're a member of the family."

"I take it then that you don't remember treating me like a long-lost relative last night?"

She shook her head.

"Or about how Mary and Sam are trying to find me?"

"I don't know any Mary or Sam. I see you around the bar. You work for the owner. You make a pretty good cosmo. That's it."

"We don't know each other."

"No," Morgan said quickly. Too quickly.

"Even though you come into the bar a lot."

"Right."

"And I serve you drinks."

She looked embarrassed. "It's just that…" Her voice trailed off, and a trace of pink appeared on her cheeks.

"What?"

"Fine," she said with a little huff of breath. "You're…Do you not know?"

"Know what?"

"I can't believe we're having this conversation," she said under her breath. "You're…Well, you're a scary dude."

"I am?"

"That's what I always thought. I mean, I've seen you toss men out of the bar who were twice your size. Whenever there's any kind of a scuffle, you're there breaking it up. I don't even know why they hire a bouncer. As soon as you show up things either get quiet or someone gets carried out."

"You haven't seen the news this morning?"

She shook her head.

"Well, when you do, you may want to go with your original inclination to throw me out."

"Are you in some sort of trouble?"

"You might say that."

I told her about the murder charge and breaking out of jail without elaborating as to my method.

To my surprise, my story seemed to make her calmer.

By now, Noah had jumped back into my lap.

"I'm not a murderer," I finished after Noah finished headbutting my chin to his satisfaction.

"I know," she said quietly.

"How do you know?"

She pointed to her temple. "Psychic, remember?"

"Seriously."

"I am being serious. Being psychic is a lot of things. But among them…" She paused, searching for words. "Okay, do you know what an aura is?"

"My aura's a mess."

Her eyes widened. "How do you know that?"

"I—I feel like you told me."

She stared unblinkingly back at me for a long time. Noah went still, ears and eyes swiveling to his mistress.

"Because you're a Traveler," she whispered.

And it all came back to me.

I sank back into the chair, trembling as the memories flooded back.

Dead Travs. In my house, my trunk.

Live Travs, outside a burning warehouse, lounging around a room that both was and wasn't Central Station.

Sam in his lab, explaining parallel universes.

Sam picking two kidnapped girls and me up in his Prius. Another Sam frantically jabbing at his tablet as I lunged at him.

Morgan pulling me away from Grymzin on the sidewalk outside The Kremlin.

Morgan in a two-handed stance, firing a Double Eagle.

An older Morgan telling my fortune.

Morgan by my side as we fired at an approaching army of Trav Beckers.

And Mary.

A tide of regret surged into a knot in the back of my throat as I realized how much I had kept from Mary. I had told myself again and again it was to protect her. But in the newfound honesty of this mental data dump, I realized it was me I was protecting. I hid my new reality from the woman I loved so that I myself could pretend it didn't exist. By shutting Mary out, I could keep from facing it myself.

And look where that had gotten me. Exiled and amnesiac, leaving Mary behind, probably with the body of some random Trav to explain my disappearance.

The doorbell rang.

"Client?" I asked.

Morgan frowned. "I don't have any appointments this morning. Excuse me."

She walked over to the door. I reached down and petted Noah some more.

But my relaxation was short-lived, because at that moment, Morgan cried out, "Trav Becker!"

I dashed to the door, fumbling for my gun, ready to deal with whatever had caused her to call me.

But she wasn't calling me at all. She was just repeating what her visitor had said.

"Do you know him?" I heard as I swung the door open wide to reveal a teenaged girl standing on Morgan's tiny porch.

"Sophie?"

Her eyes lit up the instant I came into view. She pushed past Morgan and threw her arms around my waist.

"Oh God, Mr. Becker! Is it really you?" She buried her head in my chest, sobbing. "I knew you weren't dead! I just knew it! But you've got to help us! He's hurting Sam!"

I stroked her hair. "It's okay, Sophie. It's okay."

Only then did I realize the impossibility of what was happening, even by my standards. I disengaged her tight grip just enough to pull back and examine her.

"You know me," I said.

She nodded so hard her ponytail nearly flew straight up in the air.

"But you can't know me," I continued. "Not here. Unless…"

"Unless I Traveled," she finished impatiently. "That's what I did! We needed you so badly, and I wished so hard…"

"Wait," I demanded. "You did this?"

"Of course! I'm like you. Morgan said so."

"Wait, what?" Morgan asked.

"Not you," Sophie said, irritation taking over her tone. But then she caught herself. "Oh. I'm sorry. That wasn't very nice. You were asleep the whole time you were with us. You can't really know what's going on. You see, Trav is…"

"I know enough," Morgan interrupted. "More than I want to, in fact."

The girl turned back to me. "But you remember me. Morgan…our Morgan said they probably made you forget everything."

"It's coming back. But that doesn't matter now. You said someone was hurting Sam?"

Her head bobbed again. It would have been funny if she hadn't worn such an earnest look. "And Morgan. And Mary."

Mary. She hadn't given up on me. "What kind of trouble?"

"A Trav found us. One of the bad ones. He could be taking them away right now. Or something worse. We have to go back!"

"I don't think you will be going anywhere," a new voice said.

In the tumult, Morgan hadn't gotten around to closing the door. But she'd been standing quite close to it.

Close enough for Bilol Grymzin to grab her with the hand that was not pointing a gun at me as he pushed his way into the room.

Morgan twisted in his grip. I could see her muscles tighten. I tensed, ready to take advantage of the diversion. And that's when Amy Harper appeared in the open doorway. She placed her own gun on Morgan's temple.

"Don't."

Morgan slumped and allowed herself to be guided to the center of the room. Without taking her eyes off Morgan or me, Amy closed the door. Grymzin collected my weapon.

"Well, isn't this cozy," Amy said, taking in the three of us. "Do you have a secret family you've never told us about or something?"

"It's not like that, Amy."

She shrugged. "You could be running a secret Amish bakery for all I care."

"How did you find us?"

She held up her phone with her free hand.

"You put a location app on my phone?"

"You didn't complain on those nights I had something special waiting for you in the bedroom."

She said this last with a smirk in Morgan's direction, who curled her lip in distaste.

"It wasn't me," I muttered. "I was in a parallel universe at the time."

"I don't know what that means," Amy said, "and I don't care."

Realizing that Amy had access to my phone made a light bulb went off on my head.

"You sent the video of Sam's murder to the cops."

She raised an eyebrow. "Yeah, I thought you were smarter than that. Why the hell were you carrying that around on your phone anyway?"

But before I could answer, she held up her hand.

"Never mind. Like I said, I don't care." She inclined her head toward Grymzin. "Am I done here?"

Grymzin grunted.

"That's it?" I asked. "You're just going to leave? You realize he's going to kill us, right?"

Her eyes turned hard. "We had some fun. Didn't mean anything. Maybe if you would have told me what your real game was, things would have been different."

"I don't understand."

"Give me a break, Trav. There was no way you were on board with Anton Kaaro. Cop or not, you're a straight arrow. If you would have brought me in, I might be helping you rather than him."

She looked at Grymzin again. "No offense."

The big man shrugged.

"Seems more likely you would have just ratted me out," I said. "Since that's what you did."

She shrugged. "Sorry it ended up like this."

And she left.

"I would have thought you had better taste," Morgan said softly, then turned to Sophie. "I'm sorry you had to hear that."

I would have reminded her again that it wasn't me Amy had been talking about, but we had bigger problems than the sexual proclivities of the local Trav.

"Bill, we both know how this ends," I said. "I'll go with you. But Morgan and Sophie aren't part of this. Anton doesn't like innocents to get hurt."

"He also does not like to leave witnesses."

"If we leave, they won't witness anything."

"Do you think I'm stupid?" he sneered. Then his face broke into a grin, his piggish eyes black dots sunk into his head. "Besides, watching them die will hurt you. For a few moments, at least."

He waved Morgan and me to stand near Sophie, who was trembling. Her eyes welled up. Morgan and I both put an arm around her and she buried her face in my side.

"Jesus, Bill," I said. "She's scared to death. Is this how you get your jollies? Torturing kids?"

"The more you talk, the longer she's scared." He swung the gun slightly toward Morgan, but not so much that I wasn't still covered, too.

"Over there." He pointed to our right.

Morgan disengaged from Sophie. As she slowly moved aside to give him a nice clear target, I had a sudden flashback to the last time I had been in mortal peril, a whole six hours ago.

"This would be a good time for a misfire," I whispered to Sophie. Her eyes went wide as my meaning sunk in. She screwed them shut, her mouth tightening to a thin line as she concentrated.

I closed my eyes too, focusing on Grymzin's pistol and calling on whatever force it was that governed the universe to shift causality in my favor.

He squeezed the trigger. But I couldn't wait. I had to make my move whether our trans-dimensional mojo worked or not. I whipped around, hand scrabbling for the drawer handle on the little table next to Morgan's sofa, breathing another prayer to the Multiverse that she kept her Desert Eagle loaded.

There was a click followed by an angry grunt. I snatched up Morgan's gun and swung back to face the Uzbek.

I almost made it.

Grymzin was no slouch. He saw my move out of the corner of his eye and brought his gun to bear while I was still trying to get into position.

Sophie and I had no time to wish a second misfire into existence.

Morgan leaped at Grymzin in the exact instant he fired. And this time his round fired true. Right into Morgan's chest.

19

Break on Through

S OPHIE SCREAMED.

Morgan's forward momentum carried her another step toward Grymzin. He couldn't help but spare a glance in her direction as she collapsed at his feet.

Which gave me the opening I needed. I glared hate into his tiny eyes as I fired. The force of the 50-caliber rounds drove him back as I ground my teeth, compulsively squeezing the trigger again and again. Round after round plowed into Grymzin's chest. He slammed into the wall then sank to the floor.

I dashed over, kicking his gun away, then turned toward Morgan. Sophie knelt beside her, and together we gently rolled her onto her back. Sophie pillowed Morgan's head in her lap while I lifted her shirt to look at the wound.

"Oh, no," I muttered.

It was bad. I don't know what kind of dum-dum rounds Grymzin used, but I had seen assault rifle wounds that didn't look this awful.

Morgan groaned.

"It'll be okay," I said. "Just lie still. We'll get help." I reached for my phone, but before I could dial 911, Morgan convulsed in pain.

"Oh my God!" Sophie shouted. "Do something! We've got to help her!"

I reached for a sofa pillow, which I placed over the wound.

"Put pressure on this," I directed Sophie.

Morgan coughed and bloody froth tinged the corner of her mouth. She touched my wrist.

"Don't waste your time," she whispered. Her bleeding stomach pulsed with a fit of wet coughs.

"Fuck that," I snapped. "Stay with us. We'll have the ambulance here before you know it."

She smiled wanly and gave her head a gentle shake. The screen on my phone finally came to life. I frantically pushed the emergency button.

"There's nothing you can do here," she said. "But there is hope for that other Morgan." She reached up and grabbed my shirt collar with a strength she shouldn't have possessed.

"*Save her,*" she whispered. Her grip fell away from my neck, and her head lolled to one side.

"Morgan!" I cried.

But the only response came from my phone.

"911. What's your emergency?"

I stabbed the disconnect button even though I knew it was too late. And sure enough, it immediately began to vibrate as the operator followed standard procedure and called me back.

Sophie wrapped her arms around Morgan's head. She rocked back and forth, huge sobs bursting from her slim form.

I put my own arms around her.

"Shh," I whispered.

Noah the cat appeared. He sniffed Morgan's hand, then looked at us.

"Blert?"

"I know, buddy," I said. "I'm sorry." Sophie reached out and gathered the cat to her.

We stayed like that for a few minutes. But much sooner than I wanted to I pulled away, gently moving Morgan's lifeless torso out of Sophie's lap.

"What are we going to do?" she whimpered, holding the cat tightly.

"We have to go," I said gently.

"Go? We can't just leave her!"

I sighed, holding up my phone, still vibrating with the unanswered call. "I don't want to either. But as soon as the 911 operator answered my location popped up onto her screen. The cops will be here any minute."

I powered off the phone and stuffed the Desert Eagle into the back of my pants. Putting my arm around Sophie, I gently guided her toward the door. She still carried the cat in her arms. It seemed to calm her, so I didn't object. I turned back one more time to survey the grisly scene. I hated to just leave Morgan sprawled and still leaking all over her floor, but she was right. There was a Morgan, not to mention a Sam and a Mary, who were still in danger.

I looked at Grymzin. If I had gone with my first impulse and taken him out yesterday when I had the chance Morgan would still be alive. Anton had warned me that the big man wouldn't give up. My healing memory provided a highlight reel of other Morgans who had paid the price for getting involved with Trav Becker. But at least those women had known the stakes and gone in willingly. This one hadn't done anything except let me into her house, and this was where it had gotten her.

"Goddamnit," I muttered. I was just stumbling from crisis to crisis and people were suffering because of my complete inability to get ahead of the situation.

And this is just an Uzbek thug who I knew was coming after me. What am I going to do against Trav Becker? Or a dozen Travs?

But there was no time for beating myself up. I needed to get Sophie out of here, and we had to figure out our next move. I led the sobbing girl out, softly cursing my ineffectiveness.

I got Sophie and Noah into the car and pulled out, taking a circuitous route away from the scene, one that avoided the likely routes squad cars would take.

"Where are we going?" Sophie said, coming out of a sniffle.

"I'm not sure. I'm mainly just trying to stay out of the way of the cops." Then something occurred to me. "How did you get here? We...I didn't get a chance to hear your story."

Her tale came out slowly, first interrupted by sobs and sniffles, but as she got into it, her voice got stronger and the angry redness began to fade from her cheeks.

"And after all that, you hopped an Uber?" I asked. "You're a pretty cool customer."

That brought a hint of sunshine to her face.

"But tell me again how you even knew to seek out Mary in the first place," I continued.

"I don't know," she replied slowly. "Something was just wrong. Whenever I would mention your name, my parents would change the subject. And not in that stupid way adults do when they think you can't tell exactly what they're doing. It was like they didn't even realize it. Like...like the thought of you was too slippery to hang on to."

Which was about the best description I'd heard of how the universe kept people from perceiving the dissonant effects of shifting between streams.

"And then when I saw Mary was coming to my school," she continued, "I had to see if she did it, too."

I patted her on the knee. "Well, you were way ahead of the rest of us. And the longer I was gone, the more the memories would have faded. I have a lot to thank you for."

She gave me a sad smile, but then her eyes got wide again.

"We have to get back! There's no telling what that other Trav is doing."

She was right. Mary, Morgan, and Sam could be hurt. Or worse yet, spirited away to some out-of-the-way stream where my recovering powers wouldn't be able to find them.

It was a strange feeling. Every time I reached back into my memory, I found more and more content there. But it wasn't coming back fast enough. And there was a giant hole in one critical area.

"Tell me again what you did when you Traveled here," I said.

"I don't know how to explain it," she said slowly. "When the other Trav showed up, I was so scared, and all I could think of was wishing that I knew where you were so I could bring help. Why? How do you do it?"

I sighed. "That's the thing, Sophie. I don't remember. It's one of the things that hasn't come back yet."

"Oh no! What are we going to do?"

"I don't know," I replied grimly. My knuckles turned white on the steering wheel as I dug deep into my mind for the thousandth time. The answer was there, I knew it. Given time I was sure everything would come back to me.

But time was the one thing we didn't have. Every minute we wasted here was another minute my friends and the woman I loved were in danger. I was so close to them but also far away.

"Wait," I whispered. "Maybe that's it."

"What's it?" Sophie asked.

I hung a left turn, sharp enough to make us both lean right.

"Where are we going?"

"Back to the scene of the crime."

It was late enough in the morning that Building 231 had opened for the day, but again the building was mostly empty. I held open the door to Sam's lab for Sophie, cat still in her arms, and followed her in.

Noah jumped down and began to explore.

"So, what now?" she asked, hands on hips.

I gave a helpless sigh, then had a thought. I put on the glasses. "Mike, any ideas?"

"Are you asking if I can suggest any methods for you to travel to a parallel universe?"

"Well, yeah."

"Not without data from observing such a transfer."

"You're saying you can only suggest how to travel to a parallel universe after having seen it done?"

"Yes."

"That's a big help."

Sophie watched this exchange with confusion.

"Sophie, meet Mike," I said. "In this stream, Sam was working on artificial intelligence instead of trans dimensional cosmology."

"Hello, Sophie," Mike said.

Sophie's eyebrows shot up. "Artificial intelligence? Like Alexa?"

"Geez, don't get him started on Alexa," I warned. I thought about going back to text mode, but wearing the glasses the other day had given me a headache.

I handed them to Sophie. "Why don't you two get acquainted?"

Sophie accepted the glasses but didn't put them on. Instead, she stared at me without blinking for a long time, a searching frown etched into her face.

"Music," she said softly.

"What?"

"Music," she repeated. "Morgan said that music had something to do with how you shifted between streams."

And then I remembered that she had said the same thing to me in the bar.

"Mike," Sophie said, "Can you play music?"

"What kind?"

"Pull up my favorites playlist," I said.

"I have some headphones," Sophie offered.

But there was no need. A moment later Al Stewart's voice drifted from a speaker in the ceiling.

Sophie listened for a minute, then rolled her eyes.

"What?"

"Mary can't understand your fascination with him."

"Al Stewart? She always said she liked him."

"She was being nice."

Sophie looked at me expectantly as the music played, but when I didn't start to glow, spout incantations, or demonstrate other signs of superpowers, curiosity about the AI living in the eyeglasses got the better of her. She put them on, then plopped down and sat cross-legged on the floor. She began a whispered conversation with Mike while Noah made himself comfortable in her lap.

I suddenly realized I was swaying on my feet. Getting arrested and nearly killed, followed by little sleep and nearly getting killed again was taking its toll. I needed to figure out how to get back to Mary, Morgan, and Sam, but doing it sitting down all of sudden seemed like a great idea.

So, I did. My eyelids began to droop as Al Stewart sang about a woman mourning the loss of her boyfriend, a WWI pilot lost in battle.

Mary wore a man's leather bomber jacket, the kind with the sheepskin collar, much too large for her. She stared at a cream-colored envelope with black borders.

"No," she said in a whisper that transformed into a sob. "He can't be gone."

"He is gone," hissed Trav Becker in a German accent straight out of Hollywood. He wore an SS uniform. As he came into view, I saw that Sam and Morgan were tied to chairs behind him. They were dressed as French partisans, Morgan in slacks and a beret with a kerchief knotted around her throat, and Sam in a khaki shirt soiled with dirt and blood. He had a black eye and blood encrusted his nose and upper lip, which sported a razor-thin mustache, William Powell-style.

"Wrong war," I said. "He was singing about biplanes. I would have gone with the Red Baron."

Trav's head snapped around.

"About damn time!" he crowed, German accent disappearing. "I thought I was going to have to start the cutting."

He reached out, but his hand went through me. We both watched as it disappeared into my chest.

"What?" he mocked. "Scared to come all the way through?"

I surged to my feet. From what seemed like a long ways away, I heard Sophie's voice.

"Trav! What's the matter? Who are you talking to?"

"I don't have all day," Nazi Trav snarled.

I hadn't consciously been aware, but my dream had been in black and white, just like a World War II movie. Suddenly, like those old promos for colorized movies on cable, a rainbow washed across my vision and the scenery changed.

Trav's uniform disappeared and was replaced by a loud Hawaiian shirt and pork pie hat. I blinked. This outfit was more ridiculous than the uniform, and for a second, I thought I was still dreaming.

But the knife looked real enough, as did the blood on Sam's face, although his mustache had disappeared.

I balled my fists and lunged forward.

He smiled and swung around, bringing the knife to bear. "Finally."

The lab where Sophie and I stood grew indistinct as I focused on the version before me.

"C'mon," Trav taunted, gesturing with his fingers. "Show me something I haven't seen before."

"Wait for me!" came a voice, and I felt a touch on my arm.

And then I was fully in the lab with them, the fog that had hovered around the edge of my vision clearing.

A triumphant grin split Trav's face as I appeared. Sam was tied to a chair just as he had been in my dream, bleeding from his nose. Morgan stood pressed against the wall, next to...

Mary.

My hand went to the Desert Eagle tucked into the small of my back, but the other man quickly stepped away from Sam and grabbed Mary by the wrist. He laid his knife on her graceful neck.

"Ah-ah," he admonished. "Let me see them both."

I raised my hands, palms out.

"Very good." He looked at Mary. "See? That's the advantage we have. I know what he's going to do in every situation."

But then he frowned.

Sophie popped into view behind me, one hand on my elbow, the other still holding Noah.

Seeing his mistress, the cat jumped to the floor and made a beeline for Morgan, which took him right into Trav's legs.

"Goddamnit!" he snarled, kicking at the cat.

But taking his eyes off Mary was a mistake. She grabbed hold of his knife hand with both of hers, pushing it away from her throat. Like a ballerina, she let her momentum carry her around in a half turn.

Snapping her leg up as she spun, she kicked him right in the balls.

He dropped the knife, clutching at his crotch. By that time I was in front of him. I snatched the Desert Eagle from my back and swung it underhanded, connecting with his chin. His head snapped up and he swayed back and forth, blearily trying to focus on the barrel of the oversized pistol, which I now pointed right at his bleeding nose.

His hat tumbled from his head, revealing a knot of hair gathered tightly underneath it.

I whipped the gun back up and clipped his chin savagely again.

"That's for pulling a knife on Mary," I said as he dropped like a sack of potatoes.

Once he was down, I kicked him in the stomach.

"And *that* is for the man bun. Not to mention that shirt. What hell-stream did you come from, anyway?"

With Manbun Trav now down for the count, I rushed to Sam.

"Are you okay, buddy?"

"Yeah," he said as I untied him. "It's not as bad as it looks." He pulled up the hem of his shirt and dabbed at his bleeding nose.

"It was like Darth Vader and Han Solo in *Empire*. He seemed to think that hurting us would attract your attention."

"He was right." I turned to Morgan. "Are you okay?"

She nodded. "He hadn't had a chance to get to me yet."

And then a small blur in blue jeans lunged past me and Sophie wrapped her arms around Mary's waist.

"I'm so sorry I left you!" Sophie cried, "I didn't know what else to do! All I could think of was that Trav was the only person who could help us. But it took me forever to find him, and there were these people with guns…" She looked at Manbun's unconscious form, "…other people with guns. And Trav didn't think he knew how to get back."

"Shh," Mary said, stroking the girl's hair. "It's okay. You made it. He made it. And you did great. If you wouldn't have gotten back when you did, I don't know what would have happened. We're all okay, and it's because of you."

Sophie disengaged herself from Mary's arms, still sniffling a little. She watched me as I approached them. I slowly crossed the room, afraid that if I rushed to her, Mary might change into smoke and disappear like the fog from my dream.

"Hi," I said.

"Hi, yourself."

Five feet away.

"Other people with guns?" she asked.

"It's been a busy day."

"Apparently."

I took a step toward her. "So, um…There are parallel universes."

Four feet away.

"So I understand."

Three feet.

"Sorry I never told you."

"You were waiting for the right time?"

Two feet.

"Something like that."

I was now close enough to take her hand. When I did, the dam broke. Tears welled up in both our eyes as I pulled her into my arms. She buried her face in my shoulder as hers shook.

"I should have kicked *you* in the balls," she whispered in between sobs.

"I deserved it."

She pulled away just enough to look at me.

"Why didn't you tell me?" she asked.

"I…"

"You don't have to hide the truth from me. Do you think I'm too fragile?"

"Believe me, I do not think you're fragile."

Manbun began to stir. I gave him another kick in the head. "And neither does he. Kickboxing class seems to be going well."

"I've had a lot of time on my hands lately."

Morgan picked Noah up, and he head-butted her chin. "You showed up at exactly the right time," she murmured. Sophie joined her in petting the cat. I could hear him purr from where I stood.

"Well, this is all very touching."

I whipped around, bringing my gun to bear on the speaker.

"What the hell?" Sam blurted.

I could understand his reaction. It's always a shock to encounter another version of yourself. Even one stooped with age, a patch covering one eye. What remained of this Sam's shock of red hair was white and poked out from under a ball cap in a Doc Brown-style cloud. His voice was a hoarse rasp.

"Come with me if you want to live."

20

Neutron Dance

"NICE TRICK." I jerked my head in Manbun's direction but kept my gun trained on the newcomer. "How do we know you're not with him?"

"And you couldn't come up with a more original line?" Sam put in. "We're supposed to trust you because you've seen *Terminator*?"

Old Sam shrugged. "I've had a lot of time to watch movies."

While the Sams sniped at each other, I had time to study the new arrival more closely. The tablet he held in his remaining hand looked familiar. A pair of black, thick-rimmed glasses, twin to the ones Sophie still had, protruded from his shirt pocket. But what clinched things was his ball cap. It bore the logo of the movie *Buckaroo Banzai*.

"What the hell happened to you, Gear? And where's Buck?"

The partner of the Trav Becker who had started all of this shook his head. "Not now. There's no time." He indicated Manbun. "When he doesn't report in, another one will come looking for him."

"Where can we go?" Morgan demanded. "They can track us anywhere."

"I've got a place," Gear replied.

"What about him?" I pointed to Manbun.

He shrugged. "Leave him. Where we're going, he'll have a hard time following."

"Then let's go."

"Everyone?" His gaze swept across my friends, lingering on Mary and Sophie.

I considered it for about one second, which also happened to be just long enough to see Mary's eyes flash.

"All of us," I said to Gear.

He shrugged again and raised the tablet.

"Whenever you're ready," I said.

And suddenly we were somewhere else.

"You've gotten a lot better at this," I observed. The last time I had been dragged between streams under someone else's power, I'd puked my guts out.

"Where are we?" asked Sophie.

"Oz," Gear replied.

"God, please spare me from these boys and their code names," Morgan muttered.

We examined our surroundings. We were in a good-sized open space. The floor was covered with 1960s-style tiles in black (faded to gray) and white (now beige). Two wide doors near us opened into a commercial kitchen. At the other end of the room was a small stage raised about two feet from the rest of the room. Sophie put it together first.

"We're in a school."

Gear nodded. "My elementary school."

"Your school?" I asked, unable to keep the incredulity out of my voice.

"I hated elementary school. I figured it was the last place The Boss would look."

"This is like the Treehouse, though?" I asked, referring to the uninhabited version of Central Station where I had first met The Rangers. "No people?"

"Well, there are people, just in a different quantum state than us."

He was poised to continue but I held up my hand.

"I don't need to know the math."

We stood in one of those combination gym-lunchroom-auditorium combos, common to schools built in the middle of the last century. Some of the cafeteria tables were unfolded and lined one wall. Piled on top were computers and other less familiar-looking gadgets. A wooden desk covered with books and papers occupied a corner.

Near the kitchen doors were several pieces of furniture that looked like they had been scavenged from a dorm room. A single bed, hardly more than a cot, squatted against the wall alongside a couple of beat-up dressers and a stained couch.

Gear looked around, apparently realizing for the first time that the room's only chair was being used to store a pile of laptops.

"Sorry. I don't have many guests. I think there are some chairs in Mrs. Wilbur's room."

This was directed at Sam, who immediately nodded and motioned to Sophie. "Can you give me a hand?"

She followed him through a door near the stage end of the room.

Morgan was still looking around the room. "Mrs. Wilbur?"

"My kindergarten teacher."

Gear, who I noticed had also acquired a significant limp to go with his other infirmities, hobbled over to a refrigerator right outside the kitchen door. He opened it and produced a bottle of water.

"Help yourself," he said, jerking his head toward the fridge.

I got bottles out for everyone. Sam and Sophie returned a couple of minutes later dragging several wooden chairs. Fortunately, they were regular-sized. I had a sudden vision of a teacher conference at my elementary school with my parents wedged into kid-sized chairs, knees nudging their chins as they tried to focus on whatever the teacher was saying.

We sat silently in a circle sipping our water.

"So what happened to Buck?" I asked quietly.

Gear sighed. He pulled off the Banzai hat and ran a hand across his freckled scalp. He didn't return the cap to his head, just held it in his lap. He stared down at it as he spoke.

"They hit us right after we sent you away. Subjective time on our end, hardly an hour. We hadn't even had a chance to treat our wounds. There were dozens of them. It was a massacre."

"Dozens of Travs?" I asked. "How is that possible?"

He shook his head. "I'm not quite sure. But I think The Boss figured out how to harvest Travs from orphan streams."

"Orphan streams?"

"Streams of causality that aren't different enough from others to maintain themselves. Let's say in the morning you put on red socks in one stream and blues socks in another. That difference isn't enough to build an entire reality on. One of them peters out after a few nanoseconds. The Boss must have figured out a way to pull a near-infinite number of Travs out of those streams. It gives him almost limitless manpower."

I shuddered at the thought of hundreds of versions of me all goose-stepping to the orders of The Boss, the original Sam who'd spent the last decade trying to impose his will on the Multiverse.

The hat trembled in Gear's hands.

"Back to what happened to you," I said gently. "How did you get out?"

"I was lucky," he said bitterly. "They appeared in one of my labs and opened fire the instant they saw me. Hit me in the knee. I went right down."

He pointed to the eye patch. "Shrapnel or a ricochet caught me in the eye. There was blood everywhere. They thought I was dead. I damn near was. I couldn't move, couldn't see. But I could hear."

He closed his single eye and his lips stretched into a pained grimace. "They didn't speak, just mowed down everyone they saw. When the guns jammed, they finished with those goddamned swords."

His voice dropped to a hollow whisper. "They got everyone. Buck, O'Connor, Dick, Fay, Gwen…"

Morgan gasped. "Gwen? But she was…"

Gear's voice broke. "They didn't care that she was pregnant."

He took a long swallow of water and collected himself. "Anyway, I laid there until they left. Grabbed a few necessities and came here. It's a stream at the very, very end of what my instruments could see, and time flows much slower here."

He turned to me. "It's been, what, a week, two weeks for you? It's been more than ten years for me."

"Why come out now?" I asked.

"There wasn't any reason to as long as you were on ice," Gear replied. He held up the tablet. "This was still set to track your nanomachines. But I didn't dare go after you. I just had to hope eventually you'd find your way back."

"But you were the one who wiped my mind in the first place!"

"Yeah. Sorry about that." He looked contrite. "Buck never intended that to be a permanent solution. But he couldn't take the chance of The Boss getting hold of you again. And it's a good thing he did what he did or you'd be dead just like everyone else."

"You don't know that."

He shrugged. "It doesn't matter. What does matter is that now you're the only thing standing between The Boss and his plan."

"What is his plan?" asked Sam.

"The way I understood it," I said, recalling the one conversation I'd had with The Boss, "he believed everything Buck and the Rangers did to try and keep the time stream together was just a Band-Aid. He said the only permanent fix was a complete reset."

I looked at Gear for confirmation. He nodded.

"Well, which is it?" Sam demanded.

Gear sighed, his face suddenly weighed down by every one of the couple dozen subjective years he had on Sam and me.

"The Boss is right," he said quietly.

"What?" Morgan exploded. "What about all that stuff you told us about how important it was to heal the rifts in all the streams?"

"We were doing the best we could with what we knew at the time," he snapped.

"But you were wrong," she said.

"Not completely," he said. "Remember, I've had a lot of time to work on this. Much longer than I did when Buck and I were just starting out. Back then, we were just trying to keep the Opposition from killing every Sam he could find. The Boss had a huge head start on us. I was writing code and building devices as fast as I could. And then we were focused on recruiting and training the Rangers."

"What do you know now that you didn't then?" I demanded.

"Well," Gear began. "It was Morgan...Fay," he clarified, "who put us on the right track. She was the first one who realized that Trav's abilities weren't related to my research but were a natural talent. And he couldn't have been the only person ever to manifest that talent."

"I remember this." I turned to Morgan. "You told me the same thing. That seers, prophets, witches, wise men, anyone out of history who was credited with supernatural powers actually just had the gift of being able to perceive data across the streams, seeing how things might be and then trying to steer toward that outcome."

She nodded. "I remember," she said softly. For the first time, I noticed her face was pale and she was shivering a little. She had wrapped a blanket from Gear's small bed around her shoulders.

"But that's only part of it," Gear continued, warming to his topic. "Why don't we have prophets and seers today? Or wizards? It's almost like magic worked at one time in history but doesn't anymore."

"Okay, I'll bite," I said. "Why not?"

"Well, everyone here is familiar with the Many Worlds theory of cosmology."

"Ya think?" Sam snorted.

"Quiet, Junior," Gear replied mildly. "Yes, we have each personally experienced parallel universes. But there's a problem with that theory. A huge one."

He looked around at each of us, but when none of us spoke up he continued.

"Where do you put all of them?"

"All of what?" Morgan asked.

"The parallel universes. You're creating millions of them every minute."

"Wait," I interrupted. "Didn't you just say that not every parallel universe is discrete enough to continue? That some streams peter out. That's where The Boss is getting his army."

"Sure," Gear shrugged. "But you're still talking about hundreds of millions of new streams coming into existence every day."

"Isn't the universe infinite?" Morgan asked.

"Of course not," Gear said. "Nothing is infinite. Generations of geniuses, Everett, DeWitt, Einstein. Every one of them took infinity for granted. Now, make no mistake. Space is big. Really, vastly, mind-boggingly big…"

He paused, peering at each of us in turn.

"Really? Nothing?" he asked.

We all just stared silently back at him.

Sam finally sighed and answered. "Yes, we've read *Hitchhikers Guide.*"

"I should hope so," Gear huffed. "Anyway. Space is really big. But it's not infinite. And with every minor decision on every Earth creating a new parallel reality, the dimensions pile up. Fast. Eventually, the quarters get kind of tight. It's not 'distance' in the actual sense, but whatever you want to call the space between the different streams gets smaller. And they start to rub up against each other."

He rubbed his hands together to illustrate this point. "And what happens when things rub together?"

"You mean like static electricity?" Sophie asked.

"Exactly. Well, energy, at least. So now we have more and more dimensions pushing closer and closer together. And the friction causes an energy buildup. And it turns out, this energy can be tapped by people who are sensitive to it, creating—"

"Prophets. Seers," Morgan offered.

"More than that," Gear said. "I'm talking about channeling the actual energy into physical manifestations."

"Magic," Sophie breathed.

"Exactly. Our legends of magic come out of a time when some people could wield power that seemed supernatural. In fact, you could make a case for just about any legend having some basis in fact. Monsters, gods who walked among us—"

"A flat Earth you could sail off the edge of," interrupted Sam.

"On the back of a giant turtle?" Sophie offered with a giggle.

I rolled my eyes. "Nerds," I muttered. "Nerds in every dimension. Look, I think I see what you're leading up to. All that energy has to go somewhere. Like when you scuff your shoes against a carpet and then touch a doorknob."

Gear nodded. "More like what happens when the ice crystals in clouds rub against each other. Think of the biggest lightning bolt you've ever seen, but multiplied by millions of times across a billion realities."

That shut us all up.

"And that could happen?" Mary finally asked.

"Has happened," Gear corrected. "Hundreds of times throughout history."

"Wait a minute," Mary said. "I can buy prophets foretelling the future and maybe even the occasional witch casting spells that actually worked. But you're talking about a cataclysm of Biblical proportions. Again and again. I think people would notice that."

Gear shrugged. "The energy discharge doesn't have a physical manifestation. But I've done the math. It's a cycle you can predict. The energy builds for a long time, then is expended in a flash. A giant spark which pops all these bubbles in spacetime except for one."

"And the cycle starts all over again," Morgan finished.

Gear nodded.

"How long do these cycles last?" I asked.

"Normally, hundreds of years," he replied. "That's why tales of the supernatural disappear into legend."

"I guess I don't understand what the problem is," Morgan said. "Resets are natural phenomena, right? That aren't even perceived by most people. What's the harm? Besides Trav losing his abilities, I guess."

"Which I am totally fine with," I said. "So, what's the problem?"

"I guess if you're okay with Nature randomly picking which particular bubble of spacetime survives the reset, sure," Gear said.

Now it was my turn to shrug. "That's how it's been for thousands of years. Why mess with it?"

Gear looked at Sam helplessly. I could almost see the light bulb go off in my friend's brain.

"We mess with stuff," Sam said slowly. "It's what we do."

"Exactly," Gear said. "You might be willing to let the chips fall where they may but The Boss isn't. Don't you get it? This is what he's been working toward all along. Making sure that he gets to pick the stream that survives the collapse."

"Can he do that?" Sam asked. "I can't even imagine the amount of computing power it would take to predict, let alone direct, an occurrence like that."

Gear slapped his knee in exasperation. "That's what I've been trying to tell you. What do you think he's been doing in Arkham all this time? He's had years to figure this out."

"But why?" Morgan asked. "What can he possibly gain?"

"He gets to rewrite reality in his own image," Gear said.

"But does he really?" Morgan threw up her hands. "You're talking about him like he's a supervillain. But he's you." She pointed at Gear and then at Sam. "And you. Neither of you are megalomaniacs. What makes you think he is?"

"He's nuts," Gear said simply. "We've always known that."

I thought about Sam Markus and all the versions of him I had met. The differences between them were striking. The Sam I knew, like Gear, wanted nothing more than to be left alone in his lab. But the Sam who had gotten me into all of this, the one I had tagged Sam Zero, like The Boss, had no reservations about throwing Travs at each other, ginning more up as needed.

"I don't know if nuts is the right word," I said, "but The Boss is driven in a way that's different from either of you. He believes he's saving the world and that it's okay to eliminate anyone standing in his way. But we're missing something."

"What do you mean?" Morgan asked.

"What's his endgame?"

Sam and Gear looked at each other in discomfort.

"What?" I asked.

"Nothing," Gear said.

"No," Mary said. "You two know something you're not saying. Spill it."

Gear sighed. "We don't *know* anything. But we hate the direction our society is going."

"You do?" I asked. "News to me."

Sam looked at me. "I don't talk about it much, but the attitude of the average American toward science is insulting. Take climate change, for instance. It's settled science. There is no debate."

"There's lots of debate," Morgan objected.

"Only among the ignorant," Gear snapped. "And that's what we mean. People refuse to believe evidence."

"And experts," Sam said. "Sometimes…We think that the world would be better off with scientists in charge."

"That's what this is all about?" I demanded. "All the killing, all the tragedy? All because science doesn't get enough respect? That's insane."

"Well, what did you expect?" Sam retorted. "You've met The Boss. Didn't you say he was crazy?"

"Would it be totally bad?" Morgan asked. "Haven't we all wished we could wave a hand and fix the world?"

"But it wouldn't be fixed," Mary said grimly. "Just broken in a different way."

"Exactly," Gear said. "No one should have that kind of power. And not only that…"

His mouth snapped shut.

"What?" I asked.

"Well," he began, "The Boss isn't going to take any chances on anyone interfering with his new world order."

"What do you mean? Didn't you say all the Traveler powers disappear after the reset?"

"But he'll only feel safe if you disappear along with it," Gear finished.

"Can he do that?" Sophie asked.

"Like I said, he's been working on this for years. I wouldn't bet against him."

There was silence as we all chewed on this for a moment.

Finally, I spoke. "This doesn't change anything. Our goal is the same it's always been. Stop The Boss. Fortunately, we're in a place where he can't find us, and also where time passes more slowly. We have time to plan."

Gear looked a little embarrassed. "Well, that's the thing."

"What do you mean?" I asked.

Gear turned toward Sam. "You can design an equation for the coherence of non-equilibrium quantum systems in a steady state, right?"

"Of course," Sam replied with a little bit of sneer. "Did you think I didn't go to college?"

"Don't get uppity. You see, this stream is unique. It's unlike any others in my experience, even places like the Treehouse or Arkham. Here, the coherence doesn't have a correlation with the population landscape. It's a non-monotonic relationship."

Sam's eyes widened.

"That's crazy." He shook his head in disbelief. "The quantum superposition would be in a continual state of flux. You couldn't calculate the density matrix."

"Not from outside, at least. Which is what makes this a great hideout. But there is a point in the curl flux where the diagonal elements align—"

"And might make the stream detectable by the Opposition," Sam finished.

"Exactly," Gear agreed. "I haven't worried too much about it before. The Boss thought he wiped us all out. I have some software on the drawing board that would enable me to manipulate the coherence by hand. That would re-introduce randomness to the curl flux and hide this stream even better. But The Boss wasn't looking for me so it was kind of down the list of priorities."

Sam frowned and started to say something, but I interrupted. "What you're saying is that the program that will hide us doesn't work yet, right?"

"It's almost ready," the old man said defensively.

I shook my head. "Not good enough. Manbun was unconscious when you showed up, but The Boss has surely put two and two together."

Gear nodded. "You can bet he's looking for us."

"Then we need to be ready to bug out."

Gear nodded. "We can leave any time after I finish backing up my data." He turned to Sam. "Help me up."

Sam pulled Gear to his feet and followed him over to the table with the computers. They mumbled quietly to each other as they poked at keyboards and pointed at screens.

I heard a stomach rumble from Sophie's direction.

"Excuse me," she said, blushing.

"Look at us. Child abusers." I called to Gear. "Got any food?" He pointed behind us.

Sophie, Mary, and Morgan turned toward the kitchen. I did too but was interrupted.

"Trav," Gear said, "hang on a minute."

His eyes darted toward the kitchen and I realized he was waiting until he was sure the women were out of earshot.

"What?" I asked. He didn't reply so I primed the pump.

"What is it that you didn't want them to hear?"

"Executive committee," he murmured.

"I don't understand."

"That's what Buck used to call it. When there were things he just wanted to talk over with me, or Parker."

Parker had been the most senior of the Rangers.

"What about Fay?"

Gear shrugged. "Buck protected her whenever he could. It was hard enough keeping her safe the way things were."

Fay was the eldest of the Morgans who were a part of the Rangers. In my brief exposure to her, she'd appeared to be an equal partner in the group's leadership.

"Eventually, you'll understand," Gear continued. "You've been on your own for most of this. You haven't had the chance to work on a team. It's not like anything else you've ever experienced. When your partners know you as well as you know yourself it saves time on everything. It's like a giant shortcut. You don't have to speak. The whole is greater than the sum of the parts."

"I've been a cop," I shot back. "It's not like TV where the hero is some lone wolf. All our work is done by team."

"It's not even close to the same thing," he said irritably. He gestured at the equipment scattered along the table. "How do you think I was able to come up with all of this? Put six Sams in a room together, and there's no telling what we'll come up with."

"He's not wrong," Sam put in without looking up from the screen he was examining. "What they accomplished would have taken me years working by myself."

"You'll have to put together your own team," Gear said. "A team you can trust implicitly. Buck always said, who can you trust more than yourself?"

He had a point. Mary, Morgan, and Sophie had been put in enough danger because of me.

"So, you're saying I need to recruit my own team of Rangers? How am I going to do that?"

"The multiverse may not be infinite, but it's big enough. There are hundreds, thousands of Travs out there who will join up if asked. You'll find them just like Buck did. And it will probably be a lot easier for you."

"Easier? Why?"

"The closer we get to the Collapse, the more energy builds up."

"I know. You just told us that."

"But we don't know its effects."

"Yeah, we do. *Boom.* All the streams collapse down into one."

"I mean its effects on you."

"I don't understand."

"Your Traveler power. It will get stronger. And the power may manifest itself in new ways."

"Maybe that's a good thing," I said.

"But you know what they say about absolute power," Sam said.

"But you know what they say about absolute power," Sam said.

"Yeah, yeah," I replied. "We'll burn that bridge when we get to it. But I have to tell you, Gear, I don't see myself going out and playing Trav recruiter."

"Why not? It worked for us."

"Did it? Then why isn't it The Boss who is hiding out in Mrs. Wilbur's room?"

"Fuck you," the old man snarled. "Buck saved your life. And you're going to betray everything he stood for? What he died for?"

"Gear, I…" I began.

"No!" he snapped. "Don't you get it? This is how he gets you."

"What do you mean?"

"The Boss," Gear replied, his voice hollow. "That's how he starts. He convinces you that you're smarter than other Travs, that there's a better way. Next thing you know, he's pulled you in so deep there's no getting away."

I put a hand on his arm. "I'm not going to the other side, Gear. I promise."

"At least tell me you'll think about," he begged. "You're going to need all the help you can get, or else…" His voice trailed off.

"Or else what?"

Gear sighed. "You realize you two are an anomaly, right?"

I frowned. "What do you mean, anomaly?"

"You and Sam kept things together in your stream without going in the direction that either Buck or The Boss took. It was kind of a third branch."

The Boss had said as much to me. And I had later said pretty much the same thing to Buck when I spurned his offer to join the Rangers. At the time, I had thought I could just opt out of their war. Of course, we all knew how that had turned out.

"So? We started a third branch. What of it?" Sam asked.

Gear sighed in that way you do when you've told someone the same thing over and over. "What is the defining energy force in the universe?" he asked.

Now it was Sam's turn to frown. "The Second Law of Thermodynamics," he ventured. "A closed system will maximize entropy. Entropy is the defining force."

"The universe tends toward disorder? That's your answer?" Gear challenged.

"What other answer is there?"

"Inertia," Gear said simply. "At the core of all this, that's what we're fighting. The flow of time resists efforts to change it. If you damn up a river for a hundred years then tear out the damn, the river will revert back to its original course even though it's been decades. The Boss isn't the only one we're fighting. The Multiverse *itself* resists the changes."

"You make it sound like a living being," Sam said.

"Maybe it is. I don't know. But what I do know is that you've introduced variables into the equation."

"Variables?"

At that moment, there was a crash from the kitchen and we all jumped, but the noise was followed by titters of feminine laughter.

"Do you want to know how many times I've seen you and Mary together?" Gear asked.

I didn't answer.

"None," he said flatly. "Mary and you breaking up is a consistent event throughout nearly the entire continuum."

"That's…not possible," I said.

"Believe what you want," Gear shrugged. "I've only looked in on about a hundred streams. And in every one, you two are either broken up, or—"

"Or what?"

He looked down, suddenly unwilling to meet my eyes. "Or she's dead."

Great. Now realized that I not only had to keep The Boss's crazy plan from succeeding. I also had to keep the Multiverse from killing my girlfriend in the process.

"Just…just get this stuff ready to go," I said.

Two Sam Markuses were suddenly two too many. I turned and headed for the kitchen, feeling very, very tired.

I spotted a coffee maker on a table near what must have been the cafeteria manager's office. Taped to the side of the device was an index card with brewing instructions, not to mention a couple of decades worth of coffee drips. This had to be the source of java for the entire school. I read the instruction card.

"Jesus," I said.

"What?" Morgan asked.

"Think we can drink ninety cups of coffee?"

"Oh, for God's sake. Go help Sophie. I'll take care of this."

She stood up, but then swayed, putting a hand on the back of the chair for support. Her head bobbed and her eyes were glassy.

I put out a hand to steady her. "Are you okay?"

She shook her head, then waved me off. "Y-yeah. Just stood up too fast. Go. I'll take care of this."

"Are you sure?"

"Of course."

I looked at her uncertainly.

"It's fine. Sam's not the only one who can do math."

I didn't want to leave her, but she stared me down until I left her to it.

Sophie had filled a bowl with water for Noah who lapped daintily from one edge. The girl wandered over to a walk-in pantry and poked her head in.

"There's like, a hundred boxes of Cheez-Its in there," she said.

"Sam's favorite food," I said. "It was the only thing that got him through grad school."

I pulled open the refrigerator door and grabbed Greek yogurt, bread, and a package of hot dogs. I also found a giant can of peaches which I opened using a large can opener mounted at the end of one of the prep tables.

"Not exactly USDA standards," I said to Sophie, "but it will have to do."

Sophie began feeding hot dogs into a microwave a couple at a time. A few minutes later, the smell of something very close to coffee drew me back across the room. As I approached, Mary and Morgan halted a soft conversation they were having. I was glad to see that the color had returned to Morgan's face.

Mary filled a mug with "Millie" scribbled on the side and handed it to me.

"Anything I should know?" I asked when they didn't resume their conversation.

"Don't flatter yourself," Morgan said. "Just because two women are talking doesn't mean a man is the topic."

"If you must know," Mary put in, "we were comparing maintenance schedules."

"Maintenance sch— What?"

"Our cars are exactly the same. Gray CR-Vs. Didn't you ever notice?"

"I guess not."

Sophie came around the corner. She was doing her best to balance two trays that contained a couple of hot dogs each, a mound of Cheez-Its, and some peaches.

"Will they want coffee?" she asked.

"God, no." I pulled two Cokes from the refrigerator and added them to the trays. "Don't even mention coffee in Sam's presence."

I took the trays from her and delivered them to the Sams. They glanced up as I set the plates in front of them, grunted in unison, and then proceeded to each pick up a handful of Cheez-Its, crush them between their fingers, and sprinkle the fragments over their hot dogs. They topped the mixture with about a quart of ketchup and continued an animated discussion around mouthfuls.

"It's all there," Gear said. "Do you understand the file structure?"

"Mmmph."

"Good."

Gear peered up at me. "The data's almost all backed up." He pointed to a hard drive that rested vertically in a dock.

"How much longer?" I asked.

"Half an hour maybe."

"Okay. Do you need anything else?"

"More Cheez-Its," Sam said.

I sighed and walked back into the kitchen, returning with a full box that I tossed to Sam. He bobbled the catch, of course, and the box skidded across the floor.

"Hey, be careful with those!" Gear warned.

"Why? You're just going to crush them anyway."

I left them to their grumbling and grabbed my own frank. It was topped more conventionally with mustard, onions, plus the very last bit of pickle relish I had managed to scrape out of a jar from the back of the fridge.

As I finished, I noticed that Morgan and Sophie were now by themselves.

"Where's Mary?" I asked.

Sophie suddenly became very interested in the last few bites of her meal. Morgan looked at me for a long time before speaking.

"She left."

"I can see that. Do you know where she went?"

"I think you should look for her," Morgan replied.

"Okay…"

I looked at the two women, but neither seemed interested in continuing the conversation.

It didn't take a trained investigator to follow this trail.

21

Not While I'm Around

I FOUND MARY in a classroom several doors down the hall. She didn't look at me when I came in. Instead, she stared at a bulletin board that had something to do with fractions.

"Hey," I said.

She nodded but didn't turn.

"I never really got a chance to say thanks," I continued.

"Thanks for what?"

"For not giving up on me."

"That was Sophie."

"That's not the way I heard it. Sophie may have started things, but you refused to let go. Did you really stare down Morgan's gun?"

Even though she was faced mostly away from me I could see a small smile curl the edges of her lips. "That may not have been my smartest ever move."

"Pretty amazing, if you ask me." I reached for her. She let me pull her into my arms, but kept her own folded in front of her.

"What's the matter?"

She sighed and pushed away. "It's just a lot to take in, you know? Parallel universes. Groups of Sams and Travs all fighting each other. A universe that is getting ready to undergo a cataclysm that no one but us will notice. And…"

"And what?"

She looked at me for a long time, chewing on her lip. "Morgan told me," she finally said.

"Told you what?"

"That you didn't start out in our universe. That the Trav from my…what do you call it, my stream? That he was dead."

I didn't say anything, but a big ball of acid-flavored tension began to surf in my stomach.

"Do you know what the worst part of it is?" she continued. "I did notice the difference. Just about a year ago, you changed. It used to be, you were so closed in. Most nights, you'd be three drinks in before you quit staring into space. You'd cancel plans at the last minute. Whenever I would ask you what was going on, you'd mumble something about work. I finally decided it was just part of being in a relationship with a cop. Then one day, everything changed. You became the most considerate, attentive boyfriend ever. I didn't ask any questions. Why would I? But now I know why."

"I lost you once." I hooked a nearby chair with an ankle. Using it for a footstool, I perched on a nearby desk as I tried to find the right words.

"In the stream I originally came from," I began, "I was in a bad place. Adam was dead and it was my fault. You tried, you really tried to stay with me but I made it impossible. I drank like a fish. I quit calling. When you would come over I'd just pick a fight. Finally, you gave up. And I don't blame you."

I took her hands and enfolded them in mine.

"And then I came to a place where you'd never suffered for my mistakes. Where I hadn't completely screwed my life up. So after Sam and I defanged Sam Zero we decided to just stay."

If I thought she would be flattered, I was so wrong. Her eyes flashed.

"I was the prize you got for saving the universe?" she demanded.

"No, it's not like that at all. I told you, it was a second chance. I wasn't going to lose you again."

"It wasn't your choice!" She jerked away, folding her arms again.

"What was I supposed to say?" I demanded. I put my fingers to my head in the universal phone gesture. "'Hi hon, this may be hard to believe, but I'm not actually your boyfriend.' Maybe I should have shown you his body. That would have been a fun date."

She whirled to face me. "Did you think I couldn't handle the truth?"

I ran a hand through my hair. "Look. I didn't ask for any of this. It took a long time for me to believe it myself. And then I was just trying to survive it. Yeah, maybe you were the prize.

"Not you physically." I rushed on before she could object. "The prize, the goal, was a normal life that *included* you. Telling you, bringing you into this insanity, would mean that I was acknowledging it was my permanent life. I just wanted to be quit of the whole thing. And that was before I even met Buck and Gear. Once I saw what this war had done to them I knew I'd made the right call. I would have done anything to get my regular life back."

"But it wasn't your life, was it?" she exploded. *"It was somebody else's!"*

She closed her eyes and took a deep breath. When she spoke again, her voice had dropped to a whisper.

"The Trav I knew, the Trav I loved, even though he wasn't perfect, is dead. Has been dead, for months. And I can't even mourn him." She flipped her hands in my direction. "Because you're right here!"

"That's right," I replied. "I am here. And I'm just me. I love you the same way he did. How could I not? We're the same person."

"Then what about Morgan?"

"Morgan?" My confusion must have shown on my face. "What about Morgan?"

"Have you talked to her?"

"Morgan? There hasn't exactly been time."

"You need to. Something's not right with her. Maybe it's still the residual effects of having her memories tampered with, but something's going on. And…"

"And what?" I prompted.

Her lips tightened. "Trav, I'm not blind. There is a connection between the two of you."

"Not like that. Not in the way you mean."

"Maybe not. But that's not true for other Travs and Morgans, is it? I saw both your faces when Morgan asked about, what did you call her, Gwen? She was a Morgan, wasn't she?"

I nodded.

"And pregnant. If I'm understanding all of this correctly, there's a pretty short list of potential fathers."

"One Trav said I was from the Mary-verse," I acknowledged. I'd hoped that might lighten the moment a little, but no luck.

She snorted in frustration. "Don't you see? You can't have it both ways! You tell me you're the same as my Trav, but there are Travs who have made different choices. We're defined by our choices. They're what make us who we are. If different Travs make different choices, *they are different people.* Which brings us right back to where we started. You're not the Trav I fell in love with. And I'm not your Mary."

I didn't know what to say. She was right. I'd met, what, a dozen Travs? And I had no problems telling them apart, whether they wore identifying ball caps or not. And there had been a moment when Morgan and I had come close to being…close. That moment had passed, and we both seemed to be okay with that, regardless of the Trav-Morgan shipping that the Multiverse seemed to be engaged in.

"I've never pretended to understand the physics of all this," I said slowly. "And I can't speak for any other Trav but me. It's true, most of the ones I've met have been with Morgan. I can't explain that. But there is one thing I have in common with your Trav. He loved you. I love you. We'd do anything to—"

But before I could finish, a half dozen sharp, metallic coughs erupted from down the hall.

Gunfire.

22

Something's Coming

MARY AND I tore down the hall and burst into the cafeteria. Trav Becker stood in the middle of the room, gun in one hand and sword in the other. Smoke curled up from one of the computers. Sam was trying to keep a table full of equipment between him and the gunman. Morgan had pulled Sophie behind another of the tables. Gear stood in front of the women, fumbling with a gun.

Trav turned as he heard the clatter of our approach. Mary was in the lead and I watched in horror as he swung his gun up to take aim at her.

Without thinking I pointed at the barrel of Trav's gun. Time stopped as he pulled the trigger from point-blank range of the woman I loved.

And it gave an empty click.

"Fuck!" Trav snarled. He swung his sword to bear. But we'd bought Gear just enough time. He swung his gun up, and before Trav could take a step, put three rounds into the chest of my twin.

Who had just enough time to look a little surprised before collapsing.

Gear kept his weapon trained on the man as he went down.

"Is everyone all right?" I asked. The other four nodded.

I carefully approached the body. Blood was beginning to seep from underneath it. I rolled it over.

"Good shot," I said as Gear limped over. This gave me a clear view of his weapon.

"What the hell is that?"

Gear's "gun" was a bizarre contraption that only bore a passing resemblance to a firearm. It looked like an honest-to-God ray gun right out of a 1950s serial. Brownish-gray, almost copper in color, the barrel was half again as long as Morgan's Desert Eagle. Adding to its sci-fi look were three discs which encircled the end of the barrel about a half-inch apart. It looked like a toy, but the holes in Dead Trav's chest gave it a certain respectability.

"Flash Gordon having a sale?" I asked.

Gear looked quite proud of himself. "Pretty cool, huh? Guns don't work very well when all you Travs show up and start flinging Traveler power all over the place."

Which was why The Opposition carried swords. I'd found that out the hard way in my first encounter with them. And for the first time, I thought about the odd coincidence that in the Purgatory stream of my exile, Leon Martin was an expert fencer, not a swimmer. That idea needed some extra thought, but Gear was still speaking.

"It took me forever to devise a way to suppress the quantum chaos you guys bring with you."

"I guess you figured it out," I replied dryly.

"Hadn't had a chance to test it before now. We were lucky."

"Speaking of Traveler power, I thought Mary was a goner," Sam said. "Did you have anything to do with that?"

I looked at him. "I...Maybe? It all happened pretty fast."

"I don't know, man. There was no way he was going to miss. You just stood there and pointed. That is some serious Jedi mojo."

I pointed to Gear's ray gun. "I'd rather have one of those. You got any more?"

He shook his head. "It's a prototype."

"How did they find us?" Mary asked.

"Hard to say," Gear shrugged. "Like I said, The Boss has had decades to study how the Multiverse works."

"It doesn't matter," I said. "Our superposition has been super-detected."

"Grab your stuff," I said to Gear. "We gotta go."

"He shot up my rig before the backup was done," the old man objected. "I'll have to boot up another box to see how much data we have."

"Then you better get started," I said. "Sam, give him a hand."

Sam nodded.

"Why now?" I muttered to myself.

"What? Morgan asked.

"Why attack us now?"

"Isn't it obvious? He's after you."

I shook my head. "That can't be it."

"But The Boss said it. You're special. He needs you."

"Why?" I repeated, throwing up my hands. "He's already won. What am I going to do to him? He's taken out the Rangers. I'm not much of a threat."

"Maybe he's not taking any chances."

"But why attack us here? It would be smarter to hunker down, put the whole Trav army on defense, and keep us from getting anywhere near him until he does whatever it is he's going to do. Remember when we hit Arkham with Buck? They weren't expecting us and it still went south. I can't even imagine going up against him when he's waiting for us. No, he should be sitting tight, keeping to his plan."

Ever since Gear had told us his story, and his theory about what The Boss's plan was, something had been bothering me. Something Sam had said.

We like to meddle.

Maybe The Boss had a master plan to rewrite the universe exactly as he wanted it. But what if things didn't go as planned? It wasn't like Sam Markus to put all his eggs in one basket. There had to be a backup plan in case the Multiverse didn't organize itself the way he wanted. If what Gear said was true, none of The Boss's tech would work after the change. So, he was just going to sit back and live with it if things didn't work out his way?

We like to meddle.

It was hard to imagine The Boss just letting the Traveler power discharge into nothingness. Granted, getting rid of Travs had been job one, but how could The Boss live with the knowledge that this power existed and he couldn't access it?

I looked over at Sophie who was seated cross-legged on the floor. Her chin rested in her hand, torso folded in a way only a teenager's did. I remembered Manbun's shock when she had popped into existence behind me. What if The Boss had found out there was a way to rid himself of Trav Becker but keep the Traveler power?

"Oh no," I whispered.

"What?" Morgan asked.

But before I could explain to her, a song started to run through my head. Specifically, the ominous, rumbling introduction to "In The Air Tonight."

This was no ordinary earworm. To paraphrase Mr. Collins, I could feel something coming. And that wasn't good.

I had used music as a focusing device in the past to help me pick out the particular person or stream I needed to get to. I'd never had a song pop into my head before, but I knew instinctively that I shouldn't ignore this.

I cocked my head. It was crazy, but the volume of the music in my head got louder when I faced the stage at the south end of the room.

"Trav, what is it?" Mary asked.

"We gotta go," I said.

"What do you mean?" Gear asked.

"I seem to have acquired an extra sense," I replied, more calmly than I was feeling. The music pounded and was now joined by a cloudy image forming in my head as well.

"Get your stuff gathered up."

Morgan hurried over to Sophie. Sam continued stuffing computer components into his messenger bag but now at double time.

Gear appeared next to me and grabbed my arm. "Trav, about the guys from the orphan streams."

"What about them?"

"They're not fully formed personalities like you or the Rangers. They do what they're told. And don't much care whether they live or die."

Great. An army of Trav drones.

"Mary, Sophie!" I called. "Let's move! We're going to have company!"

I turned back toward the stage. My augmented senses displayed a view that my brain resolved as spinning tunnels of light, horizontal cyclones boring through the darkness that lay behind the wall. One tunnel was nearer than four others.

I didn't stop to question if these new manifestations were further confirmation of Gear's theory about the energy buildup causing my powers to mutate.

"Ray gun!" I snapped. Gear shrugged helplessly, pointing toward a table on the other side of the room near where we'd covered Dead Trav with a sheet. The mouth of the lead circle was getting bigger. It would intersect with the back wall of the stage any second now.

No time. I vaulted over the circle of chairs where we'd held our coffee klatch, leaping onto the stage, desperately searching for something I could use as a weapon. A tall wastebasket full of baseball bats rested in one corner. I hadn't picked up a bat in years. There had been a department softball team for a while, but the municipal league had switched over to sand volleyball, which I couldn't abide.

These days, my main baseball experience was rooting for the Cardinals. Like old rock and jazz music, it was an affectation I'd inherited from my dad.

And the swing I made as I snatched a bat from the stack was pretty dismal, even by Little League standards. If anything, it was more of a cricket swing, starting low and swinging up, rather than across.

But it did the trick, connecting with the face of Trav Becker just as he popped into view.

He went down without making a sound. I wound up again, just in time to smack the second Trav as he appeared a moment later.

I felt rather than heard the appearance of a third behind me. I whirled around, but not in time. The hilt of his sword arced toward my head. I swung the bat up just in time to partially deflect the blow. The blade's edge missed me, but the flat side smacked into the side of my head. I went down on one knee, seeing stars.

I looked up helplessly as he checked his swing, changing his direction to come back around with a blow that would certainly separate my head from shoulders.

But instead connecting with my clavicle, his blade skittered along the edge of a wooden staff that appeared out of nowhere. Mary whipped her weapon around, holding it in front of her in a two-handed grip. It was longer than Trav's sword, lessening his advantage slightly. But only slightly. And Trav was no slouch. He grinned and lunged for her.

But now Sophie got into the act. Tucking her head, she sprang for his legs, doing a monkey roll right into his ankles. He toppled over and a love tap from my bat sent him to dreamland as well.

Sophie popped to her feet and grinned as we looked at her in shock.

"Six years of tae kwon do," she said.

Before any of us could reply, another Trav appeared. He was more prepared than the others. He danced out of reach of Mary's staff, ducked under my swing, and booted me in the stomach.

He spotted Gear. Before I had the chance to wish for a Trav-induced probability jam, my doppelgänger drew his pistol and snapped off four quick shots. Only two fired, but that was enough.

Gear dropped like a stone.

I snatched up the sword Trav Three had dropped and lunged at Number Four. He swung his pistol toward me, pulling the trigger. I flicked my wrist at his gun.

"I don't think so," I snarled. He pulled the trigger twice. I didn't even duck, so confident he would misfire. Before he could go for his sword I ran him through.

I didn't stop to pull my blade from his chest, just let the Trav drone slide to the ground as I dashed to Gear's side.

Sam cradled the old man's head in his lap. Bright, arterial blood flowed from his thigh, a sure sign one of the bullets had nicked his femoral artery.

"Mary, Morgan, see if you can find me some towels or something," I called.

"First aid kit in the desk," Gear wheezed.

Sophie darted over and returned with a medical kit that would have done any ER proud.

"Nice," I said.

"Nearest doctor is in another universe," Gear mumbled.

I put pressure on the wound and the bleeding finally slowed. A little bit of color returned to Gear's face. I rocked back on my haunches.

"Saved your ass, I did," he murmured. A pleased chuckle burbled from his lips. It was accompanied by some pink foam.

I grabbed for my belt. "I'll make a tourniquet," I said. "We'll get out of here and get you to the hospital."

Gear shook his head. He looked at Sam. "You know where it is, right?"

Sam nodded and ran back over to the table to grab his bag and a backpack he'd been stuffing with instruments and hard drives.

"We gotta go. Now!" I called to the women. They rushed over.

"Help me with him," I said to Mary, jerking my head at Gear.

"I said *no*," the old man snarled.

Sam had arrived back with Gear's ever-present tablet. The old man snatched it from his young double with surprising strength.

"There are more on the way, right?" he asked me.

I looked back at the stage wall. With my new extra-dimensional vision, I could see at least eight more light circles bearing down on our stream.

"Yeah," I said softly.

He began doing something with the tablet.

"We're not leaving you behind," I warned.

Gear's face was the color of paper but his eyes were calm. "We'll have to time this exactly right," he said to Sam, who nodded.

"No," I growled. "We're all going, *now*. There's no time."

Gear smiled. "That's where you're wrong. I can give you all the time you need."

I studied the old man for a second, trying to decide if he was delirious.

"Remember what he said about working on an app to modulate the coherence of the stream alignment by hand?" Sam interrupted.

"Can you hide this stream and buy us some time?"

"I can buy you time," Gear said. "Just not that way." He lowered his head, shifting position with a grimace, and went back to the tablet.

"At least let us get that wound wrapped," I said.

Gear started to object but Morgan had already dropped to her knees beside him, first aid kit in hand.

"Now explain to me what you intend to do," I said.

"No time, remember?" Gear said, not looking up. "Explain it to him, Junior."

"Remember what he said about working on an app to modulate the coherence of the stream alignment by hand?" Sam said.

I nodded.

"He's going to dial the coherence as far as it'll go. Time will run so slowly here that we'll not only have time to get away, but The Boss will lose contact with his team."

"But what happens to you?" I asked Gear.

"I keep bleeding. Just *real* slow." His impish smile took years off his face, and he looked so much like his younger version it made my chest ache.

"We'll come back for you," I promised.

"Take your time."

"Nice," I replied. "Okay, what do we do?"

"Wait for them to get here," he said. "The instant they do, you guys jump out. As soon as you're gone, I slow things down." He chuckled. "For The Boss, it will be instant radio silence. It'll drive him nuts."

"Hopefully, he'll waste a bunch of time trying to punch through," Sam said.

I shifted my vision to gauge the arrival of The Opposition. "They're almost here. Everybody, grab what you need and gather round."

Sam put a tablet that was a twin to Gear's into his messenger bag. Morgan made a beeline for Gear's ray gun.

Gear grabbed my arm. "Trav. I'm sorry about earlier. Maybe you're right. Maybe you can find another way. Just be careful. The Boss has been manipulating Trav Beckers since you were in short pants. Don't underestimate him."

I gripped his hand with mine. "I won't. I'll find a way to surprise him."

The old man nodded. "You'll have to. Now go."

I joined the rest of the group. Mary still held the staff she'd used so effectively in one hand. She draped her other hand protectively over Sophie's shoulders.

"Where'd you get the quarterstaff?" I asked.

"The proper term is Bo staff," she sniffed, "Apparently, Mrs. Peterson was a hiker," she said.

"Or a ninja," I replied, "I see you took that stick fighting class we talked about. Think I can start late?"

"If you behave, maybe I'll give you remedial lessons," Mary replied with a small smile. A small kernel of hope flared in my chest. I turned my attention back to the rest of the group.

"All right, everyone, get in close. We need to be touching."

I'd never tried to bring a group this big through before or to shift locations in space as well as stream. I'd once shifted out of a moving car and nearly gotten run over. Which is what can happen when you appear in the middle of the street two feet off the ground and going thirty-five miles an hour. Now was not the time to repeat that mistake.

But if Gear was right, power was not going to be a problem. As my inner eye watched the approach of the Trav drones, I gathered everyone close. I could now feel a slight but discernible tug in the direction of the stream from which we'd originally come.

Like before, there were no lights or sounds. One second the little stage was empty, the next, two groups of three Travs stood there, back-to-back, swords and guns at the ready.

"Now!" cried Gear.

With my arms enfolding our little group, I herded them forward.

As the school disappeared and Sam's lab swam into view, I heard Gear crow in triumph.

"Hello, boys! What's the rush? You all need to slow down."

23

Help

PROPELLED BY MY push in the other dimension, our party stumbled forward into Sam's lab. I sagged back against the wall and tried to recover from the sensory dissonance of the shift. My powers may have increased, but pulling that much mass had left me feeling like my body had been turned inside out.

"Are you all right, buddy?" Sam asked.

I nodded. "Just let me catch my breath."

"Are we sure they won't follow?" Morgan asked.

"By our measure, time in that stream has pretty much stopped," Sam said. He tapped his tablet. "The code to speed it up again is in here. But until we do that, they're like flies in amber."

"We have a little time," I said. "Probably not as much as you and Gear think, though. Anything one Sam can think of, another one will also figure out."

"Then what's next?" Mary asked.

"We can't stay here," I replied. "It's the first place they'll come looking."

Mary frowned in thought for a moment, then said, "How about the theatre?"

The Capitol Theatre had begun its life as a movie house in the 1920s. One of those huge, single-screen theaters that sat nearly two thousand. It featured one of the first air conditioning units west of the Mississippi.

After it had closed, the orchestra had run a capital campaign to update and remodel it. Mary taught at the symphony school and had keys to the building.

"It's…God, what day is it?" Mary asked.

Sam looked at his phone, then went over to his computer. After a second, he gave a satisfied grunt.

"It's Sunday."

"That's perfect. The orchestra is off until Tuesday and there aren't any rentals this week. The building should be pretty quiet."

I nodded. "Works for me."

A few minutes later, we breathed the fresh air of a crisp, Midwestern fall day.

"I don't think we'll all fit in my car," Mary said.

"That's okay," I said. "I have someplace I need to go first."

"Are you sure it's wise for us to split up?" Sam asked.

I pointed to the gear that Sam had brought with him from…well, Gear. "How long will it take you to get that stuff up and running to the point where it will do us some good?"

Sam gave me a derisive look. "Are you kidding? I barely understand any of this. Gear had years of subjective time to work on it. And before that he had a whole crew of Sams who could practically read each other's minds. I don't even know where to start."

I nodded. "I'm going to get you some help."

He looked at me skeptically. "Does this mean you've come around to Gear's point of view? You're going to find us some more Sams and Travs?"

I shook my head. "Maybe this is Trav hubris, but I still think if we go down the same path Buck did, we lose. We have to chart a new path."

"A new path?" asked Morgan. "How are you going to do that?"

"There's someone who's never been a part of this" I replied. "Like us. Well, not like us at all. But I know neither The Boss or Buck ever recruited him."

Sam tumbled to it first. "Oh no. Tell me that's not what you're thinking. There's a reason he is where he is. He's just like The Boss!"

"And you yourself said he was years ahead of you in the research. Who better to help you now?"

"But he's crazy!"

"Maybe crazy is what we need right now."

"What are the two of you talking about?" Mary asked in exasperation. Morgan stayed silent. Poor Sophie just watched us with the unease any kid experiences when adults argue.

After I explained my plan, of course, everybody looked uneasy. But nobody had any better ideas.

"At least let one of us come with you," Sam said.

"It's going to be hard enough for me to get in," I said. "And you're the absolute last person who can be seen with me."

"Thanks a lot."

"Are you okay with getting everyone to the theatre?" I asked Mary.

She nodded.

"Good. Thank you. I'll meet you in a couple of hours."

"And what if you can't get in? Or get caught?" Sam asked.

I shrugged. "I'm attempting a one-man prison break. What could possibly go wrong?"

Driving Sam's Prius, I glided along a winding, two-lane road that led to the nearby burg of Okaloosa. Cruising along Main Street was like going back in time to when towns like this bustled with retail and civic activity. But here, the forbidding limestone walls of the Oakdale prison were just a stone's throw away from the town square. I pulled up to the main gate, automatically reaching into the pocket of my jacket where I normally kept my badge.

Funny thing. It was right in my pocket where it was supposed to be. Had it been there all the time, even when I was amnesiac in Purgatory? Why hadn't I ever noticed? Or had I called it into existence at the moment I needed it?

This parallel universe stuff can really give you a headache.

"Can I help you?" said the gate guard. I showed him my badge and signed his log. I let him direct me to the area of the parking lot reserved for law enforcement, even though I knew it from many visits.

Okay, time to test my power-up. Hope you were right, Gear.

Mary had tried to talk me into Traveling directly from the theater or Sam's lab, but I still wasn't confident of my ability to shift through physical distance as well as across streams. My task was hard enough as it was. I wanted to have a firm grasp on both origination and destination.

I walked down the main hallway and repeated the badge ceremony with a second guard. This was where things got sketchy. The next checkpoint was where I was supposed to fill out a form and wait for someone to bring the inmate I was here to see to an interview room. But I needed to get on the cellblock floor.

I closed my eyes and inhaled slowly. I can't explain what thoughts went through my mind. I wasn't even sure what I was asking the Multiverse to do. I had a sudden mental image of Obi-Wan distracting guards on the Death Star by creating a sound behind them.

But I didn't have to even wave my hand. As I approached, the guard's phone rang. He turned his face away from me to answer it. As he did so, the nightstick protruding from his utility belt hit the release switch for the door. He didn't even turn around as I glided past him.

Two more guards also failed to notice me. Nor did they notice an old friend who suddenly appeared as my guide. A red-outlined version of me strode confidently about ten feet in front of me. I followed him through a cafeteria, empty this time of day, then a common area, filled with about twenty inmates who became suddenly captivated by a fight that broke out on the reality show they were watching on TV.

Finally, Red Trav stopped in front of a cell door. It was ajar, as was common in the middle of the day when inmates could come and go to some extent as they pleased. The cell's occupant was stretched out on the lower bunk, a white cord running from his ears to an iPad that lay on his chest.

"Hello, Anton," I said.

"Hello, Travis," Anton Kaaro said mildly. "This is...unexpected." His expression belied his words. Ever intractable, he didn't look the least surprised to see me waltz right up to his cell in broad daylight and violation of pretty much every prison regulation on the books.

Except for the orange jumpsuit, he looked just like the version behind the desk in Purgatory except his hair and beard were just a little longer.

I started to reply but a wave of dizziness suddenly washed over me. For a second, there were two Anton Kaaros in front of me. I realized that huge amounts of Gear's interdimensional static electricity was pouring out of me in order to just get this far. The human body was not designed to function like this for very long. I needed to finish up and get going.

I must have swayed a little because Kaaro got to his feet and looked at me curiously. "Are you all right?"

"I'm fine."

"To what do I owe the honor of this visit? And why did you, *how* did you come here? It is unusual."

I couldn't help but smile. Kaaro's tone was calm, almost indifferent, but I knew he was curious.

I smiled. "Well, actually, Anton, I'm not here to see you. I'm sure it seems strange to see me just show up." I grinned even wider at him. "But that's nothing compared to *this*."

With that, I reached out to the version of this cell that I had actually come in search of. And winked out of his sight.

24

Crazy They Call Me

FROM MY POINT of view, it was the Slavic crime boss who disappeared to be replaced by Sam Markus. Prison had aged him. He resembled Gear as much as he did the Sam I knew. There were wrinkles around his eyes and his head was shaved smooth. Like Kaaro, he lay in the bottom bunk, head and shoulders propped against a pillow, reading.

I stared into the eyes of the man I had once called Sam Zero, the version of my friend who had started me on this journey more than a year before by soliciting my "help" to stop a version of Trav he claimed was killing Trav Beckers up and down the Multiverse. It was this Sam who had been behind the whole thing. Not killing Travs himself, but recruiting down-and-out versions like me to do the dirty work for him. Sam and I had stranded him in this stream, the very one we had originated from, with the incriminating evidence of a Trav Becker corpse to make sure he didn't cause any more trouble.

Sam Zero closed the book, keeping his page with one finger. He calmly looked me up and down as if people appeared out of thin air in front of him every day.

"Aren't you supposed to be dead?" he asked.

"Not for lack of trying on your part."

He shrugged. "I think the way you arranged things to stick me in here balances the scales."

"You got what you deserve."

"I can yell for the guard," he mused. "And you'll have to explain how the man I allegedly murdered is not only still alive, but managed to get into my jail cell without showing up on a dozen security cameras."

"Do that and I'll disappear long before anyone can get here."

"Then why are you here, Trav? It can't be to gloat. That's not like you."

Sam was playing it cool, but his eyes burned with curiosity. He stared at me for what seemed like a long time. Then he smiled. But it wasn't the goofy grin I knew. This smile was hard, even predatory. I reminded myself that this Sam not only had succeeded in killing multiple Trav Beckers but had spent the last year in prison. He was not the Sam I knew and trusted. Or even the one trying to remake the universe in his own image.

Of course, the last few weeks had changed me as well.

"You need my help," he said. "That's why you're here." A triumphant glint came into his eyes. "What's the matter? Did you finally realize I was right all along?"

"Let's just say I need the help of Sam Markus to hunt Sam Markus."

"Interesting." He swung his legs up and sat on the edge of the bed and gave me an appraising look. "I never had the chance to tell you this because you were busy getting me thrown in jail for your murder and everything. But you really impressed me."

"You don't say."

"Yeah, you went from suicidal drunk to superhero in record time. And look at you now, waltzing into the most secure prison in the state without even breathing hard. You've acquired some serious Traveler mojo."

"Is there a point to this?"

"Of course, there's a point. You need me. What for?"

"We can talk about that later."

"No," Sam replied. "We'll talk about it now." And he plopped back down on the bed.

"Really? You're going to stay here when I'm offering you a chance to get out?"

He shrugged. "You want my help, you're going to have to tell me what is going on. Otherwise, fuck you."

"Okay. I guess that's fair. In a nutshell, you weren't the first Sam Markus to decide to rewrite the universe. Someone else has been at it a lot longer and doing it a lot better than you."

That got his attention. I laid out the broad strokes of The Boss's plan. Sam's eyebrows went up when I said The Boss recruited Travs to help him. His solution had been to just kill them. But his eyes lit up when I mentioned the bag full of Gear's tech, and I knew I had him.

He jumped to his feet. "Okay, I'm in. I wasn't looking forward to my shift in the laundry room tomorrow anyway. What are we waiting for?"

He had no sooner stood than I was across the room. I grabbed him by the throat and slammed him into the wall. The bravado faded from his face as I squeezed. He scrabbled at my hands, but even his prison-inflated muscles were no match for my grip. His mouth worked, but all that came out was a low gurgle.

I leaned in very close. "Yes," I said softly, "I need your help. But make no mistake. Step out of line or hesitate one fucking second when I tell you to do something and I will *end* you. I don't even have to be in the same room. I wave my hand and you'll get run over by a truck. Or a piano will fall on you. Whatever I choose. Understood?"

He nodded.

I released him. He straightened his collar.

"Anything you want to take with you?" I asked.

"You're kidding, right?"

"Then let's get moving."

He gave me an appraising look, rubbing his throat. "So who else is in on this gig?"

I told him.

"Awesome!" he crowed. "We're putting the band back together!"

I don't know how long, subjective time, my conversation with Sam took, but Kaaro was still standing in the same position when Sam and I appeared in his cell. This sight completely cracked his carefully maintained reserve. His eyes went wide as he took in the sight of me accompanied by a prisoner he had never seen before.

"Hey!" Sam exclaimed as he took in his surroundings. "Anton Kaaro! You didn't tell me a celebrity lived in my cell over here." He stuck out his hand. "Sam Markus."

Kaaro shook Sam's hand automatically, which was a further measure of his shock as the Anton Kaaro I knew rarely let himself be touched.

"Hero worship on your own time," I said. "Tick tock, Sam." I started to steer him toward the door, but when I looked at Kaaro, still trying to process my disappearance and reappearance, a crazy thought occurred to me. After all, I had just gotten done telling Sam the path to success was doing things past Travs and Sams wouldn't think of doing. And what I was about to do definitely met that criteria.

"You are probably wondering if you've gone nuts," I said to Kaaro.

"*I* have a certificate," Sam interrupted proudly. "Very official. Signed by the prison psychiatrist and everything. Did they give you one, too?"

"Shut up," I snapped. Then to Kaaro. "I'll give you the short version. I'm a Traveler from a parallel universe. The Trav Becker who was undercover with you is dead." I jerked a thumb at Sam. "Sam is going to help me stop another version of him from destroying reality as we know it. I can use all the help I can get. But this is a limited time offer.

If you need time to decide whether or not this is insane gibberish, we're out of here."

For the first time I had ever seen, Anton Kaaro was speechless. His mouth opened then closed again.

I leaned in closer to him and continued quietly. "You told me once that if you saw a conflict important enough, you'd willingly enlist."

I was betting he had never uttered that phrase out loud on this stream. But if he couldn't accept the evidence of his own eyes and roll with this he was of no use.

He did not disappoint.

"I said no such..." Kaaro began. Then his eyes narrowed. "Or apparently, I did. I think I would like to know more about your relationship with...me."

"Well, you know what you have to do satisfy your curiosity." I inclined my head at Sam. "I'll tell you the same thing I told him. You fuck me over and there is no place you can hide, no amount of money that will keep you safe from me. I can pluck you out of whatever hole you crawl into or just collapse a building on top of it. In fact, I've done that to you before."

For the second time, I saw an expression on Anton Kaaro's face I'd never seen before.

He looked impressed.

He held my gaze for a moment, then nodded. "I will come with you. And help you, Travis. If only to get to know this man who has managed to surprise me not once, but twice today."

"All right then. Stay close to me. This worked when I was alone. We'll see what happens with two of you in tow."

I poked my head out the doorway. It was clear. I motioned the two prisoners out.

"He calls you Travis," Sam whispered.

"Shut up."

223

Ten minutes later we were in the car. We were waved through the gate by a guard suddenly more interested in something on his phone than who was in my passenger seat. Which was Sam, who had called shotgun.

"That was awesome!" Sam chortled once we were on the road. "I still can't believe we just walked past all those guards. And what was the deal with the big guy in the TV room? He looked right at us."

"He works for me," Kaaro said quietly. "Had I given him the proper signal, he would have freed me."

"I'm not sure," Sam said. "Trav's got some pretty big juju all of a sudden." He turned to me. "You know, if I had known you guys could do that, things would have worked out a lot differently for me."

"It's a recent addition to the repertoire," I said. "And a symptom of how close we are to things going completely to hell."

But a part of me had totally adjusted to having near-absolute power and didn't mind it much at all. *Knowing* that there were no Nation County deputy sheriffs anywhere near us, I goosed the Prius up to over ninety miles an hour, anxious to get back to town. I was pretty sure I would get a psychic warning if something happened to the rest of my Scooby gang, but I would feel better when we were all together. Even though that meant bringing a criminal and a madman to the party.

I pulled around to the back side of the theater, where there was a stage door. The streets were quiet. Mary's SUV was the only vehicle in the small lot. I texted her that we had arrived. A minute or two later the door opened and Sophie peeked out. She led us inside and up some stairs to the second floor, sneaking looks over her shoulder whenever she could. It's a measure of the level of craziness in our reality that her glances were not for the third version of Sam Markus she had met in the last twenty-four hours, but for Kaaro, who she certainly had never seen before. She held her questions, however, not saying a word as she indicated the room where the rest of our party was.

It was the theater's green room, a relaxed space with several upholstered chairs, a couch, and some cafe tables. A long counter with a microwave and refrigerator stretched from the doorway to the windows.

Sam reclined on the couch, eyes closed. Mary and Morgan sat at one of the tables, two half-full bottles of water between them. Like Sophie, they didn't give New Sam a second glance, but at the sight of our other companion, their eyes went wide.

"Trav, what the hell?" Morgan choked.

"Geez, can't a guy shut his eyes for ten minutes without—" Sam started to groggily sit up, but snapped to full attention as he too noticed the latest addition to the team.

"Are you crazy?" he demanded.

"No," New Sam said, "*I'm* crazy. We've been through this. I have the papers to prove it and everything."

No one else made a move as he made his way to Sam, smiling salesman-bright. "Call me Harvey," he said, pumping Sam's hand.

Sam, attention now diverted from Kaaro, frowned at this double. "Harvey? As in Harvey Dent?"

The other man waggled his eyebrows comically.

Sam shook his head. "You name yourself after a Batman villain and expect us to trust you?"

Harvey shrugged. "You'll get used to it. I sure as hell wasn't going to take a sidekick name like those other guys."

"Whatever." Sam turned his attention back to Kaaro and started to say something, but Morgan beat him to it.

"This is a surprise, Mr... Kaaro, isn't it?"

He sketched a small bow. "I don't believe we've met, although I have seen you before, young lady. You patronize The Kremlin."

If this was meant to intimidate her, it didn't work. She looked at him coolly. "You have a good memory. Although I haven't decided whether to be complimented or creeped out."

"This is Morgan," I interrupted. "Mary, Sophie. You've met…Harvey. Call the other one Sam."

"It will not be necessary for me to go by a childish nickname, I trust?" Kaaro asked mildly.

Before I could process the fact that Anton Kaaro had just cracked a joke, Mary said, "Can we talk for a minute, Trav?"

"Yeah," Sam added. "About you going as batty as…"

Harvey smiled and raised his hand.

I started to explain, but Kaaro silenced me with a wave. "Please. I can speak for myself."

He glanced around the room, making eye contact with each of the others, even Sophie. Morgan and Mary met his gaze without blinking. Sam couldn't keep his eyes from darting between Kaaro and me. Even Harvey's crazy grin faded in favor of a neutral, measuring expression.

"You don't know me," Kaaro began, "but Travis and I have something of a…history. A history that seems to have dimensions of which I have only recently become aware. I find that intriguing."

"That doesn't mean we should trust you," Mary pointed out.

"True," he acknowledged. "But I have as vested an interest as the rest of you in the continued health of the…what do you call it? The Multiverse?"

Harvey and Sam nodded in exact unison. They looked like the twins in *The Shining*.

"Plus, as I am cut off from my usual resources and will soon be labeled a prison escapee, I am as dependent on Travis and his…gifts, to bring about a positive resolution to this situation as you." He turned to me. "Any lingering differences I have with you can be dealt with at a more convenient time."

"He calls you Travis," Sam said.

For the first time, a hint of exasperation crept into Kaaro's tone. "Why does he keep saying that?"

"It's not important," I replied. I turned to the Sams. "Have you set up Gear's equipment?"

Sam nodded. "C'mon, *Harvey*. Let's see if we can figure out where The Opposition is hiding."

Harvey started to nod but his attention was attracted by an object on the table.

"Hey, cool! I always wanted to make a pair of these!" He picked up the Mike glasses. "Can I have them?"

"Knock yourself out," Sam said. "The server is in another dimension."

"Who cares?" Harvey replied gleefully, slipping the glasses on. He struck a pose. "Do they make me look smart?"

"Jesus Christ, shut up," Sam said. "Let's go. How much time do we have?"

"A little," I said. "We're waiting for—"

At that moment a buzzer went off.

"That's the stage door," Mary said. "I made the calls."

"Why don't you go down?" I asked.

She nodded and disappeared into the hall. Morgan gave me a questioning look.

"I'll explain when they get here." I held up a hand to forestall any further queries.

She frowned and pursed her lips but didn't pursue it. Instead, she offered Kaaro a bottled water, which he accepted.

"You're being awfully mysterious, Mary," came a voice echoing slightly from the concrete stairwell.

"And what do you mean, it's about Trav?" said another. "He's gone." Mary re-entered with two men in tow.

227

"Surprise," I said as Leon Martin and Adam Yount looked at me in shock.

"What the hell?" Leon exclaimed.

"Trav!" Adam joined in. "This isn't possible."

But then the two cops caught a glimpse of Kaaro. Adam drew his weapon from a shoulder holster under his jacket. I raised a hand, but before I could disarm him, Mary pivoted on the balls of her feet and thrust her arm forward. From nowhere, a shaft of silver metal appeared. Before Adam could react, she used it to slap his gun from his hand.

By now, Leon had also reached for his gun but I got there in time to put a hand on his arm. "Leon, please. Don't. It's okay. I'll explain everything. I promise."

"I think I can put it together," Leon said. I could see the anger and disappointment on his face. "You've been working with Kaaro all along. Is that why you faked your death?"

"That fits what you're seeing," I admitted. "I don't blame you for coming to that conclusion. But it's not that. I'll explain everything." I turned to my girlfriend. "Right after I find out what the hell this is." I pointed to Mary's staff.

She grinned. "Isn't it cool? It's collapsible." She demonstrated, stretching her arms out, covering each end with palm, and collapsing the four-foot rod down to something that fit in her palm.

"You didn't have it in Oz," I said.

"It just got here," she replied. "It's funny, because I was saying on the drive in that I had something on order that would come in awfully handy."

I turned to Sophie who suddenly had become very interested in the fabric of the loveseat where she was sitting.

"Sophie?"

"Well, you told me I should practice!" she said.

228

"Someone needs to tell me what the fuck is going on. *Now,*" Leon said, in what we (behind his back) called his "Cut The Shit" voice. "Or I start calling uniforms."

"What's the commotion?" Sam and Harvey appeared in the room's other doorway. Leon and Adam's jaws dropped.

"See?" I said, "There's a lot more going on here than you imagine." I picked up Adam's gun and returned it to him. "Let's just put away our weapons. *All of us.*"

That last was directed to Mary. She nodded and did something involving a couple of clicks to her staff, which disappeared again.

"Everybody take a breath," I continued. "I'll bring you all up to speed."

Adam looked at Leon, who shrugged. My partner returned his weapon to his holster.

I got everyone seated, although Adam and Leon perched on the arms of the loveseat near the door, poised for action.

"This had better be good, Trav," Leon warned.

"It is, boss, believe me."

I looked over my team. Two had tried to kill me. Two others were pretty sure I was a bent cop. A woman I'd been hiding the truth from for months. Two friends who had seen much more danger than they deserved. And a teenager who should have been Snapchatting her friends, not trying to master freaky powers so she could help us assault an armed camp in another dimension.

But it wasn't a team until I could get Leon and Adam on board.

"So," I began. "Have you ever lost your car keys and finally found them in a place you know you already looked?"

"Just so I understand," Leon began.

He was still a little pale after hearing my story, but a good cop lets go of his personal narrative when presented with new facts. Of course, he'd been helped by some parlor tricks Sophie and I had performed, things like predicting Adam had inexplicably put some ketchup packets in his pocket at lunch.

As an amateur magician, we didn't do anything I couldn't have duplicated by non-Traveler methods, but combined with the evidence of the two Sams, who were murmuring and quarreling behind Sam's laptop, it was all pretty compelling. Particularly when I took the two of them on a quick jaunt to Leon's house on Purgatory and showed him a collection of fencing medals and trophies in the place of Masters swim meet awards.

In general, my boss was bearing up pretty well under the revelations. Adam was still a little shook up from learning that he was dead on the Purgatory stream. But he was adjusting.

Leon continued. "These collapses, or resets, whatever you want to call them, are natural events?"

I nodded.

"They happen periodically, and no one notices except for people like you?"

"That's our theory," I replied.

"Then explain to me again why we care? Natural disasters happen. You can't predict them. You just have to be ready to pick up the pieces."

"But it's not a natural disaster," Morgan said. "Whatever The Boss is trying to do, it's artificial. And whatever it is, it's worth recruiting all the Travs he could and killing the rest, to bring it about."

"But all of that goes away during the collapse," Leon objected. "All that happens is the two of you," he pointed at Sophie and me, "lose these Traveler powers. Please tell me it's not about that."

I shook my head. "Leon, you know me better than that. If I wanted the power, I would have joined up with the Rangers. Or the Opposition. The bottom line is we don't know what The Boss has up his sleeve.

That's why we have to go to Arkham. I'm going to find out what he is up to and put a stop to it."

"And what about the reset?" Kaaro asked.

"I don't know," I admitted. "Maybe it will happen. Maybe foiling The Boss's plans will put it off for a while. Maybe the Sams can figure out a way to bring it about in some sort of controlled landing. The key is Arkham. That's where the answers are."

There was a long silence, and for just a minute I thought perhaps despite all the evidence, I'd failed to convince my boss and mentor. Getting his approval suddenly seemed very important.

"I am too old for this shit," he finally said with a heavy sigh.

The smiles told me who in the room had seen *Lethal Weapon* (The Sams, Sophie, and Mary). Morgan and Kaaro shared a confused look with Adam.

"Don't ask," my partner warned. "It's a line from some movie. Or a song from before the Carter administration."

"Quiet, youngster," Leon growled. "You in?" Adam shrugged. Leon turned back to me. "Tell me more about this Arkham."

"You won't be going to Arkham," I said. "Someone needs to stay here and protect Sophie."

Sophie and Mary had slipped out during storytime, picking this unfortunate moment to return.

"What?" the teen cried. "No! you're not leaving me! You need me. I'm the only other Traveler. What if something happens to you?"

"If something happens to me, we've probably already lost. And remember, The Boss is after you. I'm not going to deliver you right into his hideout."

Adam was shaking his head. "I don't know, man. If these guys are as good as you say, and they're powered up like you, what good are the two of us?"

"There's still a Multiverse full of Travs out there," Harvey said. He had shown up wearing the Mike glasses, even though they were no longer functioning "How about Sam and I go out and rustle a few up?"

"Absolutely not," I said firmly. "No more Travs. We'll figure something else out."

I put a hand on Sophie's shoulder. "You have to remember, you're our failsafe. If something does happen to me, you'll need a new plan. And a powered person to carry it out. If it makes you feel any better, Mary is going to stay, too."

"Like hell, Becker," Mary snapped.

I hadn't had a chance to be alone with Mary since our return, so hadn't been able to share Gear's theory that she was at risk, not just from The Boss, but from a Multiverse that favored a Trav-Morgan pairing. I would have to convince her that I was not still trying to keep her in the dark under the guise of protecting her. I opened my mouth, but instead of beginning a sentence, my jaw hung slack.

"You were saying something about needing more firepower?" Mary continued.

She stepped away from the door. Two more Mary Logans entered the room.

25

Along Comes Mary

MARY HAD CHANGED her clothes. She now wore dark jeans and a black top covered by a thick leather vest. A green scarf was tucked into the vest's breast pocket. The other two were dressed similarly, but their scarves were red and gray. Each carried a collapsing staff.

I looked at Sophie. "I don't believe you would do this."

"You told me—"

"This is way more than practice!"

"Don't you yell at her, Trav Becker!" Mary warned. "If you have a problem with what we did, you take it up with me. It's my plan. All Sophie did was what I asked her to do."

"Scarves were my idea," Morgan offered. "I still think we could use another Morgan or two, though."

"*No!*" I shouted. "No. More. Travelers."

I rubbed my temples. "*How* does this help?" I said to Mary, then turned to the new ones. "Do you know what is going on, what the risks are?"

"Enough," said Mary Red.

233

"It is a little bit of a shock when you answer the door to find yourself on the other side," Mary Gray admitted. "But she made a pretty compelling case."

"Sophie and I searched for a stream where I…she was really, really into the martial arts training," Mary explained. "Way more than me."

"We'll get you up to speed," Mary Red assured her.

"And you've gone way farther with your violin then either of us," Mary Gray added. "After all, a girl can only do so much."

"No," I said. "This is crazy. It's just more of you in danger. That is *not* part of the plan."

"He doesn't think we can take care of ourselves," Mary Red observed.

"I think we need to kick his ass," said Mary Gray.

Mary Red nodded and took a step forward, twirling her staff over her wrist.

"Wait!" Mary blocked their approach with one arm. "Can Trav and I have just a minute here?"

"C'mon, Sophie," Morgan said. "I'm hungry. There are some vending machines downstairs. Captain, Detective?" Leon and Adam followed them.

"Our compiling should be completed by now," Sam said to Harvey. "Let's check on it."

"Are you kidding?" Harvey scoffed. "I'm not going anywhere. I haven't seen a good fight in years."

"You've been in prison."

"Yeah, not as exciting as you might think. I think they put stuff in our food."

He plopped down on the sofa. Looking up at the Marys, he patted the seat next to him. "Plenty of room. Although if you want to make it a tag team match, I would totally dig that. I have been in prison, you know."

The Marys looked at each other. They went over and stood on either side of him. His eyes went wide, thinking for just a second that his

gambit had worked. Until the women extended their staffs, each grabbing one end of the other's. Quick as lightning, one staff went under Harvey's chin, the other behind his neck.

"Ggkkk!" he sputtered as they squeezed the staffs together. Mary Red and Mary Gray lifted their arms. To keep his head attached to his shoulders, Harvey had to also rise.

"We'll just be outside," Mary Gray said.

"Skglrr," choked Harvey as they led him out.

Mary turned to me, one eyebrow raised.

"Okay, I get it," I sighed. "They—you can take care of yourselves. But there's a difference between one yappy Sam Markus and a platoon of Travs with enhanced powers. You weren't there the last time. Ask Morgan. It was a massacre."

"Which is why it's going to be different this time. That's the point of the whole exercise. Why do we keep having this argument, Trav? Why won't you let me help? Don't you trust me?"

"Of course, I trust you."

"It was your idea that we take martial arts classes together. You said you wanted me to be able to defend myself. That you didn't want me to depend on the fact that my boyfriend carried a gun. Didn't you mean any of that?"

"I did. I do. It's just that…"

She peered closely at me. "Something has changed. There's another reason, isn't there? What else are you hiding from me?"

"I'm not hiding anything. We haven't had five minutes together so that I could tell you."

"We have time now."

I nodded and motioned to one of the tables. "I gotta sit. I feel like I've been on my feet for a day and a half."

After we seated ourselves I explained Gear's theory. She went pale as I began, but by the time I finished her lips were pressed together in a determined line.

"It's not bad enough that a renegade army of Sams and Travs is out to get us, you're telling me the Multiverse is, too? What did we do to deserve any of this?"

I chanced reaching across the table, gently gripping her wrist. She didn't pull away, a small victory.

"You didn't do anything," I continued. "It's on me. All of it. I could have stayed on Purgatory and none of this would have affected you. Any of you."

She smiled then. I could see the ghost of our love just behind her eyes. "You don't see it, do you? But it's as plain as day."

"What?"

"You keep saying you try to keep out of all this, but you're right in the middle of it. Don't you get it? That Multiverse inertia works both ways. Not getting involved isn't one of your options."

"But I didn't have to involve Sam or Morgan. Or you."

"And you probably would have ended up…Boss fodder."

"Boss fodder?" In spite of everything, I chuckled. "That's pretty good."

"I got a million of 'em."

She turned her wrist and squeezed my hand. "Trav. I understand. I really do. I know you. Being a cop isn't just your job. Protecting others is *who you are.* Every day, you protect people you don't even know. Of course, you want to protect everyone you love.

"In fact," she continued, "I'll bet that moving away from their core purpose is what caused all those other Travs to lose their way. I don't want you to stop being who you are. I just want you to quit feeling responsible when other people decide that protecting *you* is worth the risk."

"I can't ask you to do that."

"You're right. You can't. We're offering."

And that was when I realized where I had gone wrong for so long. She was right. It was not up to me to deny her the right to join the fight. Even if it cost her, and me, everything. That was the deal I accepted when I took up the badge. And now Mary was now just as much a protector as me.

God, I loved her.

I smiled. "I understand. Thank you. For coming after me. For knocking me up side of the head. Hell, for going out and recruiting a set of Avenging Angels to help us."

"We decided to go with Valkyries."

"Fair enough. But seriously, I broke your trust. I know that however this turns out, it's not going to be the same for us. Maybe the inertia is just too much to beat. When this is over, I'll give you some space, like you asked. You deserve it."

"Oh no, you don't, Trav Becker. You don't get out of this that easily. Yeah, I'm still pissed. And you have some major groveling ahead of you. But we can take care of that *after* we save the universe."

She stood up, rounded the table, and slid into my lap.

I looked in her eyes, hardly daring to breathe in her scent and revel in the heat of her nearness. "I...you want to..."

"Yes, you dope. How can I not love the man who literally rewrote the fabric of reality so we could be together?" Her eyes narrowed. "But I'm not sure what I am going to do about the biggest transgression of your secret life."

"Secret life?"

"If a girl's boyfriend is going to be a superhero, she should at least get to see him in spandex once in a while."

"I'm not sure that would be good for anyone."

She took my face in her hands and drew me to her lips.

"Fuck inertia," she whispered.

And then we didn't say anything for a long time.

But through the roar of blood rushing in my ears, I could still hear Mary's voice. Voices.

"Remind me again. Why didn't we end up with him?"

"Ours obviously weren't as smart."

"They might be salvageable. I kind of need a project."

"You have a project. Saving the Multiverse."

"Pish tosh. How long could that take?"

26

Let's Go

"WHAT WE CALL Arkham is a version of the Building 231, the Physics Building at the university," I said.

I stood in the front of the green room, marker in hand, next to a whiteboard Mary had liberated from some corner of the theater administrative offices. I drew a rectangle, labeled it "AR," and slashed in some lines to represent the nearby streets.

I looked over our motley assembly. Sam and Harvey were sprawled on the couch, dividing their attention between me and their laptop. Sophie sat at one of the cafe tables with Noah on her lap. The cat had demonstrated his talent for finding us wherever we landed once again.

Morgan and Kaaro sat at Sophie's table. Kaaro had somehow managed to exchange his orange jumpsuit for his normal uniform of matching dark gray pants and shirt. I didn't want to know how he'd done it. Leon and Adam had arranged their chairs so they could watch me and keep an eye on the crime boss at the same time. The new Marys perched on a loveseat while mine leaned against the window ledge.

I drew a big X at the bottom of my sketch. "Last time, we tried a frontal assault on the Broadway side and it was a complete disaster. They were waiting for us. None of our weapons worked. It was a bloodbath."

"We can help a little with that," Sam piped up. "We've made some progress with the PBG."

Seeing our blank looks, he explained. "Probability Bubble Gun. We worked from Gear's prototype and have managed to jury-rig a couple of modules that generate a similar quantum field." He held up a small metal box. "All in this compact container. Attached to your weapon, it should suppress the ability of the Travs to screw up your fire."

"Nice," I said.

Sam grinned. "Yeah, it's amazing what you can do with a Raspberry Pi."

"A what?" Morgan asked.

"Tiny little computer," Sophie explained.

"Is that a breath mint tin?" Adam asked.

"You get me a machine shop, I'll get you something sexy in matte black," Sam said defensively. "This will do the job."

"How will you attach it?" I asked.

Harvey held up a roll of duct tape.

"Of course. We have two of them?"

Sam nodded.

"I'll take one," I said. "Morgan, you get the other. It'll look fabulous on your Desert Eagle. Anton, you take the original prototype."

Sam laid Gear's Buck Rogers gun on the table in front of him. Kaaro's look said, *You've got to be kidding,* but he picked up the weapon and examined.

I flipped the marker end to end in my hand. "The Boss has claimed that he can anticipate any idea, any plan Sam or I can come up with. So the floor is open for ideas from anyone else on how to get in."

Morgan stood up heavily and held her hand out for the marker. "Last time, I snuck in through the side door." She made a mark on the right side of the picture. "It's in the alley next to…what is that building?"

"Beach Hall," Sam supplied.

"They surely buttoned that up after you all escaped," Leon said.

The room fell silent as we stared at the whiteboard, the hum of the refrigerator the only sound in the room.

"Um."

Sophie cleared her throat.

"What about the roof?"

I looked at the sketch, then around the room. Mary caught my eye, giving me an amused look.

"We did a field trip once to go up and look through the telescopes," Sophie continued.

"Two-dimensional thinking. Gets you every time," someone said. Mary Gray reached over and squeezed Sophie to her. The girl beamed.

Adam raised a hand. "Do you have to have already been in a place in order to Travel there?"

I looked over at Sam, who grinned. Harvey gave a barking laugh, and I couldn't help but join in.

"As a matter of fact, I have been there," I explained.

"Finnegan would be proud," Sam said.

I drew two circles to represent the small observatories located on the roof and also indicated the location of the door.

"What if the door is locked?" Morgan asked.

"That will not be a problem," Kaaro said.

"Okay." I brought the room back to order. "Ingress is covered. Next issue. The Boss has got to have a control room, a main office, someplace. We aren't going to have time for a general search. Neither Morgan or I, or for that matter, Sophie, ever got off the first floor of the building. Am I right, Sophie?"

She nodded. Once again, I marveled at the young girl's resiliency. We were talking about the place where she had been held after being kidnapped. Veteran cops would have been in PTSD counseling for months after what she'd been through. But here she was, pissed off that she couldn't go back.

"Sam's lab?" Mary asked.

Sam shook his head. "Too small. And not secret lair-y enough." He turned to Harvey.

"What?" The other Sam demanded. "What are you looking at me for?"

"Because you're the closest thing to an evil genius we have handy."

Harvey folded his arms, glaring at us stubbornly. But a minute later, he puffed out a breath and rolled his eyes.

"Fine. There's a computer lab on the 4th floor," he said. "It was one of my favorite spots during undergrad. The workstations have beaucoup processing power, way more than most labs. The internet just screams. And there's a bunch of task lighting. Smart bulbs that change color. Turn off the fluorescents and you get a definite Batcave vibe. It's kind of cool."

"It's where I'd go," Sam agreed.

"And it's two floors from where we'll be entering," I said. "The Batcave it is. We have to go right past it anyway, so it's worth a shot. If it's a dead end we'll just keep going down until we find what we're looking for."

Morgan raised a finger. "You haven't mentioned yet who gets to go on this little jaunt."

I didn't reply at first. Not only was this going to be the least popular decision I'd be making, like all of my decisions, it was suspect. Were Manbun and The Boss sitting around a table at this very moment predicting my every move?

It was a paralyzing feeling. But I had to go with my gut.

"Morgan and me, of course," I began. "The Marys. Anton. Sam and Harvey."

"Wait," Adam interrupted. "You're taking *him?*" He pointed at Harvey.

"I want Harvey where I can see him," I simply. I looked at my watch. "I want everyone to get some rest before we move out."

"Like that's going to happen," Morgan murmured.

"You'll be surprised. We've all been running at full speed for days. Even if you don't sleep, get horizontal and try to recharge. There are plenty of dressing rooms. Showers in some of them if that will help relax you. I want to move out in six hours."

Everyone got to their feet, seeking out the various dressing rooms they'd appropriated for their use. But I had some tasks to complete before I could rest. And one of them needed to be accomplished now.

Morgan had risen slower than everyone else. Standing up seemed to take just about every bit of energy she had.

"Are you going to be okay?" I asked.

"Yeah," she said.

I raised an eyebrow.

"Just tired," she amended. "Like everyone else."

I nodded. "Can I talk to you a minute?"

She shrugged. I sat down and she did the same with a grateful look she tried to hide. But even though I'd requested the conversation, she was the one who started talking.

"Were you and Mary able to talk things out before all hell broke loose?" she asked.

I was unable to completely suppress a smile.

"I'm glad," she said.

"But she's worried about you," I said.

"Me?"

243

"Yeah. She's pretty perceptive. She can see something's bothering you. I can, too."

Morgan sighed. "When we were with the Rangers, this all seemed so doable. Intrepid team of Travs, Sams, and Morgans out to save the universe. Meeting Fay was a shock, but it was also exciting. She was a force of nature, and I thought, *Someday, that will be me.* It made me feel so alive and strong. Then seeing what she had with Buck."

I opened my mouth, but she had only paused to take a breath.

"Trav, they did something to my *mind.*"

A shiver rippled through her petite frame. "It wasn't like with Mary where they just relied on the Multiverse to fill in the gaps. They actually got inside and wiped my memory." She grabbed my hand. "Trav, my mind is the only thing I have. Sam has his equations, his formula. His reality is grounded in what he derives from physics. But my reality is what's inside me. If I can't trust my memory, I don't have anything!"

I covered her hand with mine. "But you got your memories back."

"Did I?" Her eyes were haunted. "I'll never know what they took. And you know what's terrible? When we had to leave Gear behind, part of me was happy that I wouldn't have to see him anymore and pretend that what he did to me didn't bother me."

"I'm sure he didn't realize it was going to affect you like that."

"I know. It wasn't his fault. At least not totally. But ever since I—"

She made quote marks with her fingers.

"—woke up, I just can't escape the feeling that I didn't get everything back. And the Traveling! Is it harder now for everyone? That last time, I thought I was going to vomit."

"I've had those moments, too," I assured her. "Remember when I came through with the Rangers? I threw up all over the place."

"That's right," she smiled wanly. "I thought those guys were never going to stop kidding you." But then her smile faded, as did mine.

Mentioning the Rangers made us both remember their fate, dead at the hands of The Boss and his Trav army.

"Look," I finally said, "don't overthink it. Everything will come back. It did for me."

She nodded. "Yeah, you're right. I guess you went through the same thing." She squeezed my hand.

"Thanks. Oh God, I'm sorry. You were the one who wanted to talk to me, and here I just went on and on. What did you want to talk about?"

"I...I..." My mouth opened and closed a couple of times. "I just wanted to make sure everything was okay," I finished lamely.

She frowned, then her eyes narrowed.

"You wanted to make sure I was okay with you and Mary!" she hissed. She withdrew her hand from mine and clapped me a good one on the shoulder. "Trav Becker, get over yourself. I'm having my share of turmoil right now, but that is *not* a part of it."

"Hey, I never said it was."

"Oh, don't give me that. Tell me you weren't just a little into the idea of both Mary and me wanting you."

I reddened, completely at a loss for words. She made me suffer for about ten seconds, then burst into a laughing fit.

"Relax, Trav. I'm just jerking your chain. I couldn't resist. Any fool can see you only have eyes for her. And let me tell you something. The Rangers may have done okay with Trav-Morgan teams, but I think you and Mary together are way more than the sum of your parts."

She sighed. "But you're right about one thing. I would like to have that with someone. Heck, that's what we're all looking for. But I believe told you before, you are not my type!"

"Sounds to me like you have your memory back." I tried to look rueful but it devolved into a chuckle, which made her giggle again in turn.

She reached over the table and we both leaned into a hug. "All right," I said, patting her on the back, "But you're still not one hundred percent. Get some rest. That's an order."

She gave me a mock salute. "Yes, sir. Is somebody going to make sure you do the same?"

"Don't worry about me. Now go." She didn't put up any more of a fight, which just confirmed how tired she was.

I watched her go, wishing I was as confident as she was about Mary and me.

I didn't want anyone else leaving the theater, but I desperately needed a change of clothes and there were a few other items I wanted from my apartment. I chanced a trip home and was pleased to see my place was pretty much how I remembered leaving it. The landlord hadn't cleaned it out or anything. I guess I wasn't so much dead on this stream as simply forgotten.

I wondered absently what would have happened if I hadn't brought Leon and Adam in on the mission but just strolled in to work on Monday. Would they have thought I had risen from the dead or just grunted a good morning and gone about their day? Or had the simple fact of my return slid things back into their previous configuration?

My trip only took an hour, but by the time I returned I was dragging and ready to take my own advice. I trudged up to the dressing room I had appropriated for myself. It was the one the maestro normally used. Small, but with a nice vanity, shower, and couch with a pullout.

The soft music playing from the bluetooth speaker on the vanity should have tipped me off, but I was oblivious, switching on the light as I entered.

"Hey!" called a groggy, feminine voice. "Give a girl some warning!"

Mary had pulled out the sofa bed and lay under some blankets. She ran a hand through her sleep-tousled hair, squinting blearily at me.

She looked breathtaking.

"Uh, sorry...I didn't know you were in here."

246

"Where else would I be? I've been waiting for you. Now, come to bed. You need rest more than any of us."

"Um. Okay."

I kicked my shoes off, unbuttoned my shirt, and then stood there, still wearing my t-shirt and jeans, feeling uncertain and a little stupid.

Mary chuckled. "You're not getting modest on me now, are you, Mr. Becker?"

She rolled to her side and raised herself up on one elbow. The blanket slipped from her supple shoulders. Being a trained investigator and all, I quickly deduced that there was nothing between the sheets other than Mary herself.

"Well?"

I surrendered to the inevitable. But before I joined her, I looked over at the speaker and concentrated. The opening strains of "O Fortuna" began.

Mary's smile got even more sultry. "Listening to *Carmina Burana* gets me hot."

"I know."

She inclined her head toward the speaker. "That's a pretty good trick."

"You ain't seen nothing yet."

It wasn't a large mattress, but anything wider than a cot would have been wasted space. She kissed me hungrily, sliding her lips against mine and darting her tongue between my teeth with a soft moan.

"I thought we were going to get some rest," I whispered.

She chuckled throatily, one hand gliding down my chest past my waist. She quickly found what she was searching for.

"Oh, I don't think either of us is going to sleep until we do something about this."

She hissed in delight as I rolled over and settled in between her firm thighs. Her soft hand curled around my hardness and she guided me into place. But then I took over, thrusting deep into her with a throaty growl.

Her eyes rolled back in her head. "Yes, please," she sighed.

Afterward, she lay curled up against me. We'd generated quite a bit of body heat, but neither of us was willing to break contact. We just lay there, arms and legs delightfully entangled.

"Thank you," I whispered.

"I think I got just as much out of that as you did," she murmured, drawing little circles on my chest with her finger.

"Hey, wait," I said. "What about the groveling? You said there would need to be groveling."

"Oh, there will be, buster. As much as you can handle."

I was still chuckling as I fell into the most restful sleep I'd had in weeks.

Needless to say, when I awoke I felt like I could conquer the world. My three hours of sleep felt like eight. Mary and I showered and dressed quickly, but did stop for a couple of kissing breaks.

"Meet back here after we save the Multiverse?" I asked.

She screwed up her face. "How about my place? This is where Timothy and I work before each concert. I have to sit on that couch."

"Good point."

We were the last to arrive in the green room. There were no jokes or comments about us being late, although it was hard to miss the approving look that Mary Gray gave us.

Morgan, cleaning rag in hand, snapped her Desert Eagle back together. A little of the light had returned to her eyes. Kaaro, had somehow found a holster that fit the ray gun.

Sam and Harvey drank Cokes. My friend was trying to look nonchalant, but I wasn't having any.

"Where did you get that?"

Atop Sam's head, the straw almost crushed beyond recognition, was Manbun's ridiculous hat.

"It was in my lab," he said defensively. "I guess he forgot it."

I shook my head. "Whatever."

I tossed Leon one of the swords I had liberated from the Trav drone in Oz.

"Are you sure?" he asked, frowning uncertainly. "If you wanted a swordsman, you should have brought the other guy."

"Just a little insurance," I replied. "But you might be better with it than you think."

He shrugged and leaned it against his chair.

Harvey had asked Morgan and me for our guns before we parted. He returned them to us now. An aluminum tin that had once contained breath mints was secured to the barrel each by a giant wad of duct tape. I raised mine up and down a couple of times, testing the balance. It sucked.

"The balance sucks," Morgan said. Hers looked slightly less ridiculous, but only because her pistol was so enormous.

"We modified some holsters to fit," Sam said, holding them out. Morgan buckled hers into place. I did the same, then sheathed my sword on the opposite hip.

"All right," I said to Sam and Harvey. "You said you had a plan for finding Arkham. Now's the time. Spill."

Harvey gestured toward Sam's head with a *ta-da* flourish of his hands.

"What?" I asked.

Harvey snorted in impatience. "Don't you get it? This hat's been to Arkham. Morgan said this is how you got there last time."

I slowly nodded as I got it. The Rangers had used a pistol from Arkham as a focus object to home in on The Boss's headquarters.

"I wasn't driving last time," I said uncertainly.

"Christ, Trav," Sam said, "I'm sure they did it the same way you do everything else. You just *think* it. You're not like us. We need math. And computers. Even then it's a crapshoot. And your powers are growing exponentially. Just focus on it. You'll get us there."

Well, if there was one thing I had learned from any of this, it was that one's mental state, whether you were a Traveler or not, actually could affect the physical world.

"In other words, I had the power all the time, I just had to click my heels?"

Sam grinned. "Let's do it, Dorothy."

There wasn't a reason to delay any longer. Leon and Sophie watched as the away team gathered around me. I caught my boss's eye.

"Keep her safe."

He nodded.

"A red shirt?" Sam asked. "Really?"

Taking a tip from Mary, I had found a long-sleeved crimson t-shirt to wear under my vest. "I didn't think it was a color any other Trav was likely to pick."

"Like we don't have enough odds stacked against us," Harvey muttered.

I turned to Leon. "And If I show up wearing any other color…"

He nodded again, making a gun-firing motion with his hand. "Bang."

"I'll try not to be disturbed at how easy you find the idea of shooting me."

But the time for levity was passed. I laid a hand on Sam's head and closed my eyes. He had been right. Whether it was my Traveling skills improving with use or the power increase he and Gear had predicted, getting to Arkham was easy.

The last time I'd made this trip it had felt like running a 5K through mud wearing cement-lined boots. Made of caramel.

Not so this time. As soon as I touched the hat an image of the Physics Building roof appeared, separated from me only by what my mind rendered as a translucent curtain. I reached forward and parted the curtain.

"Holy shit," Sam exclaimed. "That is unbelievable."

"Why? How did that look to you?" I asked.

"Like you reached out and tore a hole in thin air."

He leaned close to me, and said sotto voce, "You know, if I didn't know that the final goal was to eliminate Traveler power, I would find you more than a little scary."

"I already do."

Which made me realized there was something I had meant to tell him.

"Look," I said quietly. "You know I never asked for this. But you're right about absolute power. So, if I ever look like I'm going to pull a Frodo Baggins, you do whatever it takes to stop me. Dig?"

He swallowed hard, then nodded uncertainly. "That's Sam's job, right?"

I nodded.

"All right, gang," I announced. "Let's storm the castle."

27

In a Hot Minute

I WAVED THE others past and stepped through after them.

It had been the wee hours at home, but here it seemed to be mid-morning. The sun glinted off the domes of the university's small telescopes. I knew that if I walked past them, I'd have the same view Sam, Aaron, Finnegan, and I had the night we teased drunks with the laser.

The Marys fanned out to make sure no one else was on the roof. Kaaro went over to the door and studied the lock.

Morgan stood with her eyes shut. She swayed slightly as if the transfer had hit her harder than the rest of us.

"Are you okay?" I asked.

She nodded, but her face had gone pale again. I wished I could make things easier for her, but there was no time.

"Any cameras?" I asked as the other women returned.

The Marys shook their heads in unison. My Mary said "Nothing that we could see. There aren't any other buildings nearby. Anybody besides you would need a helicopter to land here."

"How's it going with the door?" I called.

Kaaro pulled the door open. He returned what I assumed were lock picks to a leather pouch and put it in his pocket.

"Check your comms," I directed. Leon had provided earpieces that allowed us to stay in touch. I screwed mine into my ear canal. We powered up and did a fast radio check.

There was no reason to wait any longer. "I'm on point," I said, "with Mary Green and Mary Gray."

My throat closed up at the prospect of leading the woman I loved into danger. And the cost of what I had just said wasn't lost on her. She snaked her hand down and gave mine a quick squeeze as we got into place.

"Sam, you and Harvey next. Then Mary Red and Morgan. Kaaro, you watch our six and make sure we don't lose our escape route."

I looked at Sam and Harvey. Sam was punching keys on his laptop while Harvey held it. Their job was to hack into The Boss's network so we could get a look into the surveillance system that certainly watched over the building.

"We're in," he announced. "Okay. If I was Mr. Boss, where would I put my cameras?" He frowned, pursing his lips in concentration. Then he smiled. "Gotcha."

I looked over Sam's shoulder. A dozen small windows appeared in his browser.

Things appeared to be quiet. Two Travs sat behind a desk at the building entrance, probably seeing a view similar to ours. There were several shots of empty hallways.

"Hmm," Mary frowned. "I wonder where everyone is."

"It's still early," Morgan offered. "And we have no idea what they're using for a cafeteria, mess hall, or whatever."

"We were right," Sam said. He pulled up a view of a doorway. A sign affixed to the wall next to it read "Graduate Computer Lab." The little we could see inside revealed a table with four monitors on it. A keyboard was centered between each pair. A rack was visible to the left with several rows of blinking LEDs. As Harvey had predicted, the institutional fluorescent lights were turned off and can lights in the ceiling illuminated the workstations.

"The Batcave," Sam pronounced. He pawed at the keyboard for another couple of minutes, then sighed.

"It was like we figured. I can access the peripheral system, but the good stuff is either behind a firewall I can't see or air-gapped. We'll need to be in the lab itself to access it."

"That would have been too easy," Morgan said.

"What about the stairwell on the other side of this door?" I asked. "Is there a camera there?"

He shook his head. "The first one is in the hallway just outside the Batcave."

"Okay, then." I put my hand on the doorknob. Even though we were pretty sure it was clear, I turned it quietly and opened it just enough to get a look at the other side. There was a short landing, then stairs going down to another door. I extended my Traveler senses. No ominous song melodies rang my internal alarm.

"It's clear," I announced.

I eased the door fully open. Mary Red held it as I led our party down the stairs. She blocked the door from closing completely with a half-brick she found next to the doorway. The other Marys and I got to the bottom of the stairs which widened to a width that allowed for two-way traffic. A door led to the rooms on the sixth floor. I glanced briefly through its narrow vertical window, but all was quiet. We left Kaaro there to guard the way to our exit. He moved to the corner so that he could see down the stairs and through the door. The rest of us continued down the stairs.

Two more flights of stairs brought us to the Batcave floor. The hallway beyond the door looked empty, but we knew there was a camera trained on the hallway.

"You're up," I said softly to Sam. Harvey held the laptop once again as Sam typed. A bead of sweat formed between my shoulder blades and trickled slowly down my back.

"All right," he said, a triumphant note in his voice. "Gimme just a minute to record enough footage and we'll be good to go."

Our plan was spy-movie simple. Record thirty seconds of empty hallway, and replace the live feed just long enough to sneak through.

"On TV the feed always glitches at the worst possible moment," Harvey said helpfully.

"Shut up," I said.

The thirty seconds felt like thirty hours as Sam scrutinized his display. After about a week, he finally nodded. "The loop is pretty smooth. Excellent work, if I do say so myself."

I put my hand on the door handle.

"Wait." He held up a hand. After another eternity, he said, "Okay… Go!"

I pushed on the crash bar and held the door. With a nervous look up at the camera, Mary Gray led us into the hallway. Room 416, aka The Batcave, was the second room on the right. She stepped inside.

And disappeared.

"Shit!" hissed Sam. He craned his neck around the doorway. I jerked him back by the collar.

"Be careful!"

"I know!" he growled, shaking himself free. "But I can't figure out what happened if I can't see it."

"They killed her," Mary whispered.

Harvey snorted. "Don't be ridiculous. There's no body. If The Boss had a disintegration ray, I think you'd know it. He sent her back."

"Back?" Mary Red asked.

"Back where she came from. There's a field generator in there that rejects quanta that are out of place. A Traveler rejection field."

"Then how does The Boss get in?" I demanded. "He's not from this stream any more than we are."

"That's what we're trying to figure out," Sam said irritably. "Let us think."

He chewed on his lip for a moment, muttering softly to Harvey. The rest of us watched the looped video on his computer screen, waiting for its inevitable glitch.

After a minute, Sam said, "Really? That's what you think?"

"Only one way to find out," Harvey replied, and before any of us could stop him, headed for the doorway. Just as he reached the threshold, he bent his back limbo-style and eased himself through the doorway. He even shimmied his shoulders.

Nothing happened. Now inside the room, Harvey straightened up and theatrically ran his hands up and down his body before turning around.

"Ta-da!" he said, flashing jazz hands.

"Enough." Sam said. "Can you turn it off?"

"No sense of humor," Harvey muttered. He went deeper into the room, out of our sight.

"Well?" I said.

Sam shrugged. "There's a mark on the doorjamb. We figured that was the level you had to stay under. Easy for us. We're shorter than you."

"But I'm sure The Boss just crouches down," I said.

"Where's the fun in that?" Harvey called from inside. "All clear."

We cautiously stepped across the threshold. To the left there was a device the size and shape of a data projector, right down to a big lens in the center. Harvey had blocked the lens with a wastebasket.

Sam and Harvey made a beeline for the table of computer monitors, which was opposite three tall equipment racks.

Harvey pulled out a chair, but Sam glared at him, pushed him aside, and slid into the seat. He reached for a keyboard and mouse, paused with his fingers hovering over the keys, then punched in a long string of characters. A second later, he sighed.

"Nope. Not that one."

He steepled his fingers, tapping them against his forehead. "If I was Dr. Evil, what would my master password be?" he muttered.

"Ahem," Harvey said.

"Fine," Sam muttered.

He shoved the keyboard toward his twin. While Harvey poked at it, Sam looked up. He frowned as his gaze swept a tall equipment rack in the corner.

"What the…?" he murmured.

"What?" Morgan asked.

Sam started to say something but was distracted when the computer chimed.

"Hey, I'm in!" Harvey exclaimed.

"Good work," Sam said. "What was it?"

"Pretty simple, really," he replied. A shit-eating grin overtook his face. "It just had to be all characters you could type with one hand."

"What?" I asked.

His smile disappeared. "Because I needed the other one free," he snarled. And drew a knife from beneath the table.

I scrabbled for my pistol, jerking on the grip, but it refused to come.

It was caught on the fucking mint tin.

As I struggled, Harvey grabbed Mary by the wrist and jerked her in front of him, putting his knife to her throat. Mary Red raised her staff.

"Ah-ah," he cautioned. He backed toward the door, keeping Mary in front of him as a shield. I looked desperately at Morgan, but she jerked ineffectively at her gun, stuck just like mine.

"Tough break," Harvey clucked. "All that duct tape in the way of your quick draw."

"You son of a bitch," Sam repeated. "You were playing us all along."

"Actually, I wasn't." He somehow managed to look hurt. "No, I was all in on your scheme until I got into The Boss's system. You see, he left me a message."

"A message?" Morgan asked.

"Well, not for me specifically. But he knew that any Sam who came along on a raid would sit down at that seat. As soon as I got in, there it was, waiting for me."

"What?" Morgan asked.

"A job offer," Harvey said simply. "Let's just say that after seeing how your lot works, I think I'll join the winning side."

"You're not going to get away with this," I growled. I finally got my gun free and advanced on him.

Harvey jammed the knife further into the soft skin of Mary's neck. "That's close enough. This one is kind of a pain in the ass, too."

"Fuck you," Mary snapped. "Trav, don't let him get away!"

"Oh, shut up," Harvey said. "Trav Becker would never sacrifice an innocent, let alone the woman he loves. Even if he had a room full of spares. Which come to think of it, he does. What do you think, buddy? Is it worth it? After all, you still have one left! I'm game. Take a shot."

But then this face twisted in pain as Mary raked the heel of her boot along the inside of his shin. His manic grin disappeared as her hand shot up to grab his wrist. The rest of us watched helplessly as they struggled for the knife. I waved my gun from side to side, desperate for a clear shot, but they were locked too tightly together. Finally, with a mighty shove, he pushed her away, lurching out the door, He careened off one wall before getting his balance back, and dashed toward the stairwell.

"Oh, no you don't," cried Sam. He launched himself toward the door.

"*Sam, no!*" I screamed. But it was too late. When Harvey had broken free of Mary, he'd shoved her right into the wastebasket in front of the quantum rejector, unblocking the lens.

Sam vanished.

Harvey jerked open the stairwell door and darted inside.

"Kaaro!" I called, keying my mic. "Harvey...He's getting away! In the stairwell."

"Travis," replied Kaaro calmly, "there is movement in the stairwell."

"I know! It's Harvey! Shoot the son of a bitch."

"It's not Harvey," he said. And I suddenly heard what he meant, both through my earpiece and outside our door. The slap of feet echoing against the concrete walls of the stairway.

Lots of feet.

28

Man in the Mirror

I JERKED THE projector's power plug from the wall and gave the device a vicious kick.

"Where is he?" Mary asked.

"I don't know," I said. "Maybe it sends him back to where he was most recently. In that case, he's back home waiting for us."

But what I thought was: *Or he could be back on the stream where he and I were born. Where Sam Markus just disappeared from his prison cell.*

But either way, I couldn't help him now. We had to get out without losing anyone else. And I no longer had a Sam to figure out how to get what we came for.

I kicked the projector again which turned me toward the equipment rack, a head-high array of blinking lights and whirring fans. I remembered that Sam had stared at this same rack right before the shit hit the fan.

And in a flash of insight, I knew what had attracted his attention.

"You are fucking kidding me," I whispered.

"What?" asked Morgan.

"Over there," I barked. "That big cassette. Grab it!"

She looked at me blankly for a minute, then looked where I was pointing. A black handle, about six inches tall, protruded from a dock in the center of the rack. The rest of the cassette was black as well except for two white semicircles on the side facing us. Both were generally C-shaped with the open ends facing each other. The one on the right was larger, with a thicker outline and looked a little like Pac-Man ready to gobble the smaller one up.

But this wasn't a nod to any video game.

"Goddamned nerds," I muttered

Morgan wrapped her hand around the handle and jerked the cassette free. Instantly, every light in the rack went out.

At the same moment, the door to the stairway banged open and Trav Beckers began to pour out.

I took aim, ready to take as many Travs as I could with me, but Mary Red called softly, "Wait!"

She knelt by the quantum rejector. I gave the tiniest of nods, not wanting to alert the Travs who cautiously approached us. There were six.

"Nice and easy," one Trav said. I raised my hands in surrender.

"Put it on the floor," another said.

The two in the lead reached the doorway and took a step over the threshold just as Mary Red aimed the rejector lens at them.

The front two disappeared.

Before the others could move, I squeezed off four quick shots and they dropped.

"Nice work," I said. "But can you turn it off so we can leave?"

She gave me a tight smile as she jerked the power plug out of the wall. The light in its lens faded.

"Okay, let's go!" I yelled. As I drew my sword with my free hand, a tiny voice reminded me that these Travs were just the foot soldiers. Like a spider at the center of his web, The Boss sat safe and sound while others sacrificed themselves at the altar of his psychosis.

And now I had brought him a brand-new Sam, just as dangerous as all the others. This army may not have been responsible, but they had picked the wrong time to stand in my way. My anger and misery bellowed out in a war cry as I drew my sword. Avenging angels at my side, I surged into the hallway.

Trusting Morgan and Mary Red to keep the cassette safe, Mary and I rushed the door that led to the stairs. It had fallen shut behind the Travs I shot, but I could see movement through the window. I slammed my boot against its bottom, creating a doorstop that to give us a momentary reprieve. Mary slid to a stop next to me, staff held firmly cross-body. Her eyes were steel and her jaw set firm.

"I seriously need to kick some ass," she growled. In spite of everything, I grinned.

She put her hand to the door handle. "One, two," I counted.

On three, I pulled my foot out and she jerked the door open, taking the front Trav by surprise. He stumbled slightly, which gave me the chance to grab him by the collar, increasing his forward momentum. As I pulled him past me I smashed the pommel of my sword down on his neck. He dropped without a sound.

The next Trav in line got a face full of Mary's staff and staggered back. Four more rushed down the stairs toward us and at least three more bolted up from the downstairs side. I skewered the first one that crested the stairs, pushing him into the two behind. They tumbled down, giving us enough room to get Morgan and Mary Red through the door. Mary Red handed the cassette to Morgan as she thumbed the catch to her staff.

One hand clutching the cassette, Morgan raised her Desert Eagle with the other and fired. She took a downstairs Trav out, and now the one remaining had to untangle himself from the bodies of his brothers before he could continue up the stairs. But a door slammed a floor or two down. More were on the way.

Satisfied those two could handle whatever came from below, Mary and I began to ascend the stairs.

A sharp retort with a hint of rubbery twang sounded from above us. Kaaro firing his gun. From the commotion upstairs, it was clear he had his own pile of Travs to deal with.

And they just kept coming. Three more hurtled down the stairs toward us. The two flights separating us from Anton might as well have been two miles. I drew my pistol and took out the front two, leaping over their bodies to engage the next.

But this one used my momentum against me, shoving me aside. Too late I saw his sword appear, slashing at my throat. I twisted away in time to keep him from slicing my jugular but not enough to deflect his blade entirely. The sword bit into my side. He looked past me and spied Morgan holding the cassette. But as he charged down the stairs, Mary tripped him with her staff. He sprawled headlong onto the landing. She finished him with a vicious two-handed swing.

The next two were about four steps above me. I shot the front one, nimbly ducking aside so the second wouldn't have the same chance to get past me. Fear clouded my eyes as this Trav realized he'd brought a sword to a gunfight.

But an impotent click was all I got when I squeezed the trigger. Even with Traveler mojo behind it, when the magazine is empty, the magazine is empty. I threw the pistol at his face, raised my own sword, and charged.

He parried my first blow. My blade slid along his as he attempted to rotate and get past my guard. But I spun to the side, catching his edge as it cut through the air toward me.

"They told me you didn't know the sword," he grunted, glaring at me as I parried him again, but it was much closer this time. The blow jarred my arm all the way to my shoulder and I almost lost my grip.

"I'm just full of surprises."

He brought his blade around, but I ducked and also stepped down one stair. Grabbing the railing for stability, I lunged up and forward, sliding under his guard. He gasped as I ran him through.

But I'd underestimated my own strength. The force of my strike drove him against the handrail. He teetered for a moment before tumbling over, taking my sword with him.

Which left me with just my fists, but that was fine with me. I howled again and launched myself at a Trav hurtling down the stairs, followed by another one. Before he could even raise his sword, I punched him in the face and threw him down the stairs. Mary quickly stepped over him and surged past me. His partner had no sword but instead was armed with a standard-issue police baton. He aimed it for my head but Mary blocked his arm. I smashed the bridge of his nose with the heel of my hand.

And now I had a baton. I hit the next Trav like a bus, bashing the side of his head with my baton, grabbing him by the seat of his pants and throwing him over the railing. He smashed into two Travs rushing up the stairs to take on Morgan and Mary Red.

I continued my headlong dash up the stairs and raised my baton for a crushing swipe as a pair of legs came into view.

"Wait!" Mary cried.

I dimly realized the legs were wearing gray pants, not blue jeans or black fatigues. I looked up to see Kaaro. He held a baton similar to mine in one hand. His gun lay discarded in a corner along with four or five bodies. Several more trailed down the stairs as I mounted them. He reached out his free hand, and I let him help me up to the sixth floor landing. I turned to do the same for May but she waved me off.

"Don't worry about me," she huffed. "You did all the hard work."

Mary Red and Morgan caught up to us and we hurtled up the final flight of stairs. I looked back the way we had come.

Someone was scrambling up the stairs two flights behind us.

Manbun. As I watched, he bent over and picked something off the floor.

My empty pistol.

"Fuck," I snarled. I jerked open the door. "Go, go, go!"

I followed, slamming the door behind me, even though I knew it would do no good against the type of pursuit that followed us.

But they had to catch us first. I raised my hand and the windowed wall of the green room sprang into view. Once again, I tore the curtain aside and ushered the others through.

Sophie, Adam, and Leon looked up at us, jaws agape as we appeared from nowhere. The two men closed ranks in front of the girl, then relaxed as they recognized us. I followed the away party into the green room. Suddenly the room started to spin and I sank to my knees.

"Trav!" the Marys cried in unison. I felt their arms around me.

"Oh no," Mary Red breathed. I looked absently at her hand, which for some reason, was now the same color as her scarf.

"Oh God," Morgan said. "How bad is it?"

"It's fine," I said roughly.

"No, it's not," she countered. "We need to clean this up. You need a hospital. Stitches at the least."

"No time. Manbun is right behind us." I grit my teeth and managed to climb to my feet. "He just grazed me. We gotta go."

Mary rolled her eyes and slipped my arm around her shoulders. I winced as the wound in my side stretched and reopened.

"Let's move," I said, trying not to wheeze. Mary Red and Kaaro took the lead and we staggered into the hallway.

"Wait," Adam said. "Aren't we short a Mary?"

"She's okay, we think," I said. "But we got what we came for."

I pointed to Morgan, who held the cassette.

"That's it?" Adam asked.

"It's enough," I replied. Then my head jerked as Phil Collins began to play in my mind.

"Shit. They're coming. Go!"

We launched ourselves down the stairs and spilled out onto the first floor, slamming the stage door open with a bang. Outside, I spied a dumpster. Together, Adam and I rolled it in front of the door.

The door momentarily blocked, I looked up and down the street.

"You lead," I said to Mary. "You know downtown best."

She nodded. "C'mon."

We sprinted across the street. As we rounded the corner, I heard a banging behind us. Manbun had arrived, certainly with reinforcements. If we could just get out of their sight, we might be able to buy ourselves some breathing room.

Mary led us through a small plaza that lay in between an office building and a parking garage. She turned left, running past the entrance to the garage, and finally called a halt at the next corner, putting her hands on her knees to catch her breath. Mary Red followed suit. I leaned against the wall. My wound throbbed and I took deep breaths. Everyone stood huffing and puffing. Only Kaaro, who had spent the last year in a cell, not to mention being older even than Leon, seemed unaffected by the workout.

But as the adrenaline from our flight wore off everything began to go gray. I slowly slid to a seated slouch, looking around at my friends. I knew there was something that we needed to be doing, but I couldn't seem to remember what it was.

"Trav, no!"

I smiled as Mary dropped to her knees beside me. It was always nice to have her near. Maybe she could turn on the TV and we could watch something.

"I think he's going into shock!"

I frowned. Her voice now seemed to come from a long ways away. Where had she gone? I thought she was going to sit beside me. She was trying to tell me something. But it was like being in one of those dreams where people are talking in plain English, but you can't understand

267

them. And then it was almost like there were two of her. I smiled, just watching their beautiful lips move. Best TV show ever.

But a vicious slap to my face broke through the fugue. It damn near knocked me the rest of the way to the ground.

"Trav!" Mary Red yelled. "C'mon! You have to snap out of it!" She slapped me again.

"What are you doing?" Leon was there, grabbing her arm. She shook him off.

"If he doesn't wake up, we're all finished. *Trav!*" She shook me hard.

I groaned as pain lanced through me. But it worked. My vision cleared even though I was weak. So weak.

Mary grabbed Mary Red's hand.

"Stop! You're making it worse!"

"If he faints, we're all dead," the other Mary snarled.

"All right, it's okay," I gasped. "Just hang on."

I tried to take stock of my situation. I was still lightheaded from pain and loss of blood. I didn't think I could stand. I looked at Mary, then tried to look down at the wound, but my neck just didn't seem to want to move in that direction.

"How bad is it?" I whispered.

She knelt and ran a hand through my hair. "It's bad, babe."

I nodded, closing my eyes. Was this how it ended? Me bleeding to death on an empty street, leaving my friends alone to face The Boss's apocalypse?

"Fuck no." It came out a whisper.

I struggled to a sitting position, bracing myself against the wall.

"Don't move," Mary cautioned.

I shook my head. Through the pain and jumbled thoughts racing through my head, I remembered another time I had lay wounded, life's blood leaking onto a cold floor, important work undone. Another Trav Becker had fixed things. I had never tried an advanced move like he had done. But I was no use to my friends like this.

"Sophie," I croaked. She came over, face pale as she looked at my equally white face and the blood oozing from my abdomen. I held out my good hand and she took it.

"Watch," I said. "If I don't have the strength to finish this, you'll have to take over."

She nodded solemnly.

I reached out and the various pasts and futures leading up to this moment sprang into view. My mind's eye hovered over the battle on the stairs. Several versions of the fight in the darkness were now visible. But even as I viewed those other possible paths, I could feel the window closing. It was too late.

Sophie squeezed my hand. And warmth and power flowed back into me. It seemed I could hear the girl's thoughts.

We can do this! I know we can.

But even with her lending me her strength, the pathway to a timeline where I hadn't been mortally wounded was nearly closed. I couldn't keep from getting stabbed, but if I could just...

I snapped back to reality with a gasp. I opened my eyes. Sophie still had a death grip on my hand, but there was a smile on her face.

I looked down. There was still blood. A lot of it. But it no longer oozed from my exposed abdominal wall. There was a nasty gash in my side that hurt like hell. But it wasn't fatal.

"Oh my God," Mary inhaled. "That was...I could see it change! Are you okay?"

I nodded. "Help me up."

She and Sophie helped me to my feet. I rotated my arm to loosen up.

269

"Thanks," I said to Sophie She wrapped her arms around me and hugged me hard.

The remainder of the party looked at us strangely.

"Everything okay?" Morgan asked. Mary and Sophie looked at them in shock.

"Didn't you see?" Mary asked. "Trav almost died!"

"From that scratch?" Adam scoffed. "I've seen worse at a softball game."

"It's okay," I whispered to the two women. "That's how they remember it. And that's how it should be."

"Hey," Mary Red said. "I know I'm not from around here, but does anyone else notice anything weird?"

Adam stared at her, then at her identical twin. Then at the bloodied shirt covering my minor wound. "You're kidding, right?"

"No!" she continued. "The street. It's empty."

She was right. I had spent so much time in the Oz and Arkham where we were out of phase with the inhabitants that I had gotten used to empty buildings and streets. I did a quick calculation in my head. Even taking the time manipulation in Arkham into account, by my estimation it was midday on Monday. The sidewalks should have been full of people and the streets heavy with traffic.

But we were alone.

Well, almost alone. For the first time, I noticed that Noah was trailing along a few yards behind our party.

"You should go home," I said. "Things are probably going to get kind of dicey. If I were you, I'd wait it out in a nice, warm cat bed."

"Are you talking to my cat?" Morgan asked. "Mary, I think he's still delirious."

"Sometimes I think he knows more about what's going on than any of us," I murmured. But after staring at us for a few seconds, the cat turned and disappeared around a corner.

Now we really were alone. I would have given anything to hear Sam pipe up and explain what was going on in a combination of technobabble and sci-fi movie references.

Morgan held up the cassette. "The answer is probably in here."

"What the hell is that, anyway?" Adam asked. "It doesn't look like any computer disk I've ever seen. It's huge."

I sighed. "More Sam Markus geek humor. Nobody recognizes this?"

Surprisingly, it was Kaaro who spoke up.

"*Star Wars*, yes?"

We all stared at him.

"We do not have the luxury of first-run movies in prison," he sniffed.

"He's right," I said. "It's the media cassette from the movie *Rogue One*. The one that carried the Death Star plans. I'm not sure what it is, but the instant we pulled it out, all the servers when down. I'm betting it's something The Boss needs for his plan."

But without Sam, we had no hope of actually being able to read the disc. All we could do was keep it away from The Boss.

"Why not just destroy it then?" Kaaro asked.

I thought about that for a minute. But before I could say anything, Mary spoke up.

"We should keep it. It could be a bargaining chip."

"Next order of business," Morgan said. "We can't stay out on the street. Where do we go? We're exposed here."

"She's right," Leon said. "We have to get someplace we can defend."

I got my bearings and realized our headlong flight had carried us into The District.

"I think I have an idea," I said.

Motioning Leon and Adam to watch our rear, we started down the street. Turning left, I stopped next to a weathered door.

"Ring any bells?" I asked Kaaro.

He stared at me blankly. I fished my keys out of my pocket and found the correct one. "I'm sure you could pick this lock," I continued. "But let's do it the easy way."

I slid the key into the deadbolt. It turned easily.

I passed the spot where I had cold-cocked Bilol Grymzin a couple of universes ago and started up the stairs to what on another reality stream was known as The Third Street Lounge.

29

No Parking on the Dance Floor

I LED OUR party up to the third floor. There was no lighted bar running the length of the room as there had been in Purgatory. The scratched wooden floor needed of refinishing. The only furniture in the otherwise empty room was a couple of old wooden chairs, too rickety to have been taken when the last resident departed.

"What is this place?" Leon asked.

But before I could answer we were distracted by noise from the other end of the room. The thump of a bass drum, and a flourish of piano chords.

A jazz trio warmed up in the corner of the room.

"What the hell?" Adam said.

A young man seated at the piano turned at the intrusion. Next to him, a slim fellow holding a stand-up bass pushed a long forelock of hair from his eyes. He looked at us curiously.

"They with you?" the bassist asked the drummer.

But we never heard his reply because suddenly their figures shimmered out of existence. Dust motes were now the room's only occupants other than us, swirling in the light that leaked in from a pair of grimy windows.

At the same time, I stiffened as a wave of nausea clenched my insides. It erased the memory of my belly wound as my insides churned like a toy boat in a cyclone. Dimly, I was aware that Sophie had also doubled over. She grabbed her stomach and moaned. Morgan darted over and put her arms around the girl.

"What's the matter?" Mary Red demanded.

I held up a hand, gritting my teeth until the episode passed. Sophie straightened a moment later but her arms remained crossed protectively over her stomach.

"Are you all right, honey?" Morgan asked.

Sophie nodded. "I think so," she wheezed.

"What happened?" Mary asked.

I tried to focus. For a second, there were many Marys looking at me with concern. But then all the images slammed together into one.

I shook my head, trying to clear it. "It's like the walls between the streams are coming down. It must be the beginning of the Collapse."

As if in answer, the air in the room seemed to ripple once again, and the jazz musicians flashed back into view, but just for a moment before they winked out of existence again.

Replaced by a group of Trav Beckers.

"There they are!" one cried. They surged forward. I pushed Sophie towards the Marys. They stumbled toward the door that led to the stairs.

I waved a hand at Kaaro and Morgan. "Go!"

Adam squeezed off a round, which caused the Travs to scatter. Leon, Adam, and I dove behind the bar.

"Aw, fuck," I heard Adam say. His hand cradled his midsection. Blood seeped in between his fingers.

"Let me see." I leaned over him, but he waved me off.

"It's not that bad."

"You have to go with the others," Leon said.

I shook my head.

"Don't be stupid," he said. "They need protection from the hocus pocus. Go. We'll keep this bunch pinned down so they can't flank you."

"What if they make with the hocus pocus?"

"They'll be too busy."

"Your guns will stop working soon."

Leon grinned and patted his sword. "Okay by me. I'm starting to get attached to this thing. Now go."

I looked at Adam. "Thanks, partner," I whispered.

He nodded and flashed a fierce smile. He took his hand away from his abdomen.

"See?" he said, wiping his bloody hand on his jeans, "Bleeding's already slowing down."

It didn't look to me like it was slowing down at all, but Leon waved me away.

"I'll look after him. Go."

Adam nodded in agreement. "We'll cover you."

Nodding to each other, they snuck their heads up just far enough to sight and began firing. The instant they did, I scuttled over to the stairs. The Marys, Morgan, Kaaro, and Sophie waited for me there.

"Downstairs," I panted. I ran past them, leading the way.

The next floor down was empty and dark. I ushered everyone off the landing. But when I followed, I lurched right into Kaaro, who had stopped just beyond the threshold.

"What the—?" I began, then realized that the reason everyone was still crowded near was because the room was no longer empty.

A wave of throbbing bass smacked my ears. The place was packed. A DJ perched on a raised stand a few yards away, one hand holding a headphone earpiece to the side of his head. A bunch of people jumped and writhed in front of him, fists pumping in time with the music. The crowd was more sedate near us, not dancing so much as shifting from foot to foot like you do when you're into the music but don't want to spill your drink.

I caught Mary's eye and pointed to our left. Grabbing Sophie's hand, I began pushing my way through the dancing crowd.

"Hey!" a woman exclaimed in my ear. I hadn't reached her yet, but her exclamation made my head come up just in time to see Trav Becker push her out of the way and make a grab for the cassette in Morgan's hands. He had shoved his way in between the woman and her dance partner, so I nudged the man in his direction. As I had hoped, his feet got tangled up with Trav's. My double reached out to keep from falling and grabbed the woman's hip. She slapped at his hand.

"You gonna let him get away with that?" I shouted into the man's ear, jerking my head toward where Trav and the woman were entangled.

"Hey!" he slurred and lurched toward them. "Get your hands off her, fucker!" He stood something north of six-two. Trav turned toward the sound of his voice just as the man got his not-inconsequential bulk all moving in the right direction.

This opened up a drunken oaf-sized hole in the crowd. I pulled Sophie through it, followed by the rest of my crew.

We stumbled into a space that was as empty as the other one had been full. This room had been some sort of parlor at one time. There was a fireplace along one wall and an ornate wooden border ran along the ceiling. But the formal look was spoiled a little by the fact that every single surface in the room, ceiling, floor, fireplace, and trim, was painted bright orange.

"Everyone okay?" I asked. Nods all around.

"What happened to the music?" Sophie asked.

She was right. As soon as we had stepped into the room, it had fallen silent.

"Look." Mary Red pointed back to the room from which we'd just come. The crowd had disappeared. A bare handful of people leaned disinterestedly against the wall.

"What the hell is going on?" Morgan asked.

I shook my head. "I'm not sure if this is The Boss's doing, the Collapse, or some combination of the two. But he's stuck as long as we have the cassette and Sophie."

"Exactly," came a voice.

Manbun and two other Travs appeared in the center of the room.

"Back!" I cried. The Travs charged toward us as I frantically pushed everyone through the door. As we did, I gave a small mental nudge.

We showed up in the middle of a free-for-all. The big guy's tussle with the Trav drone had erupted into a full-fledged brawl. The entire room was one big mass of elbows and fists. And not just the men. Some of the women had retreated to safe corners, but as we watched, a stout brunette bumped into a redhead, spilling the ginger's drink. With a roar that would have made Conan the Barbarian proud, the redhead landed a roundhouse punch on the other woman, who responded by grabbing a handful of fiery hair.

I flattened myself just to the side of the doorway, motioning Kaaro to do the same.

As the Trav Trio hurtled toward the threshold, I grabbed the first one by the front of his shirt and shoulder, adding some spin to his forward momentum which sent him cascading into the melee. The second one stumbled behind propelled by Kaaro, always a quick study.

But Manbun didn't follow, and when I cautiously snuck a glance back through the doorway, he was nowhere to be seen. I willed the orange room away, replaced by the empty, dusty version from our stream, and motioned everyone back through.

I cocked my ear, listening for sounds from upstairs where we had left Leon and Adam. All was quiet. I motioned to Kaaro, who moved smoothly to the doorway.

Mary Red opened her mouth to say something, but her eyes widened at something over my shoulder. I spun around.

Kaaro backed into the room, hands raised, followed by Manbun, Harvey, and two more Trav Beckers.

Manbun had acquired my PBG-equipped pistol. He gestured with it, not having to tell us to get our hands up and out in the open.

"Perfect," Manbun said, smiling. "Everyone we need, right here in one place."

"Not everyone," I said.

"Mundanes don't count," he sniffed. He motioned to Morgan. "Here's how this is going to go. You're going to give the cassette to the girl. Then she's coming with us."

He had his gun and the other two brandished their swords. They thought that had us covered. But I could tell that most of their attention was on Morgan, Kaaro, and me. Even after seeing the Marys in action in the Batcave, they seemed to have a bit of a blind spot toward her as a threat. Which was a mistake.

As one, the two women launched themselves at Manbun's companions. Mary Red swung her staff hard, connecting with the Trav on the left's wrist. He didn't let go of his weapon, but the force of the blow nearly drove him to his knees. Before he could bring his sword up, my Mary felled him with a savage swipe.

The other Trav surged toward them, sword raised. Manbun swung his pistol toward the scrum.

"Look out!" I cried, lunging toward him.

I hit him like a fullback protecting his quarterback, but I was an instant late. His gun went off a second before I got to him.

I heard a cry behind me as my hand closed on the wrist of his gun hand. Out of the corner of my eye, I could see both Marys sink to the ground. But taking my attention off Manbun brought me a stinging blow from his free hand. Colors burst behind my eyes, nearly costing me my hold on the gun.

"Typical," he sneered. "You're so predictable. Don't you get it? She makes you weak. They *all* make you weak. You'll never be able to focus as long as you're trying to protect them."

I dodged a second blow and managed to get a grip on his other hand. He tried to raise the gun again, but leverage was now on my side.

"Focus on this, you bastard," I spat, and smashed my forehead into his face. I felt more than heard the wet crunch as I broke his nose. I snatched the gun from his hand as he staggered backward.

But the blow had been just as hard on my head as his. I saw stars as I shakily brought his gun to bear.

And again, I was just an instant too late.

Freed from the Marys by Manbun's shot, the Trav who was still on his feet had grabbed Sophie and now held her in front of him, sword at her throat.

"Nobody move," he said.

I trained the gun on him. "Hurt her and you won't last fifteen seconds."

"Oh, cut the bullshit," Harvey said. "Didn't we just have this conversation? You're not going to take the chance. Hard to see yourself as the hero when it gets a little girl killed, isn't it?"

Before he could continue, I snagged Manbun by the collar and put my gun to his head.

"You're not a little girl."

He didn't even flinch. "When he shoots me, do her."

He turned his head just enough to look me in the eye but made no effort to move away from the barrel of the gun.

"Your move, Slick," he murmured.

Sophie's face was white and she was barely holding back tears. But her jaw was set firm. She met my eyes bravely.

I shook my head. "Don't worry, Sophie. No one's going to hurt you."

I lowered the gun.

"Like I said. Predictable," Manbun chuckled. He slid the gun from my hand and waved it at Morgan, who stood frozen. She looked from our tableau to the Marys. They both lay unmoving

"Give the cassette to Sophie," he continued.

She looked at me. I nodded. Morgan handed the cassette to the young woman.

"It's okay," I said softly. "He won't hurt you. They need you too much. Just do what he says."

"Smart," Manbun said. He held out his free hand. "C'mon."

Sword Trav released her and Sophie slowly made her way across the room. When she reached Manbun, he put a hand on her shoulder. I watched his eyes go out of focus, but he kept the gun trained on us.

"Don't do anything stupid," he warned. "She isn't *that* important. The Boss would probably be fine with her loss if it also took you off the board."

"Good work," Harvey said. "Let's go." He took a few steps toward Manbun and nearly walked into the point of Sword Trav's blade.

"Get that thing out of my face," Harvey said. "What the hell is going on?"

"Yeah, you're not coming," Manbun said.

"What?"

"You're done. The Boss doesn't like other Sams around."

"Now wait just a damned second," Harvey sputtered.

"Shut up," Manbun said. He flipped his pistol to Sword Trav.

"Kill them," he said. And disappeared.

Sword Trav caught the pistol and pointed it at me.

The sound of the gunshot was like thunder.

30

Moritat

TRAV HAD JUST enough time to look down at his pistol and frown before slowly sinking to the ground.

Standing behind him, still wearing Manbun's ridiculous hat, was Sam.

But with the threat eliminated, I had eyes for only one thing. I skidded across the room, dropping to my knees beside the fallen Marys. Mary had risen to her hands and knees and was putting pressure on a huge wound in Mary Red's chest with their two scarves.

"No, no," she moaned.

But we both knew there was nothing to be done. Blood no longer pumped from the wound, and Mary Red's eyes stared sightlessly toward the ceiling.

"Too slow," I whispered. "I was too goddamn slow."

"It's not your fault," Mary said, reaching her hand to clutch mine. We both bowed our heads, tears falling on the scarves, now blood-darkened to the same hue.

We became aware of another presence. Kaaro put a hand on each of our shoulders.

"I will attend to her," he said.

I slowly rose, leaning against Mary, just in time to witness Sam viciously pistol-whip his twin right across the face.

"This is all your fault!"

Sam smacked Harvey a second time. "*That's* for me having to find my way back from a stream where half the FBI is looking for an escaped murderer."

"Nob mby fauld," Harvey burbled around the blood streaming from his nose and mouth. He spat out a tooth and pointed at me. "*He* broke me oub."

Harvey shrank back as Sam raised his gun hand again, but this time I got there in time to gently lower his arm.

"Good to see you, buddy."

He shook his head. "Sorry, man. Sophie, the cassette. I was too late."

"It's okay. We'll get her back." I turned to Harvey. "How's that winning side treating you now?"

"Fug you."

"We're out of time," I said. "We have to move."

"Adam and Leon are still upstairs," Morgan reminded us.

Sam shoved the barrel of his pistol into Harvey's back, nudging him into motion, and the rest of us followed them upstairs.

The third floor was quiet. I stuck my head over the threshold, before rushing in.

The bodies of at least a dozen Travs littered the dance floor.

I rounded the corner of the bar where I had left Adam and Leon. The blood was the first thing I saw.

Leon sat on the floor, back against the end of the bar. His eyes were closed. Adam sprawled next to him, eyes open and staring.

Leon tried to hitch himself into a more upright position as we approached, his sword coming up.

"It's okay," I said.

It took him a moment to process that we were friendlies, but then he nodded, head lolling back against the side of the bar. Blood seeped from wounds in his shoulder and thigh.

Morgan and I dropped to our knees. Mary ran to Adam.

"They just kept coming," Leon whispered without opening his eyes. He gave a wet chuckle, raising the sword which was still clutched in his good hand. "You were right. I did pick up a pretty good feel for this."

He coughed, then hissed as we applied pressure to his wounds, wrapping them with strips of cloth Morgan found behind the bar.

I looked at Mary. She shook her head.

"After I got run through the second time, it was all him," Leon continued. "I didn't even realize he'd been hit again until after he got the last one. I tried to get over to him, but I was just too damned weak."

I covered his sword hand with mine. "There wasn't any more you could have done." I squeezed his hand. Leaving Morgan to work on him, I turned to the Sams.

"He's got Sophie. And the cassette," I said grimly. "What's next?"

"The Collapse," Harvey said. He had found a rag behind the bar to sop up the blood from Sam's blow. "Everything's in place. His plan all along wasn't to bring about the Collapse, just to be ready when it hit. All he has to do is wait."

As if to underscore his point, a wave of nausea hit me and the universe splintered into a million jagged pieces. The jazz trio blinked back into view, then transformed into a big band led by a short, round guy with a Van Dyke. He put a trumpet to his lips, but before he could play a note, everything shimmered again and he was replaced by a country-rock ensemble. I blinked, and dozens of versions of my friends peered at me with concern.

And then my phone rang.

I looked around for the sound until I realized it was coming from my vest pocket. I fished it out and showed my friends the picture on the screen. It was Sam's, of course.

I pushed the answer button. "How did you get this number?"

"Oh, don't act dense," said The Boss. "Calling across streams is a parlor trick. If that's the only question you have for me, I'm disappointed."

"I don't give a fuck."

"Then let's cut to the chase. Obviously, I know that you're still alive. Which means you're going to come for Sophie. Let me save you some trouble. Come now. If you do, I'll let her go."

"In return for what?"

"You know what," The Boss said with a theatrical sigh. "You. You for her."

"Why? What do you need me for? You have your cassette back. You've got a Traveler. What more do you need?"

"Well, funny thing," he replied. "You may have noticed that I have recently…increased the number of Trav Beckers in my employ."

"Employ?" I didn't even try to keep the sarcasm from my voice. "That's what you call it? More like slavery."

"Tomato, To-mah-toe. They're not complaining. But that's beside the point. I didn't just bring them in for muscle. All that Traveler energy in one place is what powers my device. It's what is supposed to get me through the Collapse."

"Is there a point to this, or are you just monologuing?"

"The point, Trav, is that there isn't enough Traveler mojo to go around. Someone is sucking all the air out of the room. You."

By now, everyone had gathered close enough that they could hear everything he said, even though I hadn't put the phone on speaker. I looked at Sam and Harvey. They both shrugged.

The Boss continued. "You've become the lithium-ion battery of Traveling. So, that's the deal. You don't have to do a damn thing. Just stand there and radiate."

"What about the rest of us?"

Another sigh. "Bring 'em along. No one here will hurt them."

"Until you delete them from your new order."

"No, you still don't get it. With you as the power source, there will be enough energy to save everybody. Isn't that what you want?"

"How do I know you'll keep your word?"

His laugh was more like a cackle. "You don't. Did you think this was a negotiation? One hour. Winter is coming, Trav. Tick tock."

The phone returned to its lock screen.

"Well, screw that," Sam said.

"There is no way he'll keep his word," Morgan added.

"I know. But if there is even a chance that the rest of you can get out of this—"

"And live in whatever world *he* has cooked up?" Mary said. "Forget it. I'd rather get erased."

"Damn straight," Morgan said firmly.

I shook my head. "He'll let Sophie and all of you go. We don't have any choice."

"The hell we don't!" Sam said. "There's got to be another way."

I turned to Harvey. "Are you going to help us? Or should we just leave you here?"

He shrugged. The crazy fire had gone out of his eyes. He looked like he was having trouble staying awake.

"What does it matter?" he mumbled. "You win, he wins. I get Collapsed either way."

"But our way hurts The Boss," Sam reminded him.

Harvey weighed this. "He is a double-crossing son of a bitch. Okay, what do you want to know?"

"Tell me about The Boss's setup."

"He has one of those anti-Trav fields set up to keep you from pulling any Traveler juju on him, and inside of that, a second quantum field that will protect him from the effects of the Collapse. That must be what he needs your power for. He's dialed in his preferred parameters for the new order. But you gotta remember, The Boss has known dozens of Travs. He reads you like a book. He wouldn't have called you if he didn't think he had every base covered."

"You're right about one thing," I replied. "The Boss has been ahead of us at every turn. He knows me better than I know myself. Whatever plan I come up with, he'll have already thought of."

And then I knew. I didn't know why I hadn't thought of it before. The Boss and Manbun might know what move I would make before I thought of it, but they had a blind spot. A beautiful blind spot.

We talked it through, and after a few minutes, it seemed like we had the bare bones of a plan.

"This is all going to be on you, Sam," I said. "Do you think you can pull it off?"

"I can't believe the Multiverse rests on me being able to quick draw a gun," he muttered. "This is so out of my wheelhouse."

"You did okay with him." I pointed to the Trav drone Sam had put down when he had leaped in.

"I had more time to aim," he said.

"You'll be fine. You have to be," I said. "What gun do you want to use?"

"Like I know anything about guns," he said. "Well, I am not carrying *that* beast." He pointed to Morgan's Desert Eagle. "And it needs to have a PBG connected to it."

He spotted my pistol, the one that Manbun had grabbed after I discarded it in Arkham, picked it up and handed it to me.

"Show me what I need to do, coach."

I stared at the gun in my hand, twin to the service Glock I had carried for a decade. How many versions of this gun had I held in the past year? Suddenly, the last thing I wanted to do was carry the same weapon into battle that rode on the hip of every other Trav Becker.

"What, Trav?" Mary asked.

I knelt at Adam's side, gently disengaging his lifeless hand from his weapon, a nine-millimeter H&K.

"Can't imagine doing this without you, buddy," I whispered, voice catching, "but maybe you can still bring us some luck."

I glanced at Leon as I did this. He nodded.

I handed the gun to Sam. "Put your Probability Bubble thing on this one. Anything we can do to change up the Trav and Sam pattern can't hurt."

He nodded. Harvey produced a pair of needle-nose pliers and in a few minutes, the task was done.

I stuffed the gun into the back of Sam's pants and draped his shirttail over it. He practiced sneaking his hand in and producing the gun.

The first time, the mint tin that contained the PBG got caught in his belt, of course. With a dark look at Harvey, Sam re-taped it and soon he was snapping the gun around pretty fast. Harvey watched him impatiently, obviously looking for an angle to get in on the con.

While Sam practiced, I took in the exhausted, bloodied faces of my friends. Morgan could barely stand. Mary and Kaaro bled from a half-dozen wounds. Leon's gaze went in and out of focus as he attempted to follow what was going on.

Suddenly it all seemed impossible. The Boss held all the cards. And how could I ask any more of the people I loved?

"Look," I finally began. "You don—"

But Mary held up her hand before I could even finish my sentence.

"Trav," she said quietly. "We're with you. All the way."

I turned to Morgan. She smiled wearily. "What? You think I'm going to miss how this ends?"

"Pretty good team to have at your back, kid," said Leon. He motioned to the bloody mess that was his left shoulder. "Sorry I can't come with." His eyes flicked toward Adam's body.

"Make them pay," he said quietly.

I nodded and turned to Sam. "Think you got it down?"

"Only one way to find out," he replied.

And so fast his hand was a blur, he whipped the pistol out and put three shots into Harvey.

31

The Turnaround

TOO LATE, I slapped the gun from his hand.

Harvey swayed a couple of times and sank to the floor. A smile spread across his lips.

"Didn't know you had it in you," he murmured. Then his face went slack, head lolling to the side.

Sam made no move to retrieve his gun, just stared into his own dead face.

"What the hell are you doing?" I demanded.

Sam didn't answer for a long time. Finally, he shook his head.

"It had to be done."

"It *had* to be done? Kill a man in cold blood? Are you nuts?"

He smiled sadly. "It would be nice to have an excuse. But no. I'm the furthest thing from crazy. Trav, think about it. There was no way we could take him with us. He was just biding his time until he could betray us again."

"You don't know that."

"The fuck I don't!" he hissed. "He's *me*. I know exactly what he was planning. He was just using us to get back to The Boss. He was either going to switch sides again or try to take The Boss's place. He couldn't be trusted. You know that!"

I shook my head. "There had to another way."

"I did what had to be done." He retrieved his gun from the floor, silently daring me to interfere.

"Tell you what," he said conversationally, "if we survive the next few hours, you can turn me in back on our home stream and I'll finish out his sentence."

"There won't be a Stream Four after the Collapse. You know that."

"You'll figure something out."

I looked at the others. Kaaro was the only one who spoke.

"We understand that this offends you, Travis. But now is not the time to debate morals. Harvey was a mad dog. He had to be put down."

"Fine," I said flatly. "We'll deal with it later. If we survive."

I closed my eyes. Sam and Kaaro were right. I knew that Harvey couldn't be trusted. We couldn't leave him here with Leon. And taking on The Boss was hard enough without having to watch our backs. I wanted there to be another way.

In the last day or so I had watched each of my friends die. There was a good chance I'd get to watch them die again.

The Boss had the obvious advantages. He had Sophie. He had his plan for the Multiverse. He had his army of Travs. He could predict every move I could possibly make.

But what he missed was that the source of my power wasn't the Multiverse. It was this bloody, fatigued group of people who never, ever gave up on me. Not even when I didn't deserve their love or loyalty. Hell, especially then.

It would be enough. It had to be.

I took a deep breath. When I opened my eyes, the splinters of reality that showed me so many different potential versions of my friends lay spread out before me. Each reality pulsed with an energy that I could see just as clearly as I could read the concerned expressions on their faces.

But now, instead of forcing my gaze to hone in on one particular version of my Scooby gang, I drew energy from all of them. The power flowed into me, filling me like cool water after a long run. I drank and drank until, with a dismissive wave, I banished the irrelevant streams.

My friends came back into view. Each one pulsed with an inner fire. No longer the simple reds and blues that I had followed in my past Travels but every color of the rainbow. Plus a few I didn't even have names for.

All except for Adam and Harvey. I didn't waste any time on the latter, but I tried casting my awareness out, searching for a stream where the big lug's aura still shone. I had healed myself. Surely, I could dial back to a moment where his injuries weren't fatal.

But it was a lost cause. The causality window was closed. He was just as dead as he was in the stream from which I originally fled. With a sigh of defeat, I snapped myself back to our local reality. My friends had stepped back and now peered nervously at me.

"Trav?" Mary said. "Are you okay?"

I nodded. "Why?"

"Um, you're kind of—"

"Glowing," Morgan finished.

I pushed aside my frustration at not being able to save Adam and managed a smile. "Believe it or not, so are all of you."

"What have you done?" Sam asked. The gun was stuffed into place under his shirt once again.

"Charged up," I replied. "Are you ready?"

"For what?"

"To take the fight to The Boss."

"Now you're talking," Sam said. "When do we leave?"

The power sang inside me. I waved a hand. The club winked out of view.

"We're already there."

We stood across the street from Building 231. The entire downtown was deserted, of course. A row of cars had been lined up along the grass and sidewalk that ran in front of the building. On my last visit, The Boss's Trav battalion had decimated the Rangers by using the automobiles as shields and firing from behind them. But the kill zone was empty today.

I cast my Traveler sense out. There was a big black *nothing* to the right of the front door, right about where the building's main lecture hall was. That made sense. There was plenty of room for both The Boss's equipment and his seemingly inexhaustible supply of near-Travs.

"We're just going to go in the front door?" Sam asked.

I shrugged. "If he was going to pick us off, he would have done so already. I guess you can just walk into Mordor."

Sam laughed and laughed as we walked up to the building's entrance.

Two Trav drones, posted on each side of the door, watched us warily as we approached. But that was all they did as I reached for the door handle and pulled it open, allowing the women to precede me, guided by Sam. This left Kaaro and me bringing up the rear.

"You're clear on how this needs to go?" I murmured.

Staring straight ahead, not deigning to look at the Travs as they fell in behind us, Kaaro nodded.

Suddenly, the heightened awareness that my Traveler power gave me shut off like a light switch. We'd entered The Boss's dampening field. Which was not all bad because the nausea that had been roiling my stomach as the Collapse approached fell away, too.

Sam led our little party to the Lecture Hall doors, then paused. A bead of sweat trickled out from under his hat and rolled down the side of his head. But the expression on his face was resolute.

"Everybody ready?" I asked lightly. Morgan smiled tightly. I put a hand on Mary's arm and squeezed. *I love you*, I mouthed.

She smiled fiercely, briefly covering my hand with hers. I allowed myself just a moment to marvel at how the woman I had tried so hard to hide this conflict from turned out to be the one I needed by my side most of all. Then I glanced at Sam and Kaaro.

The unlikely pair nodded. We were as ready as we ever going to be. I pulled open the door.

Nearly every seat in the lecture hall was filled. By Trav Becker. The Travs sat stock-still and faced the front of the room. Upon our entrance, every head swiveled in our direction. But no one spoke. Creepy as hell.

There was about fifteen feet of open floor space between where the theater-style seating of the auditorium ended and a raised dais where the lecturer held court began. Normally, there were a few rows of regular classroom chairs that filled the gap. But most of them had been pushed to the side to allow space for several tables full of equipment. It looked like the entire contents of the Batcave had been moved down here. To confirm my theory, I spotted the *Rogue One* cassette, ensconced once again in its cradle.

Sophie sat in one of the remaining chairs. Manbun stood behind her.

The Boss occupied center stage, as it were. He broke the silence with a firm clap of his hands.

"About time. C'mon, let's get on with it. The Multiverse doesn't have all day."

The Boss's vest was khaki. Unlike Harvey, he was letting his hairline recede naturally. Between that and the vest, it was almost like Gear stood in front of us. But the hard mask of The Boss's face was unlike the gentle, tired-looking man we'd left frozen in time.

Manbun had one of our Traveler-proof PBG guns stuffed into his jeans and held a regular pistol which he waved at Sam, Morgan, and me. We made our way toward the front of the room. The Trav drones watched with disinterest that verged on boredom.

We stopped about ten feet from The Boss. "Are you okay?" I called to Sophie.

She was pale and her hands were clasped together whitely, but she nodded, even finding the moxie to give me a small smile. I smiled back briefly before returning my gaze to The Boss.

"It's nice to see you three all together again," the elder Sam said. "You know, I haven't been in the same room with a Morgan and a Trav since Buck betrayed me way back when." He shook his head. "You realize it's all been a waste, right? All Buck did, all you did, was delay the inevitable. The Collapse was always going to come."

"We're here to get Sophie," I interrupted. "Not listen to you justify your actions. We have a deal. I power your gear, you protect everyone."

"You don't get it, do you?" Manbun said. "You don't call the shots here. You do as you're told."

The Boss waved a hand. "Let her go. It doesn't matter. None of this matters. You should understand by now that it's all ephemeral." He made a show of consulting his watch. "No matter what you do, in two minutes, give or take, Sophie will be back with me."

"And what about us?" Sam asked.

"Trav stays behind to power the device, of course," he replied with a shrug. "And I'm sure you realize that there is room for only one Sam Markus in the new order.

"So the rest of us just disappear then?" I gestured not just to the Trav army, but also Manbun. "Including you."

"You're not as smart as you think you are," he said. "You go, I stay. That's *my* deal."

"For what? So you can Obi-wan his pet wizard? Is that what he promised?" I pointed to the Trav assemblage. "Don't you think he'd rather have one of them, nice and docile?"

I pointed to a circle that had been inscribed on the floor with a black marker. The Boss stood within what must have been the small zone that would be preserved when the Collapse happened.

"You know, I can't help but notice he's inside the magic circle and you're not. I don't think you're getting in."

Manbun raised his weapon. "Just keep talking, asshole. Two minutes or now, doesn't make any difference to me."

"Enough!" The Boss said wearily. "Do you have any idea how many times I have heard this argument, using these exact same words?"

Manbun opened his mouth to continue but closed it at The Boss's threatening look. He motioned to a second circle drawn on the floor. This one was near the equipment rack that held the *Rogue One* cassette.

"That's your spot," he said to me. "There is just enough room in it for you to stand. Your energy will flow into the device, but the dampening field will still lie between you and the rest of us. So, if you were thinking about trying any Traveler tricks, you can forget it."

He gestured again and Manbun stepped back from Sophie's chair. She slowly rose and shakily walked toward the three of us.

As she passed Sam and me, my friend quietly moved aside to allow her to pass. This put his right side behind me, so his arm and ever-present messenger bag were now largely blocked from The Boss and Manbun's view.

Just a few more seconds, I thought.

But The Boss's Sam Markus ESP was still in operation.

"Stop!" he commanded. Sophie froze.

"Keep walking, Soph," I said quietly. I gauged the distance to Manbun.

"Sam," The Boss said condescendingly, "show me what's in your hand."

Sam raised his left hand. It was empty, of course.

"Not that hand, you moron. The one with the gun."

Sam's shoulders slumped. He slowly brought Adam's H&K into view, its barrel disfigured by the PBG box taped to it.

"C'mon, c'mon," The Boss chided. "Toss it over. What did I just say? Nobody knows how Trav Becker and Sam Markus think better than I do. I've seen you at your best and your worst. I've had every idea that you imagine is original. I *know* what thoughts are going through your heads at this instant. I even know that you, Sam, will eventually come around to my point of view. It's inevitable. Unfortunately, we don't have time to wait for nature to take its course. So I will just have to speed things along."

He raised a hand that had been behind the equipment piled on the table. He showed us a double-sided handle that he held closed.

"A dead man's switch?" Sam scoffed. "After all this, you're threatening us with a bomb? Is that the best you can come up with?"

The other Sam gave him a withering look. "You know better than that. It's not just a bomb. The switch is linked to both the explosives and my causality matrix."

He pointed underneath the table behind him which we now saw had several bags of fertilizer between its legs. "If anything happens to me, your friends not only get deleted from the stream but also die. Painfully. It's kind of a two-for-one deal."

He pointed at the small circle. "Take your place or everybody dies. Twice. Trav, face it. It's over." A frown of disappointment clouded his face. "I am giving you a solution where everybody lives. Why do you keep treating me like the bad guy?"

"Says the man with the bomb," Sam observed.

The Boss shook his head. "It's too bad there's no time to bring you along," he said ruefully. "Don't you think I used to believe as you did?

But eventually, you learn there is only one way out of the chaos. Someone has to take responsibility. Someone who has seen all the different ways it can go bad."

"In other words, play God," I said.

"I didn't ask for this," he snapped. "But I'm not going to shirk the responsibility." He looked at me pointedly. "Like some people. Enough. You don't have to like my plan, but this is the only way your friends get to live."

"Maybe it's worth it to keep you from getting what you want," I replied.

"Oh, don't be ridiculous," he scoffed. "You aren't going to sacrifice these people. You don't have it in you. Quit wasting time and toss the gun up here."

I looked at Sam. He looked one more time at the gun and then lobbed it into a soft arc. It clattered and skidded to a stop at The Boss's feet.

"You're right," I admitted. "You do know what Sam and I are going to do in any given situation. You can predict pretty much anything we'd plan." I risked a glance over my shoulder. Sophie had reached Kaaro, who was whispering in her ear. I met Mary's eye and winked.

"But we didn't make the plan."

And I sprang at The Boss, feeling the power surge through me as the energy field from Sam's gun nullified the anti-Traveler force field.

32

Back in Time

"THEY HAVE A blind spot," I'd said.

Harvey was the first one to speak. "Do tell," he said, voice dripping with condescension.

I ignored him. "Gear told me that Mary and I are an anomaly. And if you think about it, each time he's encountered her, Manbun has underestimated her."

"Yeah!" Mary said. "What'd he call me? Mundane?"

"Exactly. Even though you thoroughly kicked his ass back in Sam's lab. It's like you exist outside of his perception. I'm betting the same is true of The Boss."

"We can use that!" Sam exclaimed, catching on.

"Yes, we can." And I turned to the woman the Multiverse would never make the mistake of underestimating again.

"So, what's the plan?"

She thought for a minute. And then another. And another. Finally, a smile slowly spread across her face. Her eyes twinkled.

"Cross the streams," she pronounced.

We stared at her blankly.

"What, you're the only ones who can make geek movie references?" she demanded, turning to Sam. "The Boss has set up a field around him that nullifies Trav's powers, right?"

He nodded.

"It's got to be similar to that one." She pointed to the PBG on my Glock which still lay on the floor. "That does the same thing, only on a smaller scale. Nullifies the Traveler energy so the gun doesn't misfire. What happens if we switch it on inside his anti-Trav field?"

Sam looked thunderstruck. "I never thought of that."

"That is the idea, I believe," Kaaro commented.

Sam whipped out his tablet and stabbed at it wildly. Harvey, who had given up on paying attention and begun fiddling again with the Mike glasses, watched over Sam's shoulder.

"Well," Sam said after a couple of minutes, "one of two things will happen. Either activating one null field within another will cause them both to short out, or..."

More tablet stabs.

"Or?" Morgan prompted.

"Hang on," he said irritably. Finally, he nodded.

"Or," he continued triumphantly, "the smaller field will create its own separate field, which will nullify the null field!"

He looked at us expectantly.

"Is that good?" I ventured, trying to parse the double negative.

He rolled his eyes. "Yes, of course. Either your powers will work because the smaller field shorts out the larger one or your powers will work within the range of the smaller null field."

"Or..." Harvey nudged his twin

"*Or what?*" Morgan, Mary, and I shouted together.

"Or it won't work at all," Sam admitted.

He looked at Harvey out of the corner of his eye. For just a second, his lips compressed into a pale thin line. But so quickly I decided I imagined it, his expression changed to the familiar grin I'd always known.

"Who knows?" he shrugged. "But two chances out of three? Best odds we've ever had!"

Good odds indeed.

As I leapt for The Boss, I could feel the nullifying field fall away.

"Now, Sophie!" I cried.

And a sword materialized in my hand.

I was already moving as it appeared. I sliced through The Boss's wrist without slowing down then pivoted on my back foot, accelerating the blade. He didn't even have time to look surprised as it arced through his neck. For a long moment, his head continued to rest on his shoulders before slowly toppling to the ground, followed by the headless corpse.

I turned around just in time to see Sam execute a perfect diving catch of The Boss's hand, putting both of his own around it to preserve pressure on the dead man's switch.

Sam grinned despite the grisly display. "There can be only one," he intoned. But then his eyes widened.

I spun around. The Trav horde sat paralyzed as something like smoke billowed into the auditorium, roiling toward them. As the smoke touched each man, he disintegrated. Whether The Boss's death had cut the puppet strings or we were watching the early effects of the Collapse, I didn't know.

And didn't have time to think about it because Manbun was on the move. I swirled around to face the funhouse mirror version of myself. But he was too focused on me. Morgan took advantage of his divided attention. She swatted the gun from his hand.

"Bitch!" he spat, knocking her aside with a vicious cuff to the face. He snatched up his PBG.

"I told you. You're weak." And he swung the gun around and sighted on Mary.

"What are you doing?" I cried. "It's over! The Boss is dead. You don't have to do any of this."

"You're right," he said between gritted teeth. "You win. But you don't get to win *and* keep Mary. No happy endings."

And he squeezed the trigger.

But thinking a slap would keep Morgan Foster out of commission was Manbun's last mistake. She hurled herself at the gun just as it fired.

I arrived a second later and ran him through. The gun fell from his hand and he lurched backward, collapsing next to the equipment rack.

Morgan slowly sank to her knees. As I rushed to her, I could see blood beginning to ooze from under her shoulder. She hissed as I let her down to the floor as gently as I could. But then a small smile replaced grimace of pain and I could see the mischievous glint of the Morgan I remembered.

"Guess *I* was fast enough," she whispered. She tried to pull herself up using her good arm, but with a grimace, started to go down again. Kaaro appeared behind her, cradling her good side against him.

"Maybe I'll just stay like this for a while," she whispered, wincing again as she tried to get her wounded arm in a comfortable position.

Kaaro examined the wound. "It's very close to the artery."

Mary pulled some gauze from her vest pocket. But at the same time, a wave of nausea and heat hit me like another physical blow.

Sam stepped over Manbun's corpse and jerked the cassette out of its chassis. But nothing happened. The lights stayed on, the fans kept whirring. Whatever the cassette was supposed to do, it had already done.

My head pulsed in time with the rumbling and ground shaking which now was constant. The floor underneath my feet began to shift. I had never experienced an earthquake, but I imagined this was what the first tremors might feel like.

"Goddammit," I muttered. "So close."

"What's the matter?" Mary asked.

"Can't you feel it?" I asked.

"Feel what?"

"The Collapse is beginning."

33

In My Life

"TIME TO GO," I said. "Everybody over to the circle and huddle up. If we can all stay close, I think Sophie and I can protect us from the worst of it."

But Sophie was barely conscious. As painful as the shock waves were for me, they were hitting her even harder. Mary drew the girl to her feet and helped her to the circle.

I knelt by Morgan. Kaaro held her head and wounded shoulder against his knees. Her face was gray, but the bleeding had slowed down.

"How is she doing?" I asked.

"She is not in immediate danger, but we'll need to be careful if we intend to move her."

"No," Morgan whispered.

"What?" I asked.

"I want to stay," she said softly. Her face was twisted in pain, but she met my gaze coolly.

"You can't!" Sophie had roused enough to watch our exchange. "None of us will even exist after the Collapse!" she cried.

"Not as long as Sam keeps hold of that switch," Morgan replied.

"We don't know what effect the Collapse will have outside The Boss's circle," Mary added. "It could wipe out your memories again. Or worse."

"What about the null-null field, Sam? Won't that shield her?"

He shrugged. "Maybe. It would take me some time to do the math."

Morgan suppressed a moan as she tried to find a comfortable position. "I'll take my chances. I just can't do this anymore. My brain is like Swiss Cheese. Amnesia might be a relief."

Another wave of nausea rolled over me, the biggest one yet. Sophie swayed on her feet and Mary put an arm around her.

"Just go," Morgan said.

"I can't leave you here all alone," I said.

"She won't be alone," Kaaro said evenly. "I will stay with her."

"Are you sure?" I asked. "There's no guarantee either of you will make it through."

"I have always preferred to make my own way in the world," he said. He looked at me appraisingly and then nodded toward Manbun's body. "For most of my life, I believed as he did. That having friends, letting others close, made one weak. The Trav I knew before you took his place believed the same. But you have a strength he did not. I respect that. If I survive this collapse, perhaps the thing I'll carry with me is the memory to seek out friends."

"Look me up," I deadpanned. "We'll join a softball league or something." He raised an eyebrow. I clapped him on the shoulder, then bent forward, bringing my face to Morgan's.

"You're sure?"

She nodded. Her eyes flicked toward Mary. "You two are good together. Better even than Buck and Fay."

"Thanks," I whispered through a throat that was suddenly tight. "I'll try to live up to their example."

She reached up with her good hand and grabbed my collar with surprising strength. "But if you ever lie to her again, I will come and kick your ass, even if I don't remember why."

I smiled and covered her hand with mine.

"Noted."

"Trav!" Mary called. Sophie had more or less collapsed completely into her arms. The girl trembled in rhythm with the ripples that pulsed across my own field of vision.

With some difficulty, Morgan craned her neck so she could see Mary.

"Take care of him," she said.

Mary tried to reply, but all that came out was a choked sob.

I brushed my lips across Morgan's cheek, gave Kaaro one final nod, and stood.

"Okay, Sam," I called. "Join the party."

But he didn't look at me. The fingers of his free hand were poised over the keyboard of one of The Boss's laptops. I realized that he had moved out of the protection zone of both The Boss's circle and the null-null field we had created with the PBG device.

"Sam!" I grabbed him by the shoulder. "Snap out of it. It's time."

He didn't answer me. He poked at the keyboard and with a sigh slammed a finger on the enter key. Then he held up the dead man switch, still surrounded by the last grisly remains of The Boss's hand.

"Someone's gotta hang on to this," he said. "And that person can't be in the circle. If I let go, the whole place goes up and everyone gets deleted."

"Okay," I said quickly. "C'mon. The detonator can't be that complicated. We can disarm it."

Sam shook his head. "You said it yourself. There's no time."

"Then get in the circle! We'll take our chances! This will probably all disappear before an explosion can happen anyway. At least get in the null field."

Sam came out from behind the table where he'd been standing. "Don't you get it, Trav? That's the problem."

"What are you talking about?"

"You know what I'm talking about. I know how you feel about how I handled Harvey. You're just waiting for me to go off the deep end."

"It's not like that."

He sighed heavily, suddenly looking every bit as old as Gear. "You see, the thing is, you're not wrong. I did something you could never do."

I flicked my hand at The Boss's body. "I did the same thing."

"No. You didn't have a choice. It was you or him. Maybe there was another way. But I didn't go looking for it. Don't you see? That's how it starts. First, it's *I know best.* He mirrored my gesture toward The Boss. "Next thing you know, it's…him."

"Nobody believes that, Sam. You're nothing like him."

"Quit kidding yourself, Trav. I *am* him. Even now, a part of me is thinking through his math, trying to figure out if there is a way to salvage some of his plan."

His voice dropped to a whisper. "That's what The Boss meant when he told me I'd come around. It's what we Sams do."

"It's not," I said fiercely. "It can't be."

"Are you willing to bet the Multiverse on it?"

His grip on my arm tightened. "It's okay, Trav. It has to be me. And I'd rather go out like this than know that someday you'd be the one who'd have to put *me* down."

He nodded toward the circle. "You gotta go. Even with both you and Sophie stabilizing the exclusion zone, it's going to be a rough ride. They won't make it without you."

I pulled him into a hug and he gripped me back just as fiercely with his free hand.

"Guess it was me who was Frodo all the time," he murmured.

"No," I replied. "Still Sam. The one who did what needed to be done."

I wanted to continue, but there was something in my throat. I settled for just gripping the back of his head, touching my forehead to his.

"I love you, man," I finally managed to choke out.

"I know."

He managed to keep a straight face for about three seconds before a chuckle burbled forth.

"Geez," I said softly, "stay in one universe, will you?"

"I will if you will," he said.

Before I could speak again, he shook his head. "Just go, damn it. Before I lose my courage."

I clapped him on the shoulder and made my way over to join Mary and Sophie.

"What's going on?" the girl asked groggily. "Why isn't he coming?"

I shook my head. "He has to stay." The ground shook again. Mary reached out to steady Sophie and me. I looked at Kaaro, who still had an arm around Morgan. He inclined his chin back at me.

I gave Sam one final glance. He was giving me a thumbs up. And it was only as I tried to decipher his goofy grin that I realized it was The Boss's thumb that he had raised. He winked.

Sophie was barely conscious, head lolling on Mary's shoulder. We staggered as the floor began to roll beneath us.

"Sophie, wake up," I nudged the girl. "We need you."

She moaned, her eyes fluttering.

"We have to protect Mary. You have to help."

"It hurts," she whimpered.

"I know. But it's almost over. C'mon."

Mary and I each took an arm, helping the girl into the circle.

"Put your arms around each other," I said.

They did so but I was racked by another wave of nausea so severe I fell to my knees. I lost my group on them and fell out of the circle.

"Trav!" Mary cried.

"It's okay," I grunted, driving myself back to my feet. The room swam before me. There were now two sets of Kaaro, Morgan, and Sam. Where Mary and Sophie had stood, there were no fewer than three pairs, all staring at me in shock and concern.

"No, no," I mumbled. "Need the right ones."

Two of the Marys just continued to stare at me, but the one on the left spoke. "It's okay, Trav. Just come to us. You can do it."

It was like trying to wade through cement. I finally managed to shuffle one foot forward a couple of inches. Encouraged by this progress, I managed to drag the other one along.

I was just a few feet from Mary's outstretched arm, going about as fast a ninety-year-old after you took his walker away. Finally, my hand grazed Mary's fingers. As her hand clutched mine, the other Marys and Sophies disappeared. I surged forward, and they pulled me into their embrace. Mary freed one arm from around Sophie and reached around me, lending me her strength just as mine faded.

And then I didn't feel anything. Because Mary and Sophie ceased to exist.

Along with the rest of the universe.

I floated, suddenly unconcerned that I could neither see, hear, or feel anything. I was blind for a few seconds. Or maybe a million years. But after a time, I could once again see. Which made a part of me wish I had stayed blind. Because I could see...

Everything.

I was at the center of a nexus and radiating out was the lifeline of every Trav who had been, could have been, or would be.

Buck was there. And The Boss. I watched their doomed dance for a while. Then I studied the man I had dubbed Trav Zero desperately defending himself from Trav after Trav sent by Harvey.

I moved on to the various tendrils that represented the Rangers and the Opposition. Dozens of them. Each thread representing a life thrust into one side or the other of the war that neither side could win. Not to mention the dead-end filaments of hundreds of Trav drones.

The glowing thread at the center was me, of course. Like a dying man watching his life flash before his eyes, I saw my lifeline intersect with Trav Zero, Buck, the Rangers, Manbun, and all the others. The spot in spacetime where Gear chucked me out of the stream entirely presented itself as a glowing spot of light ejected from the main thread. Turning my attention to it created an effect like zooming in to a video frame or photo. As I got "closer," I could sense the confusion in this earlier version of myself.

His mind was a jumble and my attempt to send him calming thoughts registered as a rather odd conversation. But it was the best I could do. And while I couldn't halt the trajectory Gear had set him on, I was able to nudge him toward a stream that would give him access to some tools that I now knew would be a big help later.

That task accomplished, I looked out over the entire thread of events that led me to this moment outside of time. Seeing a few other pressure points where things nearly came off the rails, I reached in and made a few that would be (had been?) helpful. I couldn't overtly make changes to the timeline. No way to keep any Sam Markus from his inevitable slide into madness, but I now had the answers to a few questions that had always bothered me, like how a forty-year-old Billy Joel song got onto a middle school girl's computer at just the right time to provide me with deductive inspiration.

As I looked back over my past, it occurred to me that if I turned around, I could probably watch my future. It was tempting. But as I began to crane my metaphysical neck over my metaphorical shoulder, I thought of Sam.

I realized I now had the power that The Boss had tried so hard to acquire. I could pick any of the timelines that lay before me, or any that I could imagine, and make that one the foundational trunk from which all new streams would branch out into the Multiverse.

But I didn't. Instead, I faced the way I had come and watched as all the tendrils of all the Trav Beckers began to fall away. The one that I thought of as "me," with all its tragedy, comedy, and flaws, grew thicker and brighter until it encompassed my entire field of vision.

It was beautiful.

34

God Only Knows

TWO HUNDRED BUCKS guarantee, Jon. Or eighty percent of what we do at the door, whichever is greater."

The pianist took a sip from the beer I had just served him and looked at his bandmates.

"You good with that, Chris?" he asked. The drummer nodded as he scratched his beard.

"Drew?"

The bassist looked up from a notebook in which he'd been shading in the sides of an intricate abstract drawing. "Uh…yeah."

We shook hands all around.

"See you next month," I said and moved down the bar.

Mary watched me work my way toward her, toying with the plastic sword that had once pierced the garnish of her martini.

"That okay?" I asked, gesturing toward her drink.

She made a face. "Don't fish for compliments. You know you make the world's best lemon drop."

"Just want to make sure I'm keeping my standards up."

"Who knew all those drinks you mixed for me were preparing you for a second career?" she asked with a sly smile. But her lips tightened as she looked at the two musicians finishing their beers.

"Did it freak you out when they walked in? It did me. You're really going to let them play here?"

"Of course. First Friday is our best jazz night. They're jazz musicians. Good ones."

"They looked a little surprised that you hired them without hearing them."

"I have heard them."

"You couldn't have heard much over the gunfire," she said wryly.

"I feel bad that we smashed their instruments."

"Which they don't remember."

"I remember."

Although I was pretty sure that like the bar I now stood behind, their gear had come through the Collapse just fine. This version, now apparently the only version of the Third Street Lounge, showed none of the effects of the fight that Mary and I had been through.

But just because no one else remembered the battle did not mean its consequences were any less real. The absence of my friends was like a weight I carried everywhere. All the heavier since the burden couldn't be shared.

Mary touched my hand softly. "You're doing it again."

I smiled. "Sorry."

She did that a lot these days, summoning me back from the depths of my thoughts. Intellectually, I knew that I couldn't have changed how things had gone down. But that didn't make me feel much better.

"Was it worth it?" I whispered. She tilted her head, inviting me to continue. "Are things any better?"

"Of course they are."

"Not for Adam."

It was ironic. My entire journey across so many streams and so many lives had begun with Adam being dead on one stream and alive on another. But now he was gone. There were no parallel universes where Kim was driving him crazy with wedding preparations.

But at least in Adam's case there was a grave. There had been a funeral. His name was on the wall at the station that we called End of Watch. I could check on his parents as I knew he would have done for me. We could mourn him together.

Not like Sam.

I shook my head, eyes stinging. Even now, weeks after the Collapse, I still had trouble believing my friend was gone.

More than gone. Erased.

Whatever he had been doing at the computer in those last minutes before the Collapse had removed him completely from the timeline.

Unlike Adam, whose death on duty was public record, Sam Markus appeared in no death records. Or birth records. He'd never attended, let alone been hired by the university. Pictures of the two of us had been overwritten by other images. Sam Markus had simply never been.

He had sacrificed himself to keep from becoming the thing he feared the most. And it was the ultimate sacrifice. Not just his life, but his very existence.

Would the mental accommodation that kept human minds from slipping and sliding as they traversed parallel reality streams someday rob me of the memories of my friend?

I hoped not. Maybe Sam had been right. That there was no escape from the path that would lead him to becoming Harvey or The Boss. He made sure that wouldn't occur. And I would respect that choice.

Mary touched my hand. "What are you thinking?"

"I just don't want to forget them," I replied softly.

She nodded, squeezing my hand. "We won't. I promise."

"We don't know that. The universe has a lot of weight."

"Hey," she responded, lightly slapping my wrist. *"We* weren't a part of the universe's plan, and we're doing *fine."*

"That we are."

"And we're not the only ones who came out of the Collapse okay." She inclined her head toward a table across the room.

Morgan Foster was seated across from a young woman. Three other girls leaned over the seated one's shoulders. All of them stared intently at the Tarot cards Morgan had spread out in the center of the table. Morgan looked down at the cards, then raised her eyes to look at the seated woman. She said something which caused two of the friends to raise their hands to their mouths.

"That's exactly right!" One of the women exclaimed.

Morgan smiled just as a hand delivered a drink. Without taking her eyes off the cards, she slid one hand up the wrist of that hand and gave it a squeeze.

Anton Kaaro smiled and covered her hand with his before withdrawing to let her work.

I shook my head. *That* was almost weirder than Sam's erasure.

"And she doesn't remember you at all?" Mary asked.

I shook my head. "Just that I hired her for Tarot Tuesday," I said. "Which is how they remember meeting. So I am now perpetually on Anton's good side."

In this merged timeline, I had found myself once again in Anton Kaaro's employ. But the Collapse had also erased the illegitimate side of his financial empire. He was now just a tough but legal businessman. With a psychic girlfriend.

And even better, the payroll was blissfully Bilol Grymzin-less.

"You're right," I said. "It's certainly not the universe I would have written. And there are things I would change."

"You mean like not being a cop? I'll bet Leon would take you back."

"I've had enough cop to last a while."

This made her smile. "I won't say it bothers me much to have you dealing with these kind of shots instead of the other kind."

"But?"

"I just don't want you to be bored."

"Bored? I have to figure out how to make a jazz club turn a profit or Anton will turn this place into a country bar quicker than you can say Kenny G."

"Anything but that."

I started to continue but was halted by the shocked look that suddenly filled Mary's face. Her grip on my hand tightened.

"What?" I asked.

"You…You're not doing that?"

"Doing what?"

She jerked her head toward the speaker mounted in the bar's ceiling. "That."

The rumble of the bar's many conversations nearly drowned out the music, but in the lull that seems to overtake a dozen different discussions at the same instant, I was able to pick out the distinctive voice of David Bowie singing "Heroes."

I smiled, shaking my head. "Not me. Just an awesome playlist. That's over. The Traveler magic is gone."

"You're sure?" she asked.

I shrugged, spreading my hands. "Without Sam to do the math, who can be sure? But everything he and Gear said about the Collapse seems to have happened. No more red shifts. And good riddance."

"But for how long? He said that the energy starts building again after every Collapse."

"But this last go-round was accelerated by the Sams and the Travs. Without us to interfere, it could be hundreds of years before it builds to the point of producing sensitives. We'll be long gone. Sophie, too. That's what Sam bought us. A return to the natural progression."

She raised her glass.

"To Sam."

I raised a glass of water I'd been sipping on. "And Adam," I said, tapping hers.

"Heroes," she said softly.

She drained her drink, setting the glass down with a satisfied sigh. I raised an eyebrow but she shook her head.

"No, I need to go. Gotta practice. That Daugherty piece isn't going to play itself."

I nodded. "Work hard and I'll get home about the time you're ready for a break."

Her eyes smoldered. "What kind of break?" she asked, licking her lips.

"Your favorite kind."

She grabbed a handful of my shirt, pulling my face toward hers. Our lips met in the middle of the bar. I could feel the kiss all the way down to my shoes.

"You know what my favorite part of you working here is?" she breathed.

"What?"

"Nobody has to get up early."

She came back in for another kiss, giving me a tantalizing flick of her soft tongue.

"Don't be late."

She took her purse, gave me another look full of promise, and slid out from her stool, putting just enough swing into her hips to make sure my gaze followed her out the door.

"Whoa," said a guy sitting a few seats down. "You sure you shouldn't have just gone with her?"

"Tempting," I replied. I picked up her glass and swept the lemon rinds she had neatly stacked on a cocktail napkin into my hand.

"If that's how the staff gets treated in this place, are you taking applications?"

"It's not a part of the standard benefit package."

"Too bad. You been with her long?"

I smiled. "Not as long as you might think."

Mary had been putting a lot of extra practice time in. Almost as if it had been some time since she had played an extended piece. And that wasn't the only thing I had noticed since we had picked ourselves up after the Collapse.

I thought back to Mary Red's death. Both of them had gone down. I was sure that Mary had gotten back up far too quickly to have exchanged scarves.

Pretty sure.

I hadn't asked her. And I never would. After all, I had asked Mary to accept a Trav not her own. If she had made the same decision, to pick up a life worth continuing, how could I tell her that was wrong?

"Not that long," I repeated. "But it also seems like we've been together forever, you know?"

He nodded and raised his glass. I tapped mine against his and gave him a free refill as Brian Wilson's plaintive voice replaced Bowie's and sang the most perfect pop song ever written.

Epilogue

S OPHIE STARED AT the face gazing back at her from her laptop screen.

"Really? You're asking me on *Skype*?"

Even through the limited resolution of the chat window, she could see Dexter's cheeks redden.

"I was going to ask you after school, but you had your violin lesson," he mumbled.

She put on a frown, letting him hang in miserable suspense for about ten seconds, then lost it, erupting in a fit of giggles.

"You should see your face!" she exclaimed. "Of course, I'll go to the dance with you."

"Sophie!" her mom called. "I have to run to the store. You can drive. You need the practice."

"Okay!" Sophie called back, then turned back to the chat. "Gotta go."

Now it was Dexter's turn to grin. "And I gotta stay. No way I'm going out on the street while you're driving."

She stuck her tongue out at him but then grinned again, pleasantly surprised that he had found the courage to flip a little of her attitude back at her. Dex was a work in progress, but he definitely had possibilities.

She stood up, dislodging Noah from his resting place on her lap.

She stared at the cat, who stretched, and hopped back up into the empty but still warm chair. He blinked twice and settled back down, front paws tucked underneath his breast.

Sophie felt a little bad that she had somehow ended up with Morgan's cat after the Collapse, but Noah showed no evidence of any intention to leave Sophie's house. And there was also now no trace of her dad's cat dander allergy, which had always prevented pets in the past.

Oh well, she thought, slipping into her shoes, *Morgan got a boyfriend out of the deal. That sounds like a fair trade.*

She tripped lightly down the stairs, nearly running into her mom, who stood hands on hips.

"Since when did you start wearing glasses?" Mom asked.

"I think they look cool."

Mom shook her head. "When I was your age, we did everything we could to *keep* from wearing glasses."

"Geek chic," Sophie replied with a shrug. "It's a thing."

Sophie pushed the thick black frames, which had slid down her nose, back into place. Dexter had written some pretty cool code for their programming class. Maybe she could ask him to take a look at the glasses. She missed Mike.

Mom elected not to pursue the matter any further. Instead, she frowned. "Have you seen the car keys?"

Sophie shook her head. "Aren't they on the rack next to the door?"

Sophie's mom shook her head. "I looked there."

Sophie's eyes went out of focus for just a minute. She gave the minutest of nods, then walked into the kitchen, craning her neck around the corner. She grabbed the keys off their peg and gave them a jingle.

Mom appeared, attracted by the sound.

"Where'd you find them?" she demanded.

"Right on the rack," Sophie said.

Mom's eyes narrowed. "It's not possible they were in your purse from last time and you're just trying to make me think I'm losing it?"

"I would never do that," Sophie sniffed. She gave the keys another jingle. "Ready for me to drive?"

Mom gave a mock shudder. "These are the choices my life comes down to. Dementia or cardiac arrest."

Sophie rolled her eyes. "We won't have an accident."

"I know, sweetheart. You're a careful driver."

"Yup, that's why."

Sophie tossed the car keys in the air as she led her mom into the garage, confident in her abilities.

All of them.

End

Author's Note

I T IS IMPOSSIBLE to for me to reflect on the journey that is *Traveler* without thinking of Lennox Randon.

If you've had any prior exposure to my work, you have certainly heard the story of how Randon got our friend Rob Cline, and then me, to complete writing projects that had sat on the shelf for years.

Randon (he went by his last name), suffered from stomach cancer. When the group we eventually dubbed The Writing Lads began, he was in remission. Even after the cancer came back, it was easy to forget how sick he was, because he bore his tremendous burden with such grace.

I don't have many regrets in life, but one of them is that Randon didn't live long enough to read *Traitor.* I am so much richer for having known him and miss him every day.

But while Randon provided the initial inspiration for me to write these books, it was my wife Debbie who kept me going. Her attributes show up in every woman character I've ever written, with the possible selection of Amy Harper. Debbie is not a sci-fi fan, and I gave *Traveler* to her a little reluctantly. What if she didn't like it? How could I keep doing this if it wasn't something we could talk about? But when she genuinely liked it, I knew I had something.

And I definitely have Debbie to thank for not letting me quit on *Traitor.* Often (and usually after a couple of cocktails) our conversation would turn to the book. She would then demand that I get the lead out, because she wanted to know how the story ended! Without that regular encouragement, I'm not sure I would ever have finished.

And yes, she orders her cosmos with the cranberry juice on the side.

On the book production side, it fell to Rob Cline to delete the thousands of extra commas I put in my writing. He's nearly as talented an editor as he is a writer. *Traitor* is a much better book due to his hard work.

Speaking of multi-talented people, Drew Morton not only draws awesome book covers, but is also one of the best jazz bassists I know. The jazz trio that pops in and out of view in *Traitor* consists of Drew, plus pianist Jon Snell and drummer Chris Jensen, both of whom are enthusiastic *Traveler* fans. When I told Jon I had put he and Chris together with Drew, he decided to actually book that trio for some gigs! The part of the leader of the big band was played by my jazz mentor, trumpeter and composer Al Naylor.

Another musician friend, Katie Chalstrom, did some important legwork (literally). She took a break from her classes to confirm the number of floors in Van Allen Hall, the University of Iowa building that inspired Building 231. The rooftop episode with the laser actually took place, although I wasn't there. But it was a favorite story of my college friends, of whom the late John Finnegan was one.

Justin Wasson purchased naming rights for a character at an auction to benefit my Rotary club. He chose his newborn son, Dexter. Justin is a martial artist, which served as the inspiration for Sophie to take tae kwon do. It will be a few years before Dexter appreciates his role as Sophie's potential boyfriend.

As always, I'm grateful to a community of independent writers who are always there with feedback and a kick in the ass when I need it. Aaron Bunce in particular was relentless in making sure finishing this book remained one of my priorities. Aaron also supplied the title of the book during a chance meeting in the produce section of our local grocery store. You never know where inspiration will strike!

Thanks also to Heidi Hutchinson, Jed Quinn, Rachel Aukes, and Adam Whitlatch. Google them, then buy their books. You won't be disappointed.

In my local community of Cedar Rapids-Iowa City, Iowa, you should buy those books from one of our excellent local booksellers, like Terri LeBlanc and Ursla Lanphear of M&M Bookstore, and Bart Carithers of Next Page Books, and of course, the world-famous Prairie Lights Bookstore. All of them are passionate supporters of independent authors.

The Music of Traveler

MUSIC IS IMPORTANT to Trav Becker and to me. Each of us has a personal soundtrack of songs that conjure up a certain feeling, or time in our lives. Part of the fun of writing these books was thinking about songs that have been important to me, and weaving them into Trav's story.

You may have noticed that the chapter titles in Traitor are all song titles. How many can you identify? Find the answers on www.denniswgreen.com.

Here is the music mentioned in the Traveler books:

• "Trains" from *Famous Last Words* - Al Stewart

• "In The Air Tonight" from *Face Value* - Phil Collins

• "O Fortuna" from *Carmina Burana* - London Symphony Orchestra

• "Heroes" from *Heroes* - David Bowie

• "God Only Knows" from *Pet Sounds* - The Beach Boys

• "Miami 2017 (Seen The Light Go Down on Broadway)" from *Turnstiles* - Billy Joel

• "Take Five" from *Time Out* - Dave Brubeck Quartet

• "Freddie the Freeloader," from *Kind of Blue* - Miles Davis

• "I Shot The Sheriff," from 461 Ocean Boulevard - Eric Clapton

• "Too Many Nights Too Long" from *Rose of Cimarron* - Poco

• "Buffalo River Home," from *Perfectly Good Guitar* - John Hiatt

• "Birdland," from *Heavy Weather* - Weather Report

• "In The Court of the Crimson King," from *In The Court of the Crimson King* - King Crimson

• "Thunder Road," from *Born To Run* - Bruce Springsteen

I've posted a playlist of these and some of Trav's other favorite songs at http://denniswgreen.com/the-music-of-traveler/

About the Author

DENNIS GREEN'S NOVELS have dozens of 4 and 5-star reviews on Amazon. His first book, *Traveler,* ranked in the Top Ten in the 2014 Ben Franklin Independent Publishing awards.

A popular radio personality in his native Iowa, Dennis's adventures as a DJ were covered by the media not only locally, but in major markets like Anchorage and Los Angeles. He has also worked on the stage, TV, and independent film.

Dennis's writing has appeared in the anthology *Sadistic Shorts,* magazines, and his own blog at denniswgreen.com.

By day, he is the general manager of KCCK-FM, Iowa's only jazz radio station. And if it's 5:30 am, you can probably find him in the pool, working out with the Milky Way Masters swim club.

Made in the USA
Middletown, DE
25 February 2020